"I'm just re__
the merch__

He measured her coolly. "So don't bother with the gift box. I'm not buying—my daughter did the buying earlier. As I said, I'm bringing this back. Though it did cross my mind to toss it directly into the trash."

Brynn stepped into the showroom after him, making a face behind his back to hide her amusement. So he needed to make an exchange. And like most men who found themselves in a lingerie shop, this handsome stranger was out of his element and felt he had to bluster.

"I'll need to figure out your refund, sir. What exactly did your daughter find wrong with her purchase?" And who was his daughter, anyway? Brynn tried to remember.

His dark eyebrows drew together in a fierce scowl. "Wrong?" he growled. "Wrong?" His eyes raked Brynn from head to toe. "It should be against the law to sell undergarments fit for . . . for ladies of the night to thirteen-year-old girls. But since apparently it isn't—" his tone became even more derisive "—I'd advise you not to sell my child any more of these *notions,* or I'll deal out the consequences myself!"

Roz Denny has lived all over the United States, including, of course, the Southwest, so vividly described in her first Harlequin Romance, *Red Hot Pepper*. She's currently living in the Seattle area, where this second book is set. Roz has many more story ideas—and locales—to draw on!

Books by Roz Denny

HARLEQUIN ROMANCE
3032—RED HOT PEPPER

ROMANTIC NOTIONS

Roz Denny

Harlequin Books

TORONTO • NEW YORK • LONDON
AMSTERDAM • PARIS • SYDNEY • HAMBURG
STOCKHOLM • ATHENS • TOKYO • MILAN

ISBN 0-373-03122-X

Harlequin Romance first edition May 1991

ROMANTIC NOTIONS

CHAPTER ONE

THE BELL OVER THE ENTRANCE to Romantic Notions tinkled cheerfully, announcing the arrival of a late customer. Brynn Powell tore her gaze away from the column of figures she was adding to check her watch. One minute to six. Who would wait until closing time to shop on a stormy night like this?

If she hadn't already been planning to stay late and do inventory, she'd be irritated. But then, she'd been irritated a lot the past few weeks, Brynn thought, letting her gaze fall on chaotic piles of lingerie draped over every available surface in her cramped office. Altogether, it meant she'd be later than usual getting home to Kevin tonight.

Oh well, might as well let the late customer browse. Sighing, Brynn rubbed the back of her neck as she called out, "Take your time." She could hear the customer moving around in the showroom. "I'll only be a minute," she added.

Brynn reached for the telephone and dialed, then checked the stability of her loosely coiled hair. No matter how firmly she wrapped the heavy strands in the morning, the knot never seemed to last to the end of a long day.

Bzzz...bzzz...bzzz... Her home line was busy. Holding down the button for a moment, Brynn listened to the renewed fury of rain bouncing off the roof. It was typical September weather in the northwest. Shivering, she wondered if her customer had ducked inside her shop only to escape a downpour.

She dialed again, and the line was still busy. Annoyed, Brynn cradled the phone on her shoulder, then totaled the day's receipts. "Drat Kevin," she muttered, banging the receiver down.

The sudden creak of a worn floorboard behind her delivered a sharp reminder that, except for her unknown customer, she was alone in the shop on a stormy night. For a moment Brynn's heartbeat escalated.

"If you're finished dratting Kevin, I could use some help." A deep male voice cut through Brynn's mild panic.

So her customer wasn't only late but pushy, she thought, forcing a professional yet frosty smile. The back room was off limits—just as the sign over the door plainly said. And she'd let Mr. Impatient know it.

She spun abruptly in her chair, and her knees almost smacked the man who was standing next to her desk. Her gaze penetrated a dangling curtain of satin and lace, and the reprimand froze on her lips. He had the most arresting violet eyes—devastatingly sexy and framed by thick black lashes.

Men shouldn't have violet eyes. Brynn felt her teeth come together with a snap. Especially not this shade of violet and definitely not set in a thoroughly masculine face like the one staring down at her with all the intensity of a poker player. A tremor of uneasiness skittered up her spine.

She cleared her throat. "Terrible weather for shopping." Her words sounded high pitched, almost squeaky.

Ignoring her attempt at conversation, the man merely arched a brow. Then two pieces of cream-colored satin drifted past Brynn's nose and settled on her ledger with a whispery sigh. Or had *she* sighed, Brynn wondered, studying the stranger's cleft chin, his firm lips and sharply defined cheekbones.

"I have the right store, I believe," he said in a clipped, almost accusatory tone.

His declaration was bordering on testy, though something about his gravelly voice sounded . . . intimate. It was a strange combination. Brynn shivered again. She didn't know this man at all, yet she knew almost everyone in the small community of Frontage Bay. Sitting straighter, she frowned into those incredible eyes as she wrapped a stray curl around one finger.

He frowned back and waited. Droplets of rain, caught in the curve of his long lashes, winked at Brynn with diamond brilliance in the light from her single desk lamp.

Brynn felt her heart flutter upward, like a bird gone wild in her throat. If nothing else, it made her treat him with more reserve. "I trust you found the correct size?" She busied herself with the froth of creamy silk coiled on her desktop and commanded her pounding heart to settle into its proper rhythm. To equalize their positions, she stood, letting him assess her full five-foot-eight-inch height. Then, to make up for her brief lapse in professionalism, she picked up the lingerie and flashed him her most practiced smile. "Step this way, sir. I'll ring these up for you. But perhaps you'd also like to select a matching slip for your wife." She hadn't looked to see if he wore a wedding band, but it seemed a safe enough assumption given the intimate nature of his purchase.

He didn't answer, and Brynn glanced over her shoulder to find him measuring her coolly.

She gestured toward the showroom. "All right—no slip." She offered another smile. "But this must be a gift for a very special occasion to send you out shopping in this frightful weather. If you'll just follow me to the cash register, I'll total these up and let you get going. Do you need a gift box?"

"Don't bother," he growled, pushing past her and leading the way into the showroom. "My daughter did the buying earlier today. I'm just returning the merchandise. Though I must admit, it did cross my mind to toss these...things directly into the trash. This saves me wondering if she'd just dug them out."

Brynn stepped through the archway after him, trying to make heads or tails of his impassioned reply. So he needed to make an exchange. And like most men who found themselves in a lingerie shop, he was out of his element and felt he had to bluster.

"After you, sir!" She made a face behind his back and hid her amusement at finding such an intimidating man human, after all. No longer under the spell of his unusual eyes, she was better able to assess him as she made her way to the cash register. His build was rugged, rather teddy bearish, really, Brynn thought whimsically.

An executive bear, she decided, noting the fabric of the topcoat he was buttoning as he hovered near the door. It was the finest cashmere and hand-tailored to fit his broad shoul-

ders. He had the look of a man more used to taking charge—
not taking back discarded lingerie.

But wait: he'd said his daughter bought the undies earlier.
Brynn blinked in surprise. He wasn't leisurely making another selection at all; he was preparing to leave. "Just a minute, please." Her words were no more than a dry rustle.
"Wait," she tried again, louder. "I thought you wanted an
exchange."

As she spoke, he turned to face her, leaving one hand on the
ornate glass doorknob. His dark brows drew together in a
fierce scowl. "And you'd recommend something like this, I
presume?" He touched a skimpy red teddy hanging on the
nearest rack.

She glanced first at the ivory satin in her hands, then at the
red. "Red isn't for everyone," she advised.

His mouth was set in a harsh line. "You bet it isn't," he
agreed.

The man seemed to radiate some undefined hostility, and
Brynn was reduced to stammering. "Then I ... I'll n-need to
figure out your refund. What exactly did your daughter find
wrong with her purchase?"

"Wrong?" the stranger growled deep in his throat. A wave
of his hand encompassed a neat row of sheer black, even
skimpier underthings. "You should be ashamed to ask." His
voice accused even as his eyes raked Brynn from head to toe.
"It should be against the law to sell undergarments fit for...for
ladies of the night to thirteen-year-old girls. But since apparently it isn't..." His tone became significantly deeper and even
more derisive. "I'd advise you not to sell my child any more
of these *notions*, or I'll deal out the consequences myself."

Brynn absorbed his outburst in shocked silence. Still puzzled by the indignation that had suddenly blasted her from
what she'd been considering bedroom eyes, she watched as the
front door flew open under his hefty yank.

Gusts of wind blew inside, lifting the hem of a mint-green
peignoir, whipping it about a display mannequin's slender
ankles. A torrent of rain swirled over and around him, swallowing the last syllable of his threat.

Brynn's body jerked as the door slammed shut on his heels with a solid thunk. Then, just as it had when he'd entered scant minutes earlier, the bell over the door jingled merrily. The cheerful sound seemed singularly inappropriate after an encounter that had been anything but.

Clasping the lacy underthings to her breast, she dashed across the room and pressed her nose to the window, staring into the stormy darkness. She heard the roar of a car engine and watched him drive out of the mall's parking lot without so much as a backward glance. Brynn noticed that the stranger's car was sleek and dark, and as it merged with heavy traffic on the main street a light from the corner lamp post showed it to be a late-model Jaguar.

A flush rivaling the one that had heated her cheeks with healthy appreciation for his masculine good looks now burned in outright anger at the memory of his unwarranted verbal attack. "A Jaguar!" she spat, giving a toss of her head. "How appropriate for Tarzan." Brynn rammed home the dead bolt on the front door with a fury that matched the customer's arrogance.

"Of all the unmitigated gall." She stopped to examine the items. "How dare he," she fumed. "Ladies of the night, indeed ... A good many women stood in line to buy these for their teenage daughters!"

As Brynn continued to inspect the delicate edging of pink lace rosebuds, she grew more self-righteous by the second. They were tasteful. Elegant. The snippets of silk and lace came from her Sweet Dreams line. They were her own design, intended to give young girls a sense of feminine self-confidence.

"How dare he!" Brynn repeated with greater emotion, smacking each light switch in the bank of showroom lights. Only when the area around her settled into complete darkness did she feel calm enough to return to the office and her paperwork.

But even then, she couldn't concentrate. It was precisely because she *did* identify with the painful shyness of young women that she'd designed Sweet Dreams. The same reason prompted her to offer teenage girls classes in building self-esteem. *How dare he hint otherwise!*

Incensed, Brynn snatched up the telephone. First she dialed home, but when she heard the busy signal again she slammed the receiver down. What was Kevin doing talking on the phone this long? She shifted uneasily, worried about her brother being alone during the storm.

She decided to finish her accounts and leave inventory for another night, but even as she worked, her mind flipped to the stranger. *The man's a prude,* she thought. Whatever would he think about the lace and silk unmentionables she was wearing? Now *that* line of underwear was definitely provocative— and meant to be. Self-confident women, women who liked the feel of silk next to their skin, loved this particular line. He obviously didn't know that women of all ages preferred a bit of sexual fantasy over the common-sense choice every time!

Brynn toyed with a ballpoint pen, giving her anger time to abate. Before long, she was feeling sorry for the arrogant stranger's daughter. With the man's abundant good looks and obvious self-confidence, he'd probably never suffered adolescent shyness. She doubted a man like that had ever needed anything external to make him feel good about himself.

Brynn stopped fuming long enough to total a column of the day's receipts. However, she couldn't seem to rid her mind of the disturbing encounter. What would his wife be like? she wondered. Emotionally deprived? Browbeaten?

She pulled the ledger closer. As a matter of fact, who was his daughter? Brynn had been gone for only about an hour to get Kevin's medicine; apart from that, she'd handled all the sales herself.

She ran her finger down a list of entries, mentally sorting through customers, matching them with purchases. She should just forget it—except now she owed him money. Not that a man who drove a Jag would miss the money. Still . . .

Brynn frowned. Sweet Dreams weren't cheap. How could the pious oaf's child afford them on her own? Brynn drummed her fingers on the desk. Suppose the man's wife had dipped into the household funds to buy them for her daughter. What if the woman had outright defied a chauvinistic husband? Brynn built case after case and inflated each.

Then her finger hesitated alongside a cash entry, the exact cost of the two pieces in question. "The Mouse." Brynn whispered the nickname she'd attached to a shy little waif who'd been haunting her shop lately. Chewing her bottom lip, she considered it. Yes, everything fit. Including the eyes, though the waif's eyes were definitely more gray than violet.

Who was she? Brynn massaged her temples. The Mouse always trailed in behind Stacy Evans, she reflected with a smile. And she remembered thinking what an unlikely pair of friends they were. Stacy was the daughter of an old school chum, Sunne Evans. A clone of her outgoing mother, Stacy was strawberry blond, bubbly and effervescent. Surely Stacy had introduced her new friend a few weeks ago, but try as she might, Brynn couldn't recall a name.

Brynn's smile grew fondly maudlin. *Stacy and the Mouse.* On the surface, the two girls' relationship bore a distinct similarity to the childhood friendship Brynn had shared with Stacy's mother—with Brynn playing the Mouse role. Light-years ago, it seemed now. Years when she'd despaired of ever developing a figure. Despaired of developing looks. Despaired of just plain developing. Through it all, Sunne had remained a loyal confidante, and Brynn loved her like a sister. Maybe that was why she'd held a soft spot for Stacy's friend almost from the beginning.

Brynn reached for the telephone. If Sunne hadn't been her mentor, hadn't given her confidence, she'd probably never have become the person she was today. So, if the Mouse's mother was willing to risk her prudish husband's wrath by encouraging her shy daughter, the least Brynn could do was back her up. She dialed Sunne's number and listened to the distant ring.

"Hello. Coach Evans here."

"Still wearing your work hat, are you, Coach?" Brynn greeted Sunne's husband, Paul, with warm affection. A varsity basketball coach at the nearby university, Paul Evans was a laid-back sort. Acquaintances often joked that he loved sports and Sunne, in that order. Not for one minute did Brynn believe it. She admired the man's quiet strength. Paul was a fine person, a good husband and a wonderful father of two extroverted girls.

Brynn wouldn't mind finding a man like him some day. Her one and only past relationship had been with a man who'd turned out to be sadly lacking in those areas. If only there were more men like Paul Evans and fewer like the one she was trying to track down right now.... Brynn didn't finish the thought. "Is either Sunne or Stacy around?" She got right to the point of her call.

"This is a welcome surprise hearing from you, Brynn." Paul's deep voice drifted over the line. "Sunne will be sorry to have missed you. She insists you never take any time away from your job or Kevin. Not ten minutes ago, she took Stacy and Leah to the torture chamber. That's how she refers to the girls' weekly piano lessons." He chuckled, then sobering, he asked seriously, "Everything okay with you and Kevin?" His tone became guarded.

"I'm fine, Paul. And Kevin is doing as well as can be expected." Brynn twisted the phone cord. "He has up days and down days, but you know Kevin—basically he's a positive kind of guy."

Paul murmured, "Yes, I do know. He's a stoic, like your dad was." His voice held an emotional catch. "So what can I do for you if everything's fine? I've never known you to call just to pass the time of day."

She hesitated. "Well, I'm wondering whether you'd know one of Stacy's girlfriends. A quiet little girl with shoulder-length, light brown hair. Plain compared to Stacy. But she's got the most expressive eyes. Gray...lavender-gray, I'd say, if I had to define the color."

"Sure I know her, Brynn. You just described Holly Court." Paul laughed. "I couldn't have done any better, even though I know her." He paused. "Holly was here until a few minutes ago. But, hey, hasn't Sunne told you about my old college pal moving to town? He's here to help revive the Metropolitans. His name's Sam Court. Surely you've read about him in the newspaper?"

"Sam Court." Brynn tried the name, letting it roll off her tongue. She liked the sound. It was clean and simple. And powerful. "Opera?" She turned that over in her mind, too, trying to connect the stranger with the setting. Then, speaking less to Paul than to herself, she exclaimed, "That barbarian is with the Metropolitan Opera? Incredible," she murmured. "Impossible," she objected more loudly.

"Opera? Sam Court?" Paul erupted in peals of deep laughter. "Hardly, Brynn. Sunne's right. You do stay buried. The newspapers have been filled with the resurgence of Seattle's pro hockey team. We haven't had a team since the Totems. Battles over a coach, players' salaries, schedules and other things have hampered them getting a new team off the ground. For us to bag Sam Court was a real coup. Ask Kevin, he'll know."

"I'm sure he will," she acknowledged, not bothering to tell Paul that she rarely found time to read the news, let alone the sports pages.

Paul paused significantly. "I hadn't seen Sam since college. Oh, I've followed his career, of course. The Samurai has been quite successful in Los Angeles. But it's great having him move here. Like finding a long-lost brother. I sure hope they get everything ironed out so we can support this team for a while."

"Hockey? Samurai?" Brynn parroted Paul's words stupidly. She was getting much more information from Paul than she wanted. But as he went on to rave about the attributes of Seattle's new team, she had a few moments to sort through some of the pieces.

"But Brynn," Paul said, winding down at last, "I'm sure you didn't call to get a rundown on my old buddy's hockey prowess. You had a question about his daughter, I believe. I have no doubt you'll be meeting them both at our annual neighborhood Halloween party. Sunne's going absolutely crazy getting out invitations this year. You are coming, aren't you?"

"Uh-huh." Brynn's murmur was noncommittal at best. She'd been reassessing Mr. Court, trying to blend the man she'd encountered with the picture Paul was painting. She found it only too easy to cast that arrogant man in the aggressive role of hockey player. And Paul's rave review didn't alter the facts—Sam Court was rude, and his timid daughter deserved her sympathy.

Paul rambled on. "Sunne's been talking about signing Holly up for your modeling classes along with Stacy and Leah, Brynn."

"They aren't really modeling classes, Paul," Brynn pointed out.

"Well—whatever they are—Sunne is counting on you to convince Sam. So far, he's less than enthusiastic." Paul coughed. "But here I am carrying on.... What was it you wanted to know about Holly?"

Brynn digested Paul's statement slowly. She could well imagine Sam Court being less than enthusiastic about her class. Opinionated as he was about how some harmless underwear would affect his daughter's psyche, Brynn imagined he'd sooner see the child wearing sackcloth than catch her inside Romantic Notions again for any reason. Perhaps Court's wife would be more receptive to the idea of building the Mouse's self-esteem. Paul hadn't mentioned his friend's wife yet, but she didn't really have the time or inclination to get involved in the Court family history right now.

"Do you have the Courts' phone number, Paul? I owe Holly a refund. I'd like to clear her account tonight."

For a moment Paul was silent. "Uh . . . I don't think their phone's been connected yet. They've been renting an apartment downtown, but just today they moved into one of the houseboats in our neighborhood. You know—the one with all the skylights. I do believe Sunne's slipping as official town crier," he finished wryly.

"We've both been busy lately," Brynn murmured. Just now she didn't want to think of having that man as a neighbor. Sam Court was arrogant. Sam Court was rude. And worse, he had enough money to move into a half-million-dollar houseboat—near her solid, old community where all the neighbors were also close friends.

Brynn's heart sank. Numbed by the news Paul had unwittingly imparted, she muttered a quick thank-you for his help and hung up, not pleased with what she'd heard.

Blindly she picked up the receiver again. She dialed her home number, needing to hear her brother's voice. Kevin, who'd once dreamed of a career in sports and who was a sweet, caring, generous person, would never be able to consider a house in Sam Court's price range because he'd likely be saddled for life with the ever-growing expense of his medical care.

A strident ring brought her a measure of comfort. As Brynn waited, she thought about Kevin's illness. Before becoming his guardian she'd never heard the term "nephrotic syndrome." Now she knew it only too well. She knew even better the escalating costs involved in treating Kevin's kidney ailment. Insurance had long since run out, and there never seemed to be enough money to cover the cost of his dialysis. She'd been siphoning from her savings for almost a year now, and only last week Dr. Low said they had to consider a transplant. The amount of money needed for transplanting a kidney was astronomical, and although she'd been told some help would be available through the local chapter of the Kidney Foundation, the needs of patients throughout the country were always greater than the funds.

Brynn shifted the little heap of silk lingerie that had been returned by Sam Court. Its meager profit wouldn't even buy her brother a day of medicine, much less an hour of dialysis. Still, she wouldn't dream of cheating a customer.

"Hello, Mrs. Flemming?" Brynn responded to the woman who answered the phone. "Why are you still there? Is something wrong with Kevin?" Brynn held her breath while her part-time housekeeper explained that due to the sudden storm, her ride had been delayed picking her up.

"Actually, I'm glad you're staying a while, Mrs. Flemming. I have a quick errand to run. It's nearby and I promise to hurry. I'm sure Kevin's already hooked up to his kidney machine, so I'd appreciate it if you would tell him that. I'll be home as quickly as I can."

She smiled at the older woman's tut-tutting. Mrs. Flemming was always insisting Brynn worked too hard. After saying goodbye, she stood and went to the closet for her raincoat. Yes, the only honorable thing to do was brave the wind and the rain long enough to return Holly Court's money. It sounded simple enough. And it meant no leftover guilt and no further contact with the Courts. End of Brynn Powell's ill-humor. What could be easier? she thought, mustering a wry smile.

Brynn stuffed the store checkbook deep in her leather handbag before turning out the last light. Almost as an after-thought, she plucked the returned cream-colored lingerie from her desk and slid it into a side pocket of her purse. There was still an underlying hope that the oaf's wife would make him reconsider and let his daughter keep the pretty undies.

Outside, the wind hit Brynn full-force, tearing loose the hair knotted on top of her head. Rain beat against her face, and puddles sucked greedily at her polished leather heels as she rounded the corner and stepped onto the main street. She sighed, wishing she'd brought her car to work.

A young couple hurried past her, going in the opposite direction. They were huddled together under a large um-brella, chatting and laughing. The man was doing his best to keep his companion warm and dry.

An uncharacteristic longing shot through Brynn. Slowing her steps, she turned and for a moment watched the young lovers proceed down the sidewalk. She hadn't considered leaning on any man like that—physically or emotionally—since her trust in Anthony Carraras proved to be misplaced. Why should she think of it now?

Idly Brynn turned up her collar and clutched the neckline tight. Sam Court's shoulders were broad and would be nice for leaning on, she mused . . . if it wasn't for the chip they carried. A chip sticking out a mile. But then, she just might be the one to knock it off. Brynn allowed herself a tiny smile as she con-templated his reaction.

Then, bending her head to brave the wind, Brynn picked up her pace and crossed the thoroughfare, at last approaching the street that led down to the houseboat's private dock. From nowhere, another consideration surfaced, flitting briefly through her head. *Watch out, Brynn Powell, you may have met your match.*

CHAPTER TWO

SAM COURT EASED into his allotted parking place near the exclusive settlement of houseboats much later than he'd planned. He slid from the Jaguar and hunched his shoulders against a cold blast of wind, then watched his silent thirteen-year-old daughter, Holly, slam the passenger door and dash toward the gate without looking his way.

Frowning, Sam followed Holly through the driving rain. The evening was definitely not starting out the way he'd envisioned his and Holly's first night in their new home. Had he put too much stock in this move, expecting it to turn back the clock for them?

Deep in thought, he pulled out the temporary identification card that gave him access to the restricted area and flashed it at the middle-aged guard. Holly was forced to wait, and Sam could tell from the stubborn set of her jaw that she was annoyed about it. As he tucked the card away, his lips pressed together in a straight line. Well, *he* was annoyed about the way she was acting. Bidding the guard a good evening, Sam pushed the iron gate and decided he should make an effort to clear the air and get their lives back to normal. "Holly—" he started, then broke off as she ran away from him along the slippery dock.

"Don't run, Holly," he shouted. "Be careful, or you'll fall."

"Daddy! When are you going to stop treating me like a child?" She flashed him a defiant glare.

Huddled in her coat, her slender shoulders bent against the wind, she looked to him like a colt about to break the traces. Life had sure been easier when she was five, when she'd idolized him and thought him invincible. Sam's jaw tensed.

"After all," Holly continued with a toss of her head, "they've moved me into tenth-grade algebra and English at my new school."

Sam brushed past her, leading the way down the ramp where he unlocked the houseboat door and thrust it open. "Super, Muffet." Pride seeped into his tone. He hesitated only long enough to shrug out of his topcoat before riffling her wet hair affectionately, the way he'd always done.

She pulled back. "Dad...I don't want you calling me Muffet anymore."

Sam's smile faded. He slammed the closet door, loosened his tie and skirted a mound of cardboard boxes in the living room, reaching for the single lamp he'd unpacked earlier in the day.

"Okay, let's have it, Holly. I've called you Miss Muffet since you were born. Is this show of temper because I returned that damned underwear?"

She kicked the toe of one shoe against a packing crate, refusing to look up.

Leaning close, Sam stared at her. "What's wrong with your eyes?" he asked abruptly.

"My eyes? Nothing. Why?" Holly blanched as she brought a hand to her face.

"Holly Court! Are you wearing eye makeup?" Sam reached out to touch the area below her eyebrow and drew back a finger smudged with purple. He fought the knot forming in his chest. This was what he'd always dreaded having to face with Holly—an absorption in her looks, the kind of selfish preoccupation his ex-wife had had. "Go wash your face," he said with deliberate calm, "then we'll go out for pizza and a talk." Pulling out a handkerchief, he rubbed the smudge from his finger.

"All the girls my age wear eye color and lip gloss, Dad," Holly said stubbornly. "Why can't I?"

"You don't need it." Sam felt his patience slip. "Why would you want to ruin such healthy skin?" His heart constricted as he watched her lips tremble and her eyes fill with tears. Damn, but he'd always been a sucker for her tears. With teeth clamped tight, he thrust out his chin and popped open the top button on his shirt. *Not this time!*

"You didn't have to take back my pretty underwear," Holly accused around a sniffle. "That wouldn't have ruined my skin. If I hadn't been showing it to Stacy's mom when you came to pick me up, you wouldn't even have known I bought it. The lady at the shop said if she had a daughter, it was what she'd buy."

Sam turned away, leaning one hand against the wooden frame of the double glass doors. The other rested on his hip in an unyielding stance. Holly's accusation brought vivid recall of his recent run-in with the leggy blond in the B.V.D. shop. This whole blow-up with Holly had come after a particularly rough practice. One that left his bones aching. On days like today, he doubly regretted whatever it was that had driven his ex-wife down a glittering road to show biz and hoped-for stardom, leaving him to struggle with raising their daughter alone.

"I don't intend to debate this issue, Holly." Sam waved a hand toward a curving staircase. "Go change out of your school clothes. We'll eat first and discuss my reasons later."

The tears fell unobstructed down Holly's cheeks. But after a moment when neither gave ground, she whirled, dodging between the boxes, and ran up the stairs.

When she'd gone, Sam rested his forehead against the cool glass. Massaging his tense neck, he stared indifferently at the rain pelting the dark water. Did teenage girls everywhere wear enough paint to cover a ship and enough powder to blow it up? He'd mistakenly thought these arguments would be left behind in L.A.—along with the Hollywood influence.

Sam watched lights from neighboring houseboats dance exotically across the choppy waves. He'd staked a lot on this career move and he was counting on the homey community of Frontage Bay to restore his and Holly's closeness. But was he counting too much on it? Could he really bridge the gap he'd felt widening between them? Had he been wrong in coming?

A loud buzz shattered Sam's moody thoughts, and it took him a moment to realize the noise came from an intercom connecting his houseboat with the security station. "Court." His abrupt response echoed hollowly through the speaker.

"Evening, Mr. Court." The guard's reedy voice crackled with static. It triggered a revival of Sam's tension.

"I've got a half-drowned lady up here asking to visit." Something in the man's tone made Sam wary.

"I'm not expecting anyone." He clicked off, then frowned and pushed the intercom button to ask, "Who is she?" No one but Paul and Sunne Evans knew he'd moved.

"She tells me it's business," tantalized the disembodied voice—a voice insinuating all too clearly that not for a moment did the guard believe *this* story.

Sam remembered that he had a housekeeping service coming tomorrow. They must have sent a representative. "Let her through," he agreed, though still somewhat reluctantly. Releasing the intercom button, he hurried toward the door. He'd intercept the poor woman, answer whatever questions she might have, and thereby save her a needless trip down the slippery ramp.

Sam hadn't realized the wind had whipped up considerably, enough to drive raindrops through his shirt, stinging his skin. One other thing he hadn't considered, as he lowered his head and ran, was that his visitor, battling the same gale, would come charging down the short ramp without looking. He nearly bowled the woman over.

As they collided soundly, she let out a surprised yelp, stumbled and fell heavily against him. Sam grabbed for her waist in an effort to steady them both.

Straightening, he gaped at the dripping wet stranger. For a moment, Sam saw only a pulse hammering furiously in the hollow of a creamy throat. Then, as he slowly recognized the woman from the lingerie shop, his own pulse began to escalate in anger.

"You," he growled. "What are you doing here?"

"Being manhandled by a boor," Brynn Powell answered tartly, tossing wet curls out of her eyes while trying to disengage herself from Sam Court's fierce and unwelcome grasp.

But his fingers merely tightened as he continued to glare at her through a slanting curtain of rain. For an instant Sam had a fleeting desire to throw her in the murky drink and show her what *boor* really meant. It was a desire that grew stronger as his gaze lingered on her full, red lips. Lips made appealingly moist by the falling rain. He didn't need the temptation of an alluring woman added to his already overloaded circuits. With a thunderous scowl Sam thrust her an arm's length away. "I repeat," he said harshly, "what are you doing here?"

"Not enjoying your charm and personality." She brushed his hand from her waist.

Before his last run-in with Holly, Sam had been regretting his verbal attack on this lady. It wasn't like him to lash out at a stranger. Sam stepped back. Now he remembered how this attractive blonde had come across in the store. She'd looked decidedly Victorian in the midst of all that erotic folderol. And she'd treated him with insufferable calm.

Brynn stalked past a stony-faced Sam, slipping and sliding down the ramp toward his door. "I'll discuss my business with your wife if you don't mind." Throwing him a haughty look, she raised her hand to knock.

Sam bounded after her, catching her wrist before she could rap on the door. "I do mind. Whatever your business, you'll take it up with me."

Brynn angled her chin a degree higher until she was in a position to watch a raindrop travel the length of his suntanned cheek. It came to rest in the shadowy cleft of his chin. Warmth flooded her face, and she retreated into the hostility she'd conjured up.

"The uncivilized, such as yourself, may conduct business on their doorsteps, Mr. Court, but I have the good sense to get in out of the rain." With a quick twist of her wrist, Brynn broke free of his hold, delivering the knock he'd prevented.

With murder in his eye, Sam reached around her, turned the doorknob and threw open the door. "By all means, my lady," he breathed, softly menacingly, "step into my parlor..."

"Said the spider to the fly," Brynn murmured automatically, continuing the old rhyme. She sidestepped him, needing to put space between herself and the rakish violet eyes that held her own in some kind of overt challenge. A challenge she didn't want to explore.

Shivering despite herself, Brynn stepped past him into a warm wood entryway. Struggling to gain composure, she stated why she'd come. "You left my shop without Holly's refund, Mr Court. I'm here to return her money. I assume Mrs. Court advanced your daughter the cash, as you obviously did not."

"You assume a lot," Sam grated, slamming the door behind him. "Holly," he shouted over her head, forcing Brynn deeper into the dimly lit interior. "Holly, come down here please."

Brynn's eyes turned toward the curved oak staircase. She had never seen the inside of this particular houseboat, though she'd long admired its unique architecture. She'd always imagined it had a skylight in the master suite where one could lie in bed and count the stars overhead on a clear night.

Brynn brought herself up short. What had provoked such an outrageous thought?

"Obviously you know more about me than I know about you." Sam spoke from directly behind her. "Is it too much to ask that you give me your name?"

Brynn turned to comply. But no sound emerged from her mouth. Sam Court had removed his rain-splotched tie and dropped it in a puddle on the floor. Now, unself-consciously, he was in the process of shedding his wet shirt. Shrugging out of it, he stood before her, shaking water from his dark hair like a wet puppy. Before Brynn could blink, he was using his navy blue undershirt as a towel.

Her mouth went dry. Compared to the night outside, the houseboat suddenly seemed unbearably warm, and she absently began to unbutton her raincoat. Earlier, in her shop, she'd guessed the man was well-built, but to see his chest— tanned, evenly muscled and dusted in all the right places with crisp, dark hair—well, Brynn wasn't prepared for that.

The only flaw she could see in Sam Court's otherwise Adonislike physique, was a long white scar running from his left shoulder to the inside of one elbow and a second scar following the upper ridge of his collar bone on the opposite side.

Hockey! Brynn wet her lips and forced herself to think about the sport that was probably responsible for Sam Court's scars. *Ice. Skates.* Nothing more intelligent would come. She'd ask Kevin. He was crazy about the sport. Crazy about all sports. He'd been something of an athlete, too, until illness struck.

"Well, are you going to tell me your name or not?" Sam's voice held a ripple of unmistakable laughter.

"You find my returning your money amusing?" Brynn asked, still following the play of muscles beneath his skin. "Where's Holly?" She didn't like the breathless quality of her voice. Nor did she like her next thought—that Sam Court's skin looked warm. Touchable. It had been a long time since she'd touched a man's skin. Not since Anthony Carraras. Anthony, who had promised he'd take care of her forever. Anthony, who'd left a string of women holding empty promises. All at once, Brynn realized the silence in the room had lengthened and Sam Court was watching her expectantly.

"What?" Feeling a blush that started at her toes, she toyed with the belt on her coat, trying to appear nonchalant.

"Name. What. Is. Your. Name." He enunciated clearly, eyeing her with a faintly mocking smile. "Or perhaps I should call you Madame X, considering the business you're in." He threw back his head in a deep laugh that tapered off when Brynn glared at him. "Don't get huffy," he chided. "I was going to say 'Goldilocks' might be more appropriate if that was truly a blush I caught."

"Daddy," a voice called from above. "Did you want me?"

Brynn jumped, turning toward the sound as Holly Court came into sight trailing one finger along the banister of the curved oak staircase.

The teenager paused in the middle of her descent, shock registering in her eyes.

"M-Miss Powell?" She stuttered Brynn's name, darting a nervous glance from their visitor to her father, then back again. Holly nibbled at her lower lip, and her eyes grew wide and wary.

"Hello, Holly." Brynn faced the somber-looking girl directly, relieved to find some of her own uneasiness fading now that she was no longer alone with Sam Court. She could have hugged the girl. "But please...everyone calls me Brynn," she said with a smile. "Are you enjoying your new home, Holly?"

Even as she asked, Brynn studied the luxurious interior of the living room, taking in the warm, hand-crafted cedar walls and colorful stained-glass panels flanking either side of double glass doors. The interior breathed money. She cleared her throat and offered more small talk. "Moving is never easy, Holly, but you couldn't have come to a lovelier place. The bay has a charm all its own."

"Kevin would like to visit." Holly's lashes dropped, hiding her eyes.

Behind her, Brynn felt Sam's interest perk. Hers did, too. "I didn't know you and Kevin were acquainted."

"Who's Kevin?" Sam stepped out and looked from one to the other. "Is that the same Kevin you were dratting when I walked in on you today?"

Brynn didn't answer. Neither did Holly. Instead, the girl approached Brynn nervously. "Kevin's been telling me how much he'd like to sit on our deck to watch the yachts go through the passage. From his bedroom, he can't quite see the channel. I said, if it's all right with my dad, he can come over some Saturday. That is—" she frowned "—if he's feeling up to it." Her words trailed off as she glanced doubtfully at Brynn. "Of course, it would have to be okay with you, too."

"Who's Kevin?" Sam repeated, showing more than a hint of resentment. "Is he your son? And what would Holly know about his bedroom?" Sam's gaze was on his daughter, but it was plain the query had been intended for Brynn. At least, he'd finally learned the woman's name. Brynn Powell. Brynn. But had Holly called her Miss or Mrs.? Sam couldn't remember. He mulled the name over in his mind and found it to his liking.

"Kevin is my younger brother," Brynn replied softly, her heart in sympathy with Holly's self-consciousness. What was it costing the young girl to open up in front of a father who seemed to form snap judgments? And he *did* form snap judgments, if his perpetual scowl was anything to go by.

"How is it that Holly knows him? Why have I never heard of this young man before?"

Sam Court was making his authoritative presence felt. He was beginning to sound very much like a father. Brynn saw

Holly's chin lift in a stubborn way that resembled the attitude she'd glimpsed earlier in the man himself.

She didn't know how Kevin and Holly's friendship had come about. Kevin had never mentioned the girl that she could recall, but she made a logical guess in an attempt to ease the tension building between father and daughter. "Kevin has a kidney ailment, Mr. Court. Stacy Evans brings his lessons and returns them to school when he isn't able to attend. Since the girls are obviously friends, I imagine that's how Holly met him."

Brynn didn't see any need to mention the endless, painful tests involved in matching Kevin with a possible kidney donor—crossmatching, they called it. A perfect specimen of manhood like Sam Court wouldn't be interested in hearing about her agonizing wait to see if she would be the desired match. She was in this alone. Kevin had no one else.

She swallowed a sudden taste of fear and turned to see how Sam Court was reacting to the information. "Aren't you cold?" she snapped without thinking.

At first he looked annoyed. Then the look became a rakish grin and the grin spread, creating deep creases along each side of his well-shaped lips. The effect was to soften his face, so stern and forbidding only a moment before. Brynn experienced a very real yearning to touch one of the laugh lines and follow it down his cheek. Frowning, she stepped back, reminding herself she'd lingered far too long at this task. She began digging through her handbag until she found the store's checkbook and hauled it out.

"The refund, Mr. Court," Brynn whispered. "Perhaps I'll just make it out to Holly." Clearing her throat, she raised her voice. "According to my records, I owe someone in this household forty-five dollars and twenty-three cents." She pushed a tendril of hair away from her eyes and scrambled in her bag again until she found a pen. The man was a jock. A superhero, undoubtedly used to women falling all over him. Well, she would look for more substance in a man, if and when she had energy enough to pursue one.

Sam was intrigued with the way she was blushing and trying not to show it. Blushing seemed a little strange for a woman who made her living selling the things he'd seen in her shop. He studied the damp halo of gold beginning to curl around her head, remembering how she'd twisted an errant lock around and around one finger when she'd faced him in the cozy back room of her shop. Sharply, Sam reminded himself that he wasn't in the market for a woman in his life. Should that ever change, his lady of choice wouldn't hawk filmy underwear.

A cold breeze lifted the hair on his forearms, and he muttered, "Holly, do me a favor, please. Grab me a clean shirt out of my closet. Any one you can find will do."

Holly hesitated a moment, looking as if she wanted to protest. Apparently thinking better of it, she trudged up the stairs.

Thank goodness he was going to get dressed, Brynn thought. Seated on a packing crate, using her purse as a writing surface, she found Sam's unblinking appraisal unnerving.

"Will your wife be home shortly, Mr. Court?" she pressed, though she was beginning to have strong suspicions that there was no Mrs. Sam Court—at least, not in residence. When he didn't answer right away, she glanced up.

He stood silently contemplating her. Sam wasn't sure how to answer her question. He decided to remain evasive—his protective barrier against something he could feel taking shape between them. "I make all the decisions affecting my household," he said coolly. "You'll deal with me or not at all."

Damn the woman! He'd come off sounding like a tyrant. Sam watched pity break through Brynn's controlled expression—pity for his daughter. In a frosty voice, he said, "Nothing concerning my family is any of your business. I suggest you save your sympathy for someone who needs it. I certainly don't."

Brynn's eyes blazed in response. "I'd feel sorry for any teenager stuck with an intolerant chauvinist for a father, Mr. Court. Are you aware how hard it is for a girl to develop self-esteem at any age, without encountering roadblocks at home?"

"Is that right? What makes you the world's leading authority?" Sam advanced on Brynn, only to discover she'd dismissed him and returned to her writing. "It may interest you to know, Ms. Busybody, that my daughter and I rarely disagree. In fact I can count on one hand the number of arguments we've had. Which includes, I might add, today's ripping disagreement over your unholy underwear." As he spoke, Sam idly traced an old scar paralleling his collar bone. When it rained hard, as it had today, the bone ached like fury. What he needed—if this troublesome woman would ever leave—was a long soak in his newly acquired hot tub. Sighing, he closed his eyes and rocked back on his heels. When his eyes snapped open, he met Brynn's smoldering gaze squarely. Almost glowering, he strode toward the bottom of the stairs. "Holly! What in the devil is keeping you? I didn't mean you should iron one."

Brynn's gaze shifted away from the hockey player's powerful naked torso. His lack of modesty was appalling. Fumbling in her bag, she pulled out the cream-colored undies. Normally she knew stock numbers by heart, but tonight they totally escaped her. What didn't escape her was that Sam Court followed a different set of rules than the ones he set down for his daughter.

Holly's step on the stairs drew Brynn's attention. She recognized the wistful longing in the young girl's eyes, and knew that Holly's father had to have witnessed her yearning, too. He was reaching for his shirt at the very moment the girl had allowed her guard to drop. What, if anything, was he feeling now, when his daughter's disappointment was so open, so acute? Despite herself, Brynn suffered a pang for both father and daughter.

Quickly she finished writing her check. Ripping it out, she stood and tucked the undergarments back into her bag as discreetly as possible. She'd been wrong to come. Wrong to interfere. If the shoe was on the other foot—her foot—Brynn admitted that she wouldn't welcome Sam Court's coming between her and Kevin. Still, she was sure Holly could use some sort of positive comment just now. Fastening her raincoat, Brynn gave Holly a reassuring smile. "I've been sitting here thinking how pretty your hair is tonight, Holly, feathered around your face like that. Cut shorter, I think it would look thicker and have a lot of natural curl."

In the middle of Brynn's compliment, the lights in the houseboat flickered. They blinked briefly a second time, then went out altogether.

"Daddy?" Holly's voice floated through the darkness, ending on a note of panic.

"It's only the storm, Muffet. Don't move. I have a penlight in my duffel bag. I'll only be a minute." Sam's gravelly voice reached out through the darkened room. Steady and reassuring.

Brynn dashed toward the front entrance and bumped solidly into Sam. "Is the power outage confined to your houseboat?" she asked, alarm sneaking into her voice, "or is the entire area out?" Her fingers curled into the warm flesh of his arm.

"Staying put goes for you, too." Sam thrust Brynn away without answering her question.

"You don't understand. I need to telephone home." She pushed past him, her breathing ragged. "Kevin is on his kidney machine. He needs me—ooh!" She tripped over a packing crate and lost her balance.

"Daddy!" Holly had edged farther down the stairs, and the fright in her voice increased.

Catching Brynn off balance, Sam yanked her against his side. "If both of you will do as I say, everything will be fine," he said tersely. "Our telephone hasn't been connected, but all three of us will go outside and check out what's going on. Holly, follow my voice." Within seconds, Sam had assumed complete control and moved them outside into a world enveloped in stormy darkness.

In other circumstances, Brynn might have resented his take-charge attitude. And she certainly would have reacted to the feel of his body against hers. But now all her concerns centered on Kevin, stranded and possibly in danger. She stumbled going up the ramp, this time smacking her nose against Sam's broad back.

"Easy. Take it easy," he admonished, reaching for her hand. He'd given Holly the penlight to carry and had one hand clasped firmly on the girl's shoulder. As Brynn's eyes adjusted to the dark, she could see Holly pulling up the hood of a gray sweatshirt. Somehow, it reminded her that she belonged at home, finding Kevin's jacket, getting him to the hospital. Not here relying on strangers.

"Can't you hurry?" Brynn exclaimed, moving out of his warm grasp.

"And break my neck? You'd like that, I suppose," Sam muttered sarcastically. "Holly, watch your step there. Is everyone on the main dock now? Careful! Slow down. I don't want anyone getting hurt."

Wind howling off the dark bay slammed into them with a vengeance and tore at their clothing. Rain peppered them from all directions. Brynn huddled behind Sam, shivering as they crept along the slippery dock. It seemed to take forever. She could hear waves whacking against the pilings. Sam was right to go slowly. Her heel hit a crack and she twisted her ankle. She cried out, then immediately bit her lip to stifle the sound.

"Did you hurt yourself?" Sam gripped her elbow.

"I'm fine," she lied. "Please . . . we must hurry."

"We'll call for help from the gate. Look, the guard already has a lantern burning."

Brynn couldn't remember ever appreciating a sliver of light and a working telephone more. But as Kevin's illness progressed, she was learning to count even the smallest blessing.

Moments later, Sam, Holly and the guard all clustered around her as he dialed and they hovered anxiously until she finished speaking. She exhaled slowly. "Lucky thing for me, our housekeeper was delayed due to the storm," she explained. "Kevin's already on his way to the hospital. I want to thank you all for your concern. I'll just walk home, get my car and be on my way."

"Is Kevin going to be okay?" Holly's face was drained of color.

"Don't worry, Holly. Kevin's been through this before. The paramedics, bless them, know exactly what to do." Turning to Sam, she added, "The main danger comes from his heparin pump shutting down in the middle of dialysis. Heparin thins his blood. When the power goes off and the pump shuts down, all the lines carrying his blood have to be disconnected and cleared of clots and all impurities filtered out. The risk of blood loss and infection are high. But I'm confident he'll be just fine now.'' Saying it aloud reassured her as much as it did Holly.

''All the traffic signals are out. You're not walking anywhere. We'll take you to the hospital.'' Sam thanked the guard and beckoned Holly and Brynn to follow him.

''You don't have to do that. I'll need my car later to bring Kevin home.'' But even as Brynn protested, Sam hustled her up the slope and thrust her into his Jaguar.

The first thing to strike Brynn was that it smelled like new leather. Second was that she was shaking like a leaf. She hadn't realized how weak her knees were until she sank into the butter-soft leather seats. Would she have made it home up the long hill?

''Which way?'' Sam asked, glancing over his shoulder, reminding Holly to buckle her seat belt.

Brynn gave him detailed directions, uncomfortable under his direct gaze. She was relieved when at last she spied the lights of Emerald City Hospital burning in the distance like a handful of jewels displayed on black velvet. But of course the hospital had its own generator. She let a deep sigh escape.

''Does your ankle hurt?'' Sam shot her another piercing look.

''No—not much. Actually, I was thinking how kind you've been . . . considering.''

Sam allowed a tiny smile to surface as he pulled his car beneath the awning of the hospital's well-lit entrance. ''Considering I'm a pigheaded, chauvinistic boor and uncivilized to boot?'' Not giving her time to reply, he jumped out, sped around the hood and opened her door. Keeping a straight face, he motioned Holly over. ''We'll go in with Miss Powell, Holly, just to make sure everything's all right.''

''No.'' Brynn put up a staying hand. ''Don't bother coming in with me. It's a school night for Holly, and I've kept you from your unpacking as it is. I've been through this before— not a lot, but I'm no stranger to the emergency room. Oh . . .'' She paused. ''I almost forgot. Your refund.'' Brynn was somewhat embarrassed to find his check still crumpled in her hand. "I should be the one to apologize. I was wrong to infringe . . . but I didn't call you pigheaded."

Sam shut Holly's door firmly, indicating that she should remain in the car, then escorted Brynn to the entrance. Pausing under the lights, he casually helped himself to the delicate lace undies still stuffed in the side pocket of her bag. The row of tiny pink rosebuds stood out clearly as he folded them into one large hand.

"There are valid reasons why I believe Holly doesn't need these, Miss Powell. The issue goes much deeper than mere underwear. But tonight, I find that her happiness is more important than any of my reasons."

He calmly ripped the check in half and lifted Brynn's hand, curling her fingers around the pieces of paper. He held her closed fist for a moment in his own. "A wise man is one who takes a wise woman's advice on occasion, Brynn Powell. I'm the one who owes you an apology. Are you quite certain you won't need my help getting Kevin home?"

Brynn nodded, eyes widening. Her hand lay comfortably in his larger one, and for the first time, she didn't have a ready comeback.

Accepting her silence, Sam nodded. Without further comment, he withdrew his hand and returned to his car.

Holly waved goodbye out the side window as her father drove through the emergency loading zone.

Sam didn't look back once.

When she could no longer see the Jag's taillights winking in the distance, Brynn shook herself out of a stupor and stuffed the pieces of the check into her coat pocket. It was hard knowing what to make of a man she had fully intended to hate, a man who first sparked her anger, but who suddenly seemed human enough, appealing enough, to leave her tingling inside.

Abruptly, Brynn gave herself a mental shake. Tingling feelings didn't pay bills. And men like Sam Court didn't stick around when the going turned rough. How well she knew that.

With Kevin's problems, life would probably get a lot rougher before it got better. He deserved all her spare energy—and goodness knew there was precious little to spare, she reminded herself harshly, turning to go inside.

CHAPTER THREE

BRYNN KNEW HER WAY AROUND the sterile corridors of the sprawling hospital. Most of the nurses in the kidney treatment center called her by name. Because of his good nature, Kevin was everyone's favorite, and Brynn loved the hospital staff, one and all. They'd been her salvation. Brynn, without any training or experience, was thrust into the role of single parent to a chronically ill adolescent a year before. Her parents had both died in a car accident, and she'd had to deal not only with her grief but with Kevin's illness.

Tonight's visit was almost routine for Kevin, and he was always much better about taking such things in stride than she was. Once his blood tests had been completed and his condition stabilized, they left the ward. Of the two, Brynn seemed the more exhausted. Her day had started at five o'clock; it was well after midnight when a cab dropped them at home. She was dead on her feet and still had to settle Kevin in his bed before calling it a night. At least electrical power had been restored while they were at the hospital.

Finding Kevin's bed proved to be a challenge. Brynn sighed heavily as she glanced around her brother's room. When she was feeling generous, and tonight she wasn't, she would say Kevin's room looked "lived in." Now, because they'd debated the same issue so often and she was tired, she let him know she wasn't pleased with the clutter. "Messy, Kevin." She pointed to an unmade bed strewn with books, cassettes and dirty clothes. "How can you live in this...this pigpen? Did you sweet-talk Mrs. Flemming out of cleaning in here today?" Swinging her arm to encompass the lot, her gaze fell on a new poster tacked to Kevin's wall. A giant poster. She broke off in the middle of her tirade and simply stared at a glossy life-size picture of Sam Court.

"What is this?"

Kevin ambled up behind her. "An autographed picture of the Samurai, Sis. He's a defenseman on our new hockey team. Can you believe my luck? He's going to live right down the hill from us. Holly Court, his kid, is a friend of Stacy's. They brought me this poster yesterday. It rounds out my sports gallery, don't you agree? I didn't have a single hockey poster, and this one's even signed."

Brynn stepped closer. The picture didn't do the man justice. It was an action shot, but obviously posed. His helmet was off and someone had been trying to capture a macho image, no doubt. Brynn sniffed disdainfully. They'd let his hair curl over his forehead, as though he'd been sweating, and he was staring intensely at the puck. Did he bring that intensity only to the game? Brynn couldn't help wondering.

Unexpectedly her spine tingled. He would be a man of many facets, she thought, studying the print. Ice sprayed from the blades of his skates. The padding made him look bigger, yet the raw power she'd sensed when he shed his shirt earlier in his living room was missing. Still, this picture was bound to draw women. Come to think of it, he never had given her a straight answer concerning the whereabouts of his wife. To look at this shot, no one would ever guess him to be a husband or a father. Brynn suddenly realized that behind her Kevin was talking.

"So what do you think, Sis?" He was inspecting the dressing over his cannula—the implant of polyurethane tubing that, when connected to the machine, carried his blood to be cleansed.

"About what, Kevin? Is something wrong with your cannula?"

"No!" He threw up his hands and grimaced in disgust. "I'm talking about me visiting the Courts on their houseboat, maybe next Saturday. Haven't you heard a word I said?"

Brynn examined his eager face. The puffiness that had been present when she'd first returned home to take over the household had subsided, and he'd lost the telltale yellowish cast to his skin. The dialysis seemed to be working well. But this was the first time in months Brynn had seen boyish excitement in his eyes.

"If Holly's father agrees," she murmured, smoothing a lock of Kevin's fine, blond hair. It crossed her mind that she was making a mistake...but then it didn't really matter how she felt about Sam Court. Since she'd come home, there hadn't been time to allow Kevin a social life—not that she had one herself, but she didn't want to think about that now. "How did Holly happen to invite you?"

With a show of annoyance at her mothering, Kevin pushed her hand away. "Holly's new in town and kind of lonely, but she's also real smart. She's a genius at algebra. Do you know they moved her a year ahead in school? I like this kid," he mumbled. "She doesn't goo up her face or worry how she looks all the time, either. I'll bet Dad would have been impressed with her."

"Well, that's understandable. Professors like intelligence. But Dad wasn't just another egghead. Paul tells me he never missed a single one of your soccer games."

"You know, Brynn," Kevin said, turning serious, "suppose I *am* lucky enough to have spare parts surgery. I'll never be anything more than a spectator. Dr. Low said I had to be realistic. The chances of getting an injury in contact sports are pretty high, and that's a killer for someone with only one good kidney."

Tears sprang to Brynn's eyes. She reached up quickly to wipe them away. Kevin wouldn't appreciate her feeling sorry for him, and she didn't want it, either. She just wished she could be as positive as he was and as matter-of-fact about the prospect of a transplant. But then, maybe she would be, if the medical team determined that she was a fitting donor.

Kevin slid an arm around her waist. "I try not to, but sometimes I get scared thinking about my future. You know what I mean?"

Brynn's throat tightened. Pulling away, she punched him softly on the upper arm. "Hey, enough of that, okay? We Powells are tough." She walked toward the poster of Sam Court, tugging off her coat as she went. Her blood quickened just looking at the picture. "Tough," she said louder, thinking it would be all too easy to seek solace from a man of his strength. Sharply, Brynn reminded herself that some men took rather than gave, and she had no energy for another taker.

To Kevin she remarked aloud, "In order to stay tough, my man, even Powells need to sleep. Suppose you hit the sack. And no reading under the covers with a flashlight, hear?"

"I hear," he answered, reaching for his pajamas.

YAWNING, BRYNN TORE A SHEET of drawing paper from the pad and after gazing at it critically from several angles, crushed it into a tight ball and tossed it into the wastebasket.

The renaissance nightgown she'd been planning in her head for several weeks wasn't taking shape on paper. She set aside pad and pencil, stood up, stretched, then crossed the room to where an overworked coffee maker gave a final gurgle.

She poured herself a cup, then leaned against the wall to drink it. She stared at the dark liquid, seeking answers to her dilemma, but the coffee emitted no genie—only steam. Her frazzled nerves didn't need the extra caffeine this morning even though she probably wouldn't stay awake without it. She didn't like admitting that her ragged nerves were a direct result of her sleepless night. A night during which visions of Sam Court kept popping up between the woolly sheep she'd been trying to count. It had been absolutely maddening to find herself still wide awake when Kevin's alarm jangled.

Pulling a wry face because the memory annoyed her, Brynn sipped almost scalding coffee, not deriving half the pleasure she usually experienced from that first morning cup.

It was all Sam Court's fault, she fumed, for coming in here before closing. Brynn knew that blaming him for her lost sleep was unreasonable. Still, there was no denying it, the thought of him moving into her neighborhood had interrupted her sleep. And now the lack of sleep was affecting her ability to create. Or was the phone call she'd received from Doctor Low's office early that morning the real reason for her tension and hampered creativity? The bell over the shop entrance announced her first customer of the day before Brynn could decide which.

She took a hurried last swallow, considering that since her midweek ad had come out in the morning paper, it might be her last break for the day.

"Brynn? Are you back here, Brynn?" Sunne Evans poked her head around the door, nearly colliding with Brynn in the process.

"Sunne! What a surprise." Brynn gave her friend an enthusiastic hug. "I thought I was going to have to send you an engraved invitation, it's been so long," she teased. "Hey, you're just in time for coffee."

"Ah, coffee! The word is music to my ears. As usual, my house was pure bedlam this morning. I poured three cups and all three got cold before I pushed that crew of mine out the door." Sunne accepted the steaming cup Brynn handed her, closing her eyes and inhaling the aroma.

Brynn laughed. "You wouldn't trade a minute of that chaos and you know it. But isn't this your aerobics morning? What gives?"

Sunne opened her raincoat, revealing a perky red-and-white leotard and tights outfit. "I'm all ready, as you see. I just came by to gossip. We haven't done that in a blue moon."

Reclining against her work desk, Brynn stared at the floor, fearing she knew exactly what subject her old friend was about to broach.

Sunne pushed aside a stack of lingerie and helped herself to the lone armchair. She looked at Brynn expectantly.

"Oh, come on, Brynn! Aren't you going to tell me what you thought of Paul's college friend? I happen to know you met Sam Court last night, you sly little devil. You must have made a good impression, because when we ran into him at the pizza place after he'd given you a lift to the hospital, Sam agreed to let Holly take your class." She rolled her eyes heavenward. "He'd been dead set against it before."

Brynn choked on her coffee. "You never once mentioned anyone new in the neighborhood, Sunne. When you called me about adding a new student, you were positively vague. I assumed it was another girl from Stacy's music group."

"I didn't think it made any difference who she was, Brynn. And I figured you'd meet Sam around the neighborhood once they got settled into their new home. But isn't he yummy, Brynn? Famous. Rich. Good-looking. Eligible." Sunne accentuated each word. Her sales pitch was unmistakable.

"Sunne!" Brynn stalked across the room to the coffee maker and with her back to the other woman, poured herself a fresh cup. Her heart gave a funny little flip. But Sunne was only confirming what she'd really suspected all along—there was no Mrs. Court. When coffee splashed over the edge of the cup, Brynn couldn't blame caffeine for her unsteady hands. "I'm not interested in hearing about Sam Court's attributes or his marital status, Sunne."

Well, maybe that was a teensy lie. She'd like to know, but asking would only encourage Sunne's matchmaking efforts, so instead, Brynn tried for a cavalier approach. "I don't have time to think about any man in the way you mean. I already feel guilty because Kevin's lost so much. He needs any free time I have."

"Hogwash!" Sunne walked over and placed her cup on the counter. "You're cracking under the load. Since you've come home I've watched you take on more and more. You've lost weight, and if you'd look in the mirror you'd see the dark circles under your eyes. What you need, my friend, is an occasional night with a good man to loosen you up. I want you to knock the Samurai's eyes out at our annual Halloween party. I'm giving you more than a month to get ready. With your flair for design, I don't expect to see you wearing that disgusting costume you borrowed last year from Louise Cavanaugh."

"Sunne!" Brynn gasped. It was no secret how Sunne had felt about her costume. But even for Sunne, the suggestion of spending an occasional night with a good man was outrageously bold. Brynn's cup wobbled. Sunne had been matchmaking since she first learned to talk—and she really believed that her friends couldn't possibly be happy if they didn't become half of a pair.

Snatching the cup from Brynn's fingers, Sunne set it down and hooked an arm through Brynn's tense one, smiling devilishly.

"Now don't Sunne me in that tone of voice. I'm right and you know it. But if I don't scoot now, I'll be late for my class.

Never fear, I'll be back. I want you to make an appointment to have your hair and nails done, perhaps even a massage. It'll take about a month to get color in your cheeks again. Lord knows I do volunteer work all over this town—why not here?''

Brynn balked. "I'm not a project. And after Anthony, I'm not sure I want another man." She extricated herself from Sunne's hold, then with a little sigh caught her friend's sleeve. "I could use you to watch the shop this afternoon, Sunne, but not so I can pamper myself. Dr. Low's office phoned. They want me to come in later to go over the crossmatch tests. The nurse wouldn't tell me anything over the telephone. I'm so worried."

"Oh, Brynn." Sunne's smile faded. "Of course I'll help. All you ever have to do is ask. I'm not trying to minimize your situation; you know that. You're doing a great job with Kevin. I just happen to think you also need time for a personal life. I never liked that smooth-talking Carraras. But I thought he was your chance to break into the big time, so I hoped for the best." Sunne's voice failed, and she hugged her friend tight. "Oh, hey, I'll be here the minute the kids get home from school."

Brynn nodded, swallowing the lump in her throat.

Two customers came in and began browsing. Sunne stopped at the door, exchanging her worried look for a bright smile. "I'll see you at three," she said. "And I'll probably buy out the shop while you're gone. It's dangerous to turn me loose with all this new merchandise. Is Paul ever in for a treat when we go on vacation." She breezed through the door, leaving Brynn with a wink and a grin. "Chin up, my friend."

Brynn shook her head, realizing she, too, had begun to smile. Sunne always made her laugh. It was impossible to remain upset with her for long. She'd been like that as far back as Brynn could remember. Despite the reservations Sunne confessed to now, she'd been the one who first promoted Anthony's promise of a dream job at Luminaire—but then none of them had known he was quite so adept at lying. Sunne always meant well, but in this case, she couldn't possibly imagine what an evening with the man known as the Samurai would bring. "Flint striking flint, making fire, that's what," Brynn muttered, hurrying to help a waiting customer.

SAM STARED AT THE FORM Holly had given him after school. A paper outlining the points Miss—no, he supposed it should be Ms.—Brynn Powell's self-esteem classes would cover. He couldn't believe that in a weak moment last night he'd agreed to let Holly attend. Paul Evans must have poured one too many beers for him out of the pitcher they'd shared at the pizza parlor; otherwise he would have held his ground. And given this small community, he should have guessed Paul's wife would be a close friend of Ms. Powell's.

It was a simple enough form, Sam supposed, only requiring his signature and an attached check. He didn't need to see the woman again if he didn't want to, because Holly had said Sunne Evans would return the form for her. So why this vacillation on his part? he wondered.

Sam tilted back his chair and put his feet on the desk. He touched the fresh cut under his left eye gingerly before lacing his hands behind his head to begin nothing more than a mindless study of the neat grooves connecting the boards in the knotty pine ceiling. Lately he'd been plagued by a strange melancholy.

There was plenty he should be doing instead of daydreaming, Sam admitted. But he'd been at the bottom of a four-man pileup at practice and, among other things, had taken the tip of someone's blade under the lower edge of his face shield. Already his knee ached, his ribs were taped so tightly he could hardly breathe, and his left thigh was turning black and blue. The only activity he wanted right now was to relax and let the warmth and comfort of his snug new home sink into his weary bones. Times like this, he gave more than a passing thought to getting out of hockey. In California, he'd been ready. Then this new team had called with an offer that seemed to provide him with the perfect answer. It meant he could give Holly roots in a new, slower-paced community, a place with a strong sense of neighborhood and traditional values. Paul Evans had always made Seattle sound ideal. But to Sam, roots meant marriage. Or in his case, remarriage. Had he licked his wounds enough?

Surely all women weren't obsessed by beauty. Weren't some the domestic sort?

Yet he and Holly weren't doing so badly alone. It wasn't as though his place was a totally masculine domain. The housekeeping crew he'd hired had done a good job, adding a woman's touch here and there, a bit of warmth and brightness. Yes, Sam thought, smiling, he was going to like the houseboat—and Frontage Bay. Then suddenly his smile gave way to a frown.

One possible serpent in his paradise was a nasty rumor he'd heard at practice. A rumor that the team was going to be sold almost before it got off the ground. It was unsettling, to say the least. Half the reason he'd jumped at this opportunity was to build a solid foundation in a nice community while he took time to decide what he wanted to do with the rest of his life. A new team owner might see his age as a liability. Those were real problems facing him. So why was he sunk in this moody speculation over one lousy form and a woman he didn't really know? Or was it all connected with a nagging worry that somehow life was passing him by?

In L.A., one sports announcer hinted that at thirty-three, the Samurai was getting too old to play. When his body ached like this, Sam felt inclined to agree. Perhaps he should consider a coaching offer after all. He liked kids. Maybe he could get them early enough to instill a few things, like skill and sportsmanship—which had fallen by the wayside in hockey, he felt.

On his desk, Brynn Powell's form fluttered, catching his eye. Sam scowled. Dropping his feet to the floor, he grimaced as the chair snapped forward, causing him pain.

Ms. Powell's classes promised to teach his daughter things like developing a positive self-image, the art of meaningful conversation and the proper care of hair, skin and nails. Overall, her six-week course promised to stress the attainment of confidence and a sense of self-worth.

Now that was a lot of teaching, Sam mused, toying with the paper. Holly looked fine to him the way she was. But this list . . . weren't those all things mothers usually passed on to their daughters? Or was that chauvinistic thinking on his part?

A trait he possessed in abundance—or so Brynn Powell had been quick to point out to him last night.

Hell, where was all this self-flagellation getting him? He had no idea how to go about teaching Holly any of that stuff. And she'd smiled like the Holly of old when he'd given his okay for her to attend the damn course. What could be the harm in it? Before he could change his mind, Sam scribbled his name on the bottom of the paper, then reached for the checkbook he'd used to pay the housekeeping firm.

Maybe Brynn Powell would like to come teach him how to manage a home for his daughter without a full-time house-keeper as he'd had in California. Especially since Ms. Powell's form implied she was such a super woman. He chuckled to himself at the very idea.

Holly's sudden wail interrupted Sam's train of thought. His first fear was that she'd hurt herself. His heart leaped into this throat and lodged there. Running hard in spite of his own pain, he met her at the foot of the stairs. Stacy Evans was just leaving, closing the front door behind her. Sam opened his arms to Holly, wondering if the girls had just had a tiff.

"Daddy," Holly sobbed, slamming against his chest so hard his teeth rattled. "I've ruined my hair. It's just awful. Now what am I going to do?"

Sam held her at arm's length. After his heart slid back to its rightful place and resumed regular beating, his first inclination was to strangle her. At some point between the time she'd come through the door after school and this moment, Holly had chopped off every strand of her long, brown hair. What was left stuck out raggedly all over her head. She hadn't been quite accurate in her assessment, Sam realized, biting his tongue. It looked worse than awful.

Only the utter dejection in her eyes and the steady trickle of tears streaking her cheeks kept him from demanding a full explanation.

"Uh..." Sam cleared his throat. "What result did you have in mind when you started this project, Holly?"

"I told Stacy what Ms. Powell said last night about my hair, and she agreed. Only Stacy said it would look a lot better if I had it cut real short all over." Holly sobbed louder. "She said it would be simple because we found this picture in a magazine. But it doesn't look like the picture at all."

Sam felt his anger building. Brynn Powell didn't have to work at sabotage, he thought grimly, it came naturally with her suggestions. As if the woman's frivolous undies hadn't caused him enough trouble, now she'd perpetrated this.

"Get your coat, Holly," he said in a carefully controlled voice. "One of the items on your Ms. Powell's outline is a section on hair care. I think we'll start your instruction early and get that lesson first."

"All right, Daddy," Holly agreed meekly, scrubbing the tears away. "Do you really think she can make it look good again?"

Sam was about to say that she damn well better, but knowing how fragile Holly's ego was at this moment left him biting back the retort. Dammit, when he was thirteen, his free time had been spent playing junior hockey. Compared to this fiasco, his mother's job of doling out Band-Aids sounded like a treat. Then he remembered how she'd always worried about the possibility of broken bones and stitches. Strange how, these days, he had developed a new respect for a mother's role.

Following Holly out the door, Sam found himself praying Brynn Powell could salvage this hatchet job. Though he didn't know much about cutting hair, even he knew Holly's would present a monumental challenge.

Minutes later, Sam approached the lingerie shop feeling his heartbeat quicken in anticipation. On the short ride up the hill, with Holly sniffling beside him, he'd had time to think about what he was doing and why.

Brynn Powell wasn't at fault in the matter of Holly's hair, nor did her flyer indicate in any way that she cut or styled hair. Technically she could not even be counted as a friend of whom he could ask a favor...but who was counting? The only other person he knew in town was Paul's wife, Sunne. And their daughter was partly to blame. So by the time he had pulled his car into Romantic Notions' parking strip, he had at least admitted that the shop owner herself intrigued him—intrigued him enough that he'd use a lame excuse like Holly's butchered hair to make contact again.

He was downright disappointed when he walked into the lingerie shop and was greeted by Sunne Evans instead of Brynn.

"What in the world happened to you two?" exclaimed Sunne, not trying to hide her amazement.

"Me?" Sam questioned, looking startled.

"Yes, you," returned Sunne, staring first at Holly's tear-streaked face, then pointing at Sam's cut cheek. "Holly looks like she tangled with a lawn mower and you with a Mack truck. What are you guys doing here?"

Sunne Evans posed a damn good question, one Sam was still wrestling with in his own mind. Deep down he was a private man and he wasn't certain about sharing his ambivalent feelings with Paul's talkative wife.

On a spur-of-the-moment thought, Sam peeled out the paper on Brynn's classes and related a much shortened version of Holly's plight. Though he glossed quickly over Stacy's role, Sunne picked up on it right away.

Bending down, she lifted Holly's chin until their eyes met. "Honey, never take any of Stacy's suggestions to heart until you check with an adult first. I love her dearly, but she's always three jumps ahead of me. And that's part of the reason I'm putting her in Brynn's class—to see if I can channel some of that excess energy in a more...appropriate direction." Straightening, she gave Sam a wry grin. "Stacy takes after her father, of course. That child once convinced Joey Parks down the street to jump out of the second-story window with an umbrella as a parachute. Paul says we're lucky Joey landed in the rhododendron bushes, which broke his fall instead of his neck." She shrugged expansively.

Holly started to sniffle again. Sam shifted his weight to the other foot. "So Ms. Powell isn't here?"

"No. She had to take Kevin to the doctor. I expect her back anytime. Can I help?"

Drying her eyes, Holly was quick to ask in a worried voice, "Mrs. Evans, is something wrong with Kevin? He wasn't at school today."

Sam took note of Holly's abrupt transfer of concern.

"Well." Sunne chewed on her lower lip. "He went with Brynn to get the results of some tests. I'll tell you what, Holly, why don't you wait in the back room? I brought some home-grown apples. You can have one for a snack. I'll run you by the houseboat after Brynn sees what she can do about your hair. That way, your dad won't have to wait."

"I don't mind waiting," Sam interjected, not wanting to leave Holly until he was sure something could be done. And now that he was here, he wanted to see Brynn Powell again. So he could put her in perspective and forget her, he told himself as he paced while Sunne showed Holly into the back room.

Alone in the midst of silk and satin frills, Sam grew uneasy again. To distract himself, he began checking out the merchandise, something he hadn't really done on his last visit. Today, he began to study it in detail.

He paused in front of a headless gold mannequin draped in a pale lavender floor-length nightgown that plunged daringly low in front. From a side view, Sam could see wide lace panels that covered little and left less to his imagination. *Wow!* His heart raced just looking.

It was impossible to walk behind the display, but Sam wanted to see how the gown's narrow straps were connected in back and just how close to the hipline it was riding. He was having no difficulty at all visualizing the shop owner wearing that sizzler. The minute he read the sign announcing it was *the barest, by Brynn,* he began picturing the filmy creation against her opalescent skin.

"Perfect," he breathed, placing one hand on the manne-quin and tilting forward on the balls of his feet, straining to see the back view. "Perfect!"

"Find something you like?" Sunne's amused query came from close behind and a little to the right of him.

Rocking back on his heels, Sam bumped the mannequin. It teetered precariously until he reached out and held it steady.

"I was just checking out the engineering on that thing," he muttered, backing away.

Sunne's amusement turned into contemplation. "Really?" Her one word was more thoughtful than disbelieving. "Is there someone you were thinking of buying that for?"

"My mother," Sam shot back, ignoring the upward snap of Sunne's eyebrows, though he felt somewhat guilty when he thought of his plump, gray-haired mother.

"Uh, yes... Well, Sam..." she ventured with uncharacteristic hesitancy. Then, in Sunne fashion, she suddenly blurted out, "Were you planning on bringing a date to our Halloween party next month?"

"I hadn't thought about it," he said, relieved to have the subject changed. "Paul mentioned it, of course. But I'm not much on costume parties. Besides," he said, shrugging, "my team goes on the road next week."

"I thought Paul told me that particular weekend was a home game for you," Sunne cut in.

"Maybe." Sam backed toward the door. "I don't have a sitter arranged yet for the time I'm gone, to say nothing of a part-time person when I'm in town. I can't make plans until I do. Holly may have told you that she doesn't want a full-time sitter any more, and I've promised to try to work out a new system."

"Holly's welcome at our home any time—you know that, don't you, Sam?"

Sam hedged. "Holly likes staying with you. But I don't want to wear out our welcome."

"As if you could! Paul thinks of you as a brother. And I'd already intended to invite Holly to sleep over on the night of the party. The whole neighborhood is invited. It's a good way to introduce you around." She laughed. "If you don't mind meeting an abundance of hoboes, skeletons and witches."

"Everyone comes?" Sam's gaze slid past Sunne to the lavender gown. He stroked his chin with the tip of one finger.

"Everyone," she assured him, following the path of his wandering gaze. "Even if I have to hog-tie them," she murmured.

"Ah, well." Sam flushed, pulling back his sleeve to check his watch. He didn't exactly like the turn his thoughts had taken.

The bell behind him tinkled and a group of women swept into the shop, chatting and laughing boisterously. He suddenly felt very out of place. "I'll have to check my schedule and let you know. Are you sure it's all right to leave Holly here? It looks like Ms. Powell is going to be gone longer than planned."

Sunne smiled at the customers and greeted each by name before she walked Sam to the door.

"You should call her Brynn. We're all on a first-name basis around here, Sam. And you have my word, Holly will be just fine." Sunne opened the door. "Holly's dilemma will give Brynn something else to think about if Dr. Low gives her bad news today." She stepped outside, forcing Sam to do the same.

"What kind of bad news?" Sam's brows knitted.

"Brynn was hoping to be able to give Kevin a kidney. The test results were due back today. However, she was sure that if all systems were go, they'd have told her over the telephone. Since they called her to the office, she assumed the answer was no." Sunne rubbed her arms briskly, warding off the chill of the stiff wind blowing off the bay.

"She's offering a kidney?" Sam's tone was strained. The furrows in his brow deepened. "That's no penny-ante stuff. What if someday her own goes bad?"

"What if?" Sunne's eyes darkened and she shook her head slowly from side to side. "That very question can tear up a family, I'll tell you. I belong to a woman's group that does volunteer work for the Kidney Center, and I've seen what families go through when it comes to this decision. But Kevin has no one else. Brynn knows all that and more."

Sam cast a glance toward the shop window filled with frilly undergarments. When he spoke, his tone was grave. "She must have more substance than it appears." The wave of his hand signified the neon sign for Romantic Notions.

"I'm not given to discussing the private lives of my friends, Sam. But in Brynn's case, you don't even know the half of it.

She gave up a top-dollar career in New York to raise Kevin after their folks died. And before that, her money helped the family make ends meet. She's not had an easy time of it." Sunne backed into the doorway, still rubbing her arms.

"Oh, hey." Sam noticed Sunne's goose bumps and her efforts to avoid the wind. "You get back inside. You'll freeze out here with no coat. Maybe I should get Holly. I'd hate to cause the Powells more problems."

"No trouble, Sam. I'll drop Holly back by the gate on my way home. Wait until you see the magic Brynn works on Holly's hair. And wait until I get my hands on my daughter. I may shave her head in atonement."

Sam chuckled as Sunne shooed him away and closed the door before he could protest further. He shook his head. Poor Paul. The woman was a steamroller. He grinned. And Paul loved it. Suddenly his grin faded. His thoughts and his sympathy were centered on Brynn Powell as he got into his car and merged with the stream of traffic. He'd been assuming a lot about the woman's character without any real justification.

Gliding to a stop at a red light, Sam happened to see the object of his concern at the wheel of a vintage Volkswagen. She was making a left turn, crossing in front of him. Her face appeared pale, with features set as though sculpted from alabaster. His stomach tightened. The look of despair she wore, her vacant expression, touched a responsive chord in him. Sam remembered some lonely hours he'd spent pacing the floor alone when Holly had pneumonia a few years back.

The blond-haired youth seated on her right must be her brother, Kevin. Sam's view was quick, fleeting at best, and the car behind him honked loudly when he stared too long and almost lost his chance to cross the intersection.

Some part of him wanted to pop a U-turn. Some part wanted to follow Brynn Powell to her store. "And do what, Court?" He growled the question half under his breath. "Give her your kidney? Get real." The sobering statement was drowned in the roar of the Jaguar's engine.

Sam reminded himself that he hardly knew Brynn Powell— reminded himself that he had enough problems of his own, without asking for more. He drove two streets farther, then made his U-turn, tromping hard on the gas pedal. Even the sharp pain in his thigh, another souvenir from morning practice, didn't convince him to change his mind and go home.

CHAPTER FOUR

THE ROMANTIC NOTIONS SHOWROOM was empty except for the youth Sam had glimpsed in the car with Brynn. His back was toward the door, but instead of turning at the sound of the bell, the boy seemed intent on listening to an erratic flow of conversation Sam could hear filtering from the back room.

Closing the shop door with one hand, Sam pocketed his car keys with the other. Striding quickly to the center of the shop, he asked, "What's the trouble, son?"

The youth turned at the sound of the man's voice, hands thrust deep in jacket pockets.

"Oh, my gosh," Kevin burst out, staring at Sam. "The Samurai. In person!" He raked a hand through his hair, standing it in pale spikes around his head, frankly awed in the presence of an idol.

"I didn't do anything to Holly, sir. I swear!" He made a cross over his heart with one finger and raised his palm. "I just walked in there and said, 'Hello Holly.' She let out a yell, dropped her apple and ran for the bathroom, hollering at me to go away. She's locked herself inside."

It made no sense to Sam, but he was certain it had something to do with being a thirteen-year-old female—foreign territory to him. Still, he clapped one hand reassuringly on Kevin Powell's shoulder before entering the melee.

"Problem, ladies?" Sam's low question drew startled responses from Brynn and Sunne, who were making serious supplication to a closed door, behind which muffled sniffling continued.

"Sam!" Sunne crossed toward him at once. "Holly is being a regular pill."

Sam smiled, noting that Brynn Powell met his gaze without offering comment, though last evening she'd been very vocal. Now, color rose in her pale cheeks as her gaze traveled to his swollen eye.

"You didn't get in a wreck last night because there were no street lights, did you?"

He noticed her expression changed, softened, as her face registered this new concern. Sam touched his cheek, then shook his head. His stomach did a cartwheel. It was a long while since anyone had shown real concern about his injuries, though to be honest, he'd systematically kept his distance from anyone who would. "It's nothing." He fobbed it off, returning to the matter at hand. "I've never known Holly to act up in public." Closing the gap, Sam grasped the doorknob and rattled it. "Holly, come out. Let's discuss this."

Holly's sniffles lessened. "Is he gone?" Her voice trembled.

"She's talking about me, isn't she?"

Sam turned in time to see Kevin throwing up his hands.

"I didn't do anything," the teenager repeated. "I was going to talk to her about today's algebra assignment."

"It's not you, son. It's her hair," Sam explained. "Holly's embarrassed."

Kevin looked confused. "Was there something wrong with her hair? I didn't notice."

"Brynn, it's like I've been trying to tell you," Sunne broke in. "Stacy convinced Holly to whack off her hair. It looks a mess," she admitted, lowering her voice. "Do you think you can fix it?"

"I'm not a beautician, Sunne. Why not call Midge? See if we can catch her before she leaves her shop." Motioning toward the phone, Brynn chewed at her lower lip as Sunne hurried to comply.

"If this is all because I told Holly... I mean, when I suggested her hair would look nice short... Well, I'm real sorry, Mr. Court. But you must understand that I have neither the qualifications nor the license to cut hair. In my class, I touch briefly on healthy hair. That's really the extent of it. Last night I wanted to give Holly something positive to consider when she had to give back the things she'd bought. That's all I intended to do.'' She studied him seriously.

Her fine-boned face was so drawn and pale, Sam felt *he* should be apologizing for adding to her worries. There was a tightness around her mouth, and unless he missed his guess, fairly recently those large blue eyes had been shedding tears. The news she'd received must not have been good. Sam suffered another twinge of sympathy. He knew what it was like to field bad news alone.

''Excuse our interruption, please, Ms. Powell. I'll just get Holly and we'll make other arrangements.'' If she wanted to keep things formal between them it was fine by him. Less threatening, also. He didn't know what he was doing here, anyhow.

Sunne dropped the telephone resoundingly in its cradle, then dashed across the room with a smile lighting her face.

''If you two don't beat all,'' she quipped lightly, gazing first at Brynn, then at Sam. ''As I told Sam earlier, we're all neighbors, for goodness sake. Stop with all this Ms. and Mr. stuff. Sam, meet Brynn. Brynn, meet Sam. There now, you've been properly introduced.'' Sunne winked at Kevin, who was still hanging back.

''Perhaps you should be the one to teach my class on etiquette, Sunne,'' Brynn said dryly. ''Can Midge take Holly or not?''

''Oh! Did I forget to tell you that?'' Sunne made a horrible face at her friend. ''Why don't you offer Sam a cup of coffee?'' She dug her elbow in Brynn's ribs. ''I'll take Holly next door. After all, this whole mess is really Stacy's fault.''

''Ow!'' Brynn pressed a hand to her side and shot Sunne a murderous glare. ''I distinctly remember hearing you say Paul expected you home soon. You can drop Kevin by our house. And in return, he'll help carry the half of the store you bought to your car. Won't you, Kevin?''

''Sure, but is Holly all right?'' Though the sniffling had ceased, he eyed the door with some misgiving.

''She'll be fine if everyone will just leave us alone,'' Brynn said firmly.

"Okay," Kevin muttered. "I'll phone you later, Holly," he called out, his tone almost as firm as his sister's.

Sam felt a surge of respect for the boy. For the first time, he took a good look at the youth he'd expected, by all reports, to be puny and frail. What he saw was a fairly normal-looking teen. Not unlike fans he met when his team visited high schools. Except maybe Kevin Powell had better manners. He wondered if perhaps Sunne had exaggerated the severity of the boy's condition. She did seem to run toward the dramatic.

"I'll help carry packages, too," Sam offered politely, following Sunne into the showroom.

Brynn heard Kevin reply, "Thanks, but I can manage, sir."

Sam's response brought a smile to her lips. "Knights and nobles are called sir. Me, I'm holding out for sainthood. Until then, just call me Sam."

Brynn appreciated the fact that Sam hadn't treated Kevin with kid gloves. Or worse, like some others she knew—Anthony Carraras for one, who had acted as though Kevin was a leper.

"They've gone now, Holly," Brynn said softly as the bell tinkled. "Won't you please come out? A friend of mine next door is a top-flight genius with hair."

The bathroom door opened a crack. "Is Kevin gone, Ms. Powell?" Holly's breathless question ended in a hiccup.

"Yes, he's gone. But Kevin wouldn't have made fun of you, Holly. He isn't like that. Friends mean more to Kevin than how they look."

The door opened wider. With eyes puffed and red from crying, Holly approached Brynn.

Brynn hadn't really seen Holly's hair until this very moment, and now that she did, she understood everyone's concern. She understood a lot more, too. What would the stiff-necked Sam Court say if he knew his daughter was trying to impress Kevin—if he knew she had a crush on him? Brynn cleared her throat, not even daring to think about that prospect. "Let's not keep Midge waiting, Holly. The sooner she gets started, the happier everyone will be." Looping one arm around the girl's shoulders, Brynn eased her out the back door.

Minutes later, after settling things with Midge, Brynn returned to her shop. She slipped inside, then hesitated for a moment, closing her eyes and rubbing her temples, as the back door closed quietly behind her.

Sam Court's husky question startled her. "Would taking you out for dinner tonight make up for some of the trouble we've caused?"

His topcoat was slung over one shoulder, and he leaned casually against her desk with ankles crossed. He looked relaxed, a state that Brynn hadn't experienced much lately. Her hands dropped from her temples as she continued to gaze at him. He looked good. Too good. She didn't want a man in her life, didn't need the complication. Especially not a man as rigid and hardheaded as Sam Court.

"I thought you'd gone."

"I'll wait for Holly," Sam replied, watching Brynn strike out across the room. She walked with the grace of a ballet dancer. Sam smiled. As she passed him, he could see tendrils of hair that had slipped from her loose topknot clinging to her neck. He fought a sudden impulse to lift one strand and kiss the pale tender flesh beneath. He wasn't usually given to impulsiveness where women were concerned. He remained carefully still, unmoving as a statue. "The café down the street. Is it passable? We could always grab a bite there." His voice ended in an unexpected catch.

Brynn turned to face him. She had experienced a jolt of awareness when she passed him and wondered if he'd felt it, too. It was impossible to tell. His features were set and closed. The responding prickle along her arm and down her spine lingered, but he remained impassive. Not surprised, she shook the feeling away, refusing to examine it more closely.

"They serve mostly health food," she murmured, unable to meet his unwavering gaze. "But please, you go along if you're hungry. Midge will call me when Holly's finished. I'll send her to the café. I'll be here anyhow, because I have to restock some display racks before I leave." As if to prove it, Brynn grabbed a stack of peach silk from a shelf, clutching it to her breast.

Sam crossed his arms, heedless of his coat, which slid to the desktop. Bending his head until his chin touched his chest, he measured her through a thicket of lashes. "You have to eat sometime, don't you? Why not now?"

Brynn considered his offer. The doctor's news had left her at a real loss, and Sam Court's simple logic tempted her. How long had it been since she'd had dinner out? Six months? A year? For him, though, dining out was probably no big thing. Hadn't Sunne said they'd met over pizza just last night?

Reluctantly, Brynn declined. "I can't go with you." Her flat refusal didn't reveal the true depth of her struggle or her indecision. Turning away, she dismissed the man and his tempting offer, carrying out instead her self-appointed chore of stocking the showroom.

Sam followed. "Can't or won't, Ms. Powell?" he taunted, moving swiftly to confront her.

Peach silk slithered to the floor between them. Both bent to retrieve the filmy articles, but Sam was fractions of a second faster.

Brynn froze. Her fingers met his in a mingling of warm flesh and cool silk. She glanced up, startled. Though Sam was taller, he'd gone down on one knee. Now his lips were only inches from her own. Brynn watched, too stunned to move.

Sam let his heated gaze sweep slowly to her throat where a pulse hammered erratically. His eyes inched higher, fixing on her lips. The air seemed to close around them, heavy with their combined breathing.

"Brynn?" He spoke her name for the first time. He liked the way it sounded as it rolled off his tongue. *Brynn.* It was different. *She* was different from the women he'd known in California. Women who were into health clubs, ranch mink and money. Suddenly, Sam wanted to know what Brynn Powell was like when she was younger. When she was Holly's age, say...

Brynn straightened, pulling away. For her, the timing was all wrong—wrong for the type of involvement she could read in his eyes. She was facing Kevin's agonizing wait for a kidney, having been told some very hard facts about what would happen if he didn't get one, while the worst trauma in Sam Court's cushy life appeared to be Holly's shorn hair. Yet for some reason, she lacked the strength to turn and walk away, though she did carefully clamp down on her reaction.

Sam regained his composure first, recognizing her brush-off. It was a technique he'd employed himself. The heat rising in his cheeks stung the discoloration under his injured eye. At least he hadn't dropped the peach camisole he'd picked up, Sam noted with satisfaction as he watched its matching French bikini slide through Brynn's hands, ending crumpled on the floor. A slow smile twitched at the corners of his lips. For some perverse reason, he hoped he was making her damned uncomfortable. With a mocking bow, Sam offered her the camisole.

"Thank you." Her words were strained. Embarrassment battled with indignation. Yesterday in this very room he'd touted modesty; today Sam Court appeared to be quite comfortable using his suggestive smile to the fullest.

Snatching the camisole from his fingers, Brynn quickly retrieved its mate from the floor. She preferred him sanctimonious, she thought, to dealing with his lazy, sexy charm.

"I can't have dinner with you," she said tightly, returning to their earlier conversation. "Tonight Kevin goes on the machine again to make up for the time he lost last night. Anyway, you don't owe me. This is a neighborhood where people help one another." Brynn hung up the last of the peach silk, thankful that her fingers had obeyed long enough to finish the task. She straightened a row of slips that were already straight before adding tiredly, "I wouldn't consider leaving him alone."

"Nor would I expect you to," Sam cut in brusquely. "If you'll just tell me where you live, I'll meet you and Holly there. I noticed a Chinese take-out at the bottom of the hill. Is that okay? If Kevin can't have Chinese, you tell me what he can eat. I'll get it." Striding to the counter, Sam reached for a paper and pencil, which he held out to her. "Here. Give me the directions to your place."

Brynn accepted the paper and pencil; she scrawled her address and sketched a map. Until this instant, she hadn't realized how very much she needed distracting from Dr. Low's disheartening report, rejecting her as Kevin's donor. Company for dinner would allow her a few extra hours before she had to start thinking about the long waiting list on which they'd placed Kevin's name today. Finding a perfect cross-match was of vital importance. If they were lucky, a suitable kidney might show up within months. Then again, it could be years.

Brynn returned the paper to Sam. "I appreciate your asking about the food. Kevin is on a protein restricted diet, but most people never even give it a thought. Tonight, he'll have eaten early. He's extremely self-disciplined for fifteen. You won't need to worry that he'll feel slighted."

Sam nodded, accepting her statement. Folding the paper, he pulled out his wallet and tucked her address inside. He savored the compliment she'd given him. Absentmindedly he returned the wallet to his pocket. Then, with a snap of his fingers, he jerked it out again, adding, "I almost forgot. How much for Holly's hair?"

"I'm not sure." Brynn worried her bottom lip. "Why don't you stop next door before you leave? You can let Holly know what you've got planned. That way you can pay Midge direct. And have you considered that maybe Holly would rather not see Kevin undergoing dialysis?"

Sam closed his wallet. "I'll go next door right now. And don't worry about Holly feeling uncomfortable with Kevin. I can tell you, she's a trouper. Those tears today were not normal."

Brynn smiled. "Stacy won't set foot in the house when Kevin is using that machine. A great many adults I know feel the same. You should at least give Holly the option, Sam. Some of us harbor fears others might never suspect."

Just hearing his name fall softly from Brynn's lips sped Sam's heart up a beat or two. But he'd been heeding an inner discipline for so long when it came to women, he brushed the warm feelings aside and stuck to the subject at hand. "My daughter is made of sterner stuff, in spite of having a marsh-mallow heart. Why, just last night she asked if I'd let her help out in your shop after school, because Kevin told her you have more work than one person can handle."

Walking with him toward the front door, Brynn hesitated, then chuckled. "Ah, the wisdom of youth. If Holly was only a couple of years older and I had the extra money, I might hire her. As it is . . ." She let the sentence trail off.

Sam wasn't smiling, and his tone remained serious. "Maybe I should pay you to let her help."

Brynn caught his sleeve as he opened the door. "Could it be that your daughter comes by her marshmallow heart honestly?"

He grinned mischievously. "I might point out here that my reasoning is probably more selfish than altruistic. Holly doesn't want a sitter, and I refuse to let her stay by herself when my team's traveling. So far, we've agreed to disagree." He shrugged lightly. "It just came to me. This might be a solution."

She laughed. "Don't you know by now? Kids always want to do what you say they can't. If you let her stay by herself for a while she wouldn't like it. It gets lonely and boring. I know. I spent a lot of time alone because my parents both worked."

"Well, maybe," he said, looking doubtful. "But I think I'll have her stay at the Evanses' place until I can make other arrangements. Anyhow, it's my problem, not yours. I'd better head out if we're going to eat soon." The shop bell tinkled furiously as Sam slammed the door on his departing words.

Brynn held her breath and watched him swiftly cover the distance between her store and Midge's beauty parlor. He had the liquid gait of a natural athlete, she noted. Drawing back, not wanting to spy, Brynn returned to her stockroom wondering what had happened to Sam Court's marriage. He seemed a caring man. But was he divorced or was he widowed? Had Sunne ever said? Not that she had a valid reason for knowing—outside of normal curiosity about a new neighbor.

Brynn frowned and slipped into the chair behind her desk. Pulling the ledger toward her, she opened it and balanced out the day. Why had she agreed to dinner? Halfheartedly, she ran one finger down the sales column. Zowie! Sunne Evans had spent a small fortune on lingerie today.

Brynn's frown changed to a chuckle as she discovered an envelope bearing her name in Sunne's scrawl tucked between the pages. Probably a note demanding her silence on Sunne's extravagance. Though Brynn had never known Paul to deny his madcap wife anything. As it turned out, it wasn't a note. It was an early birthday card. Brynn's brow furrowed as she tapped the card lightly against her lips. Her birthday was less than two weeks away and she'd almost forgotten it. Or could she be forgetting on purpose, she wondered, as she slid the card into her purse.

She was almost thirty, and what did she have to show for the past ten years? Her face on a few pages of obsolete fashion magazines, wearing clothes that no longer held market appeal.

Sunne seemed to think giving up modeling had been hard, but what her friend didn't know was that she'd never really modeled from choice. So what *had* kept her in New York for so long, besides the money her parents needed for Kevin? Brynn grimaced. *Anthony Carraras.* It was who, not what. Anthony, to whom the perfect face and body were everything. Charming Anthony, whose lies and deceit held her back from what she really wanted, a career in fashion design. By convincing her that he had her best interests at heart, he'd kept her modeling until it was almost too late to break into design. Was his duplicity the reason she was wary of other men? Probably.

The back door opened, dispelling Brynn's moody introspection. Holly Court whirled in, seeming to dance on a puff of wind. More than ready to forget distasteful memories, Brynn crammed the ledger in a drawer and prepared to give Holly some perfunctory compliment.

The gust of wind receded, pulling the door from Holly's loose hold. It banged loudly, covering Brynn's shocked response. No longer a plain, drab little mouse, Holly Court had emerged a stunning butterfly. How would Sam Court deal with *this*? Brynn wondered, barely managing to cover her surprise.

"Do you like it?" Holly rushed to stand beside Brynn's desk, holding her breath anxiously.

Jumping up, Brynn caught the girl's hand and twirled her around. She took real pleasure in Holly's happiness. "It's lovely, Holly. *You're* lovely," Brynn corrected with a laugh. "That pixie cut accentuates your eyes and brings your delicate bone structure to life. You look positively exotic."

"Oh!" Holly's hands fluttered. "I'm so glad you think it looks good on me. Will Kevin like it, too, do you think?" The expression in her eyes remained a trifle apprehensive.

Brynn thought of her levelheaded brother and the things he'd mentioned that set Holly Court apart from the other girls he knew. Kevin wasn't impressed by beauty. Yet Brynn, observing how important her answer was to Holly, weighed each word carefully. "What matters to Kevin is intelligence, loyalty and a sense of humor. It's one of his more admirable traits."

Holly clasped her hands and nodded. "I know just what you mean. My dad is like that, too. I guess that's what really makes me feel so good inside when my friends' mothers drool over him, and I know I'm the lucky one, 'cause he's the best-looking dad in the world, and he doesn't even know it." Holly ran her sentences together in one long string.

Brynn smothered the remark that popped into her mind. She could well imagine how a roomful of women, mothers or not, would react to Sam Court's compelling masculinity. Hadn't she reacted that way herself? But didn't he know how he came across? Brynn thought he did.

"It's not quite the same, Holly," she said gently. "I'm afraid you're talking about superficial appearance, while I'm talking about deeper values."

"You think my dad's handsome, Ms. Powell?"

"I didn't say that, Holly. I said—"

"You don't think he's a hunk, then?" Holly broke in again, sounding worried.

Now it was Brynn's turn to show frustration. "Holly! Stop it this minute. We were not discussing me, or your father, or what I think about him being a hunk. We were talking generalities."

"Yes'm."

Brynn noticed Holly was barely able to contain a smug grin. It made her feel she'd come out second best at the end of round one. No wonder Sam was anxious for Holly to keep busy after school. Her double talk probably drove his lady friends away.

"Speaking of your father, Holly, he's bringing dinner to my house. If he beats us there, I don't think he can get in."

"Where's Mrs. Flemming?" Holly asked, scurrying around, helping Brynn shut off the store lights.

Brynn checked the front lock and keyed the burglar alarm before she answered. "It's a part-time job for her." She sighed. "You know, I'm really grateful to your dad for providing dinner tonight. I guess I'm more tired than I thought."

"You work too hard, Ms. Powell." Holly climbed into the Volkswagen, reached across the console and unlocked Brynn's door. "Kevin and Mrs. Evans both think so."

"Oh! What did Sunne say, Holly?" Brynn remembered her friend's joking words this morning about spending her evenings with a good man. Surely Sunne wouldn't dare say anything like that in front of Holly. But then again...Sunne dared a lot.

"I dunno exactly." Holly righted herself after Brynn took the first corner a little too sharply. "I overheard her tell Mr. Evans she hoped you weren't too tired to make a new costume for their Halloween party this year. He laughed and said if you wore the same one as last year, you'd get all the rest you needed, 'cause no one had nerve enough to ask you to dance."

"Rats!" Brynn slowed, pulling into the drive around the Jaguar parked at the curb. Slowly she guided her car up the incline. "Looks like your father beat us after all. But he must have arrived before Kevin hooked up, because he's not stuck outside. I hope Kevin takes this unexpected visit in stride. He tends to idolize sports figures."

"It'll be okay, Ms. Powell. My dad's cool. Do you mind telling me what you did wear to the Halloween party last year?" Holly took up where she'd left off as she and Brynn climbed the front steps.

"Promise you won't say anything if I tell you? In case I can't think of anything else?" Brynn studied Holly, who solemnly raised her right hand in promise.

Bending close, Brynn whispered in her ear.

"Well, my gosh!" The girl pushed open the front door, shaking her head. "I don't see why no one asked you to dance. Sounds a little weird, but after all, it was only a costume."

Brynn chuckled, because she noticed Holly, too, had shuddered as she described it—which had been exactly Sunne's reaction. Suddenly she smelled the tantalizing aroma of Chinese food and immediately lost interest in further explanation.

"Ask whom to dance when?" Sam met them in the hall outside the kitchen.

"Is Kevin already on the machine?" Brynn asked. She was trying not to think how nice it was to have someone greet her at the door with dinner already cooked. A handsome male someone, at that.

"Yes, and he's eaten. What dance?" Sam persisted. "Holly?"

Holly looked at Brynn dubiously. Brynn put her finger to her lips, reminding the girl of her oath of silence.

"Hey, Muffet, your hair looks better." Sam let out a long, low wolf whistle.

Holly closed her eyes. "Daddy, really! You said you wouldn't call me Muffet," she admonished with a toss of her new, short curls. "I'm going upstairs to show Kevin. I hope he likes it." Draping her jacket on the hall chair, she almost flew up the spiral stairs.

Brynn shut the closet door after depositing her coat. She caught the tail end of Sam's scowl as his gaze followed his daughter's shadow up the stairs.

"Don't you like her hair?"

Sam crossed his arms over his chest. He scuffed a toe lightly along the hall rug, shifting his eyes to study the pattern he'd made in the thick shag. "She looks so...so grown up," he muttered. Then, flushing slightly, he tilted his head to look at the ceiling. "I don't suppose you cover the birds and bees stuff in that class of yours, do you?" he asked hopefully.

Brynn shook her head, biting her lip hard to keep from smiling at such a masculine man's discomfort. "Are you saying you've avoided bringing up the subject of sex?" She moved past him, placing a hand on the kitchen door.

"Shh," he hissed, shoving her through to the kitchen and letting the door bang closed behind them. "Not so loud. Her old man isn't ready for these things yet. She's just a kid."

"Oh, for goodness sake, if you're embarrassed, Holly will be, too." Brynn snatched up a pot holder then stopped, noting that Sam had already set three TV trays with china, silver and stemware. "You have everything ready." She arched a brow in surprise.

"I hope you don't mind the trays. Kevin suggested bringing one upstairs for Holly. When I left, you looked so tired, I just thought you might like to relax by a fire tonight."

"Did you talk to Holly about Kevin being on the machine?" Brynn felt an overwhelming need to steer the conversation away from herself and back to the teens.

Sam responded with a nod. "It's only the woman stuff I find tough." He passed a hand over his jaw. "And she has been moody lately."

Brynn decided she would have to give Sam credit on at least two counts, anyway—allowing Holly options, and digging through Brynn's buffet drawers to find linen napkins and napkin rings. It had been a long time since she'd come home with energy enough to care how her table service looked. More often than not she'd fix a sandwich on a paper plate to avoid doing dishes. Brynn felt herself softening toward Sam. After all, it was probably normal for a man to deny that his girl child was becoming a woman, especially if he was dealing with it alone.

"Sam, if you think discussing the facts of life with your *daughter* is hard, think about me discussing them with my *brother*." Brynn used the pot holders she'd picked up to pull the dishes from the oven. Maybe he'd think the sudden warmth in her cheeks came from the hot stove.

Sam grabbed a spoon and started ladling out chow mein.

"It's just . . . could it wait a year, I wonder?" He sounded worried.

Brynn put egg rolls on each plate and gave a negative shake of her head. "If the opportunity presents itself, I suppose either Sunne or I could talk to Holly. However, I may ask you to reciprocate with Kevin. Paul said he'd handle it, but he never seems to find time."

"You've got yourself a deal." Sam stepped close and held out a spoon filled with sweet and sour pork. "Maybe you and

I should discuss personal philosophy first, though." He wagged his eyebrows.

Steadying his hand with her own, Brynn accepted the morsel. As her wary gaze met his mischievous appraisal, the scene seemed somehow too intimate. She backed away. It would be easier to discuss the subject with Holly if her father didn't keep sending out mixed messages. Their friendship was much too new for this kind of repartee.

Sam chuckled low in his throat, setting down the spoon and picking up one of the trays. "Maybe Sunne Evans will have to counsel Holly *and* you. When I helped her carry out her packages today, she didn't suffer any inhibitions talking about her plans for seducing Paul with those slinky designs of yours." He grinned. "Don't worry, Kevin was well out of earshot."

Brynn cursed the pale skin that let her blush so readily. However, Sam didn't look back, for which she was thankful. She could hear him whistling as he carried Holly's tray up to Kevin's room.

She poured each of them a glass of the plum wine he'd brought and took the two remaining trays into the living room. Then she touched a match to the dry kindling that lay waiting in the fireplace. It had been weeks since she'd had time to enjoy a fire.

And it was a thoughtful gesture on the part of a man who was little more than a stranger. But a man who set her pulse racing nevertheless. As the flames leaped and danced, throwing shadows on the wall, Brynn wondered if he considered eating by firelight seductive.

Deep down, underneath all her protestations, was she secretly hoping he did? Was she hoping Sam Court might be the man to share her joys and her sorrows? She hadn't thought she was looking for a man, a relationship. And what about him— what was *he* looking for? The thought that he might be interested in her was a sobering one. Exhilarating, too. Made her feel like a desirable woman again.

Until this very moment, Brynn hadn't realized that she'd set aside a need to feel feminine...a *right* to feel feminine. Funny, she mused, staring into the flames. Before she met Sam Court, it hadn't seemed important.

CHAPTER FIVE

SAM HESITATED in the doorway to the Powells' living room. His pulse leaped and blood raced to his head. Suddenly, he experienced another of those vague attacks of dissatisfaction. The picture Brynn Powell presented drew him like a magnet.

Shoeless, she was curled in a corner of the chintz sofa. Her plate was pushed to one side of her tray, sharing it with a large drawing pad. The clasp holding her heavy hair was gone, and she chewed thoughtfully on the end of a pencil. She looked exactly the way he'd imagined her last night. An image he'd found unaccountably disturbing.

Clearing his throat, Sam made an effort to break the spell. "Nice, homey place you have." His gaze swept the room. "I like a place to look lived in." He sauntered over. "So tell me, what are you creating here?"

Brynn glanced up from her drawing and smiled. "Lived in is a nice way of saying messy, Sam. Between running the store and designing, I never have time to tidy up. And this creation is going to be a jade silk teddy. But I doubt you'd approve."

Sam bent to look over her shoulder. "Mm! I wouldn't say that . . . as long as it's not for my daughter." Straightening, he rubbed the back of his neck and began pacing the room, pausing now and then to scan the books on the built-in shelves beside the fireplace.

Brynn's eyebrows shot up. "Teenage girls love teddies, Sam. What's your objection?"

"I happen to think there's a distinct difference between what's acceptable in a high-school locker room and in an adult's bedroom."

Frowning, Brynn made a few rapid strokes with her pencil. "Where have you been hiding, Sam? Today, age differences are less defined. And maybe you don't know it, but a thirteen-year-old—boy *or* girl—needs to be accepted in the locker room. No less than in the classroom.''

"So you've done away with all age barriers?'' It was Sam's turn to raise his eyebrows. "How many women do you see wearing patent-leather Mary Janes? Personally, I think both women and girls could look a little more wholesome.''

Brynn laughed. "Milk is wholesome, Sam. Veggies are wholesome. Women are...oh, forget it.'' She'd intended to say women were sensual human beings, but decided against it. "Speaking of food, we'd better eat before it gets cold. Besides, there's really no point in arguing. You have nothing to worry about, as far as Holly's...friendship with Kevin is concerned, anyway. He told me what he likes most about Holly is her intelligence and that she doesn't goo up her face.''

Sam retrieved his tray from in front of the rocking chair and joined her on the couch. "It's obvious Kevin missed my discussion with her over eye shadow the other night. And I noticed right away that he's a young man with firm convictions. He's also quite a talker. In case you wondered why I was upstairs so long, he was twisting my arm to speak to his phys ed class. Conned me out of twenty autographed posters, too. If that kid ever goes into politics, he's got my vote.'' Hesitating, Sam laid his fork aside. "If the truth be known, I could use a little of his fast talk now. I have a confession to make, Brynn.''

"Sounds serious.'' Brynn chewed at her lip as she looked up from her drawing. Tonight she didn't want to face anything serious. Instead, she was hoping Sam's company would help her forget Dr. Low's disheartening news.

Sam watched in fascination as the flickering firelight turned her hair into spun gold. Taking a long, steadying breath, he muttered into his wineglass, "I'm afraid I'm guilty of doing something I hate having done to me.''

Brynn treated him to a slow smile. "I see why you got along so well with Kevin. He's a master at beating about the bush. Out with it, Sam. What terrible thing did you do?''

"I know Kevin isn't old enough to drive, but I gave him tickets to my game tomorrow night. I should have checked with you first to see if you could take him.''

In the silence that followed, Brynn recognized a little cha-grin and a lot of impatience in the tense set of Sam's jaw. Across the room, the measured tick of the mantel clock blended smoothly with the snap and crackle of the fire. "Is that all?" She shrugged, stabbing a crisp shrimp with her fork. "I was waiting to hear you confess something really terrible. Granted, you should have checked with me first, but then, I suppose we're even, considering my blunder with Holly last night." Reaching over, she nudged his tray. "Now will you eat? I hate seeing food go to waste. Here, I'll go get the rest of the wine. Sounds like we could both use a second glass to-night." She paused at the door and chuckled. "I'll bet you wanted to strangle me for suggesting Holly cut her hair, didn't you, Sam?"

"It never entered my mind," he lied, watching her graceful exit from the room. Sam was finding it hard to explain the sudden burst of joy that settled in his heart. It had been years since he'd invited anyone who mattered to one of his games. Oh, he'd handed out hundreds of free tickets each season, but they'd gone to nameless, faceless fans. People who knew more about him from the tabloids and the sports magazines than he knew about himself. And he had no reason to be so happy, because he hadn't really asked Brynn. But he'd given the tick-ets to Kevin, knowing she'd likely be the one to take him.

"You didn't finish your dinner," Brynn scolded, returning with the wine. "And here I assumed all athletes were big eat-ers." Dropping to one knee, she carefully placed the bottle between them on the floor. Strictly by chance, she glanced up and caught Sam watching her with hungry eyes. Brynn felt the blood heat her cheeks.

"Is this your normal appetite?" she asked in a rush of words.

"No," he murmured, openly admiring the length of her slender leg beneath a skirt that had risen to mid-thigh. "Sometimes I'm ravenous."

Brynn's cheeks flamed. She returned to her seat and smoothed the fabric over her knees. Goodness, she wasn't normally coquettish. She was a responsible adult. No more wine for her tonight. She'd almost forgotten the art of flirting and found it easier to take a different tack. "I don't play games of any kind, Sam. And not being much of a sports fan, I'm ashamed to admit I know so little about hockey. As a friend of mine from Georgia puts it, I'm really more the veranda and mint julep type. Will your game be bloody?"

Throwing back his head, Sam laughed. He reached out and cupped her chin in one palm, then skimmed her upturned face with indulgent eyes. "It doesn't get bloody if I can help it." Heat seemed to sizzle along his arm. Sam pulled back and picked up his crystal goblet. "Some teams get rather rough at times," he admitted with a shrug. His eyes took on a teasing light. "In the stands, you'll have to watch out for low-flying hockey pucks. On rare occasions, they've been known to lose us a fan or two."

Brynn's pulse began to jump erratically. His crooked, boyish smile tugged at her heartstrings. In an uncharacteristic response, she leaned over and ran one finger hesitantly along the cut under his left eye. "Hockey?"

He jerked away from her feather-light touch so fast her hand fell to the cushion separating them. Almost idly, Sam traced a fingertip around each of hers.

A shiver ran up Brynn's spine. "Why hockey, Sam?" she asked, curling her fingers into her palm. "Don't football stars get better press and more public adulation? And," she added flippantly to calm the butterflies in her stomach, "more money?"

Sam studied her. Did prestige and money matter? *But of course they mattered.* He'd never yet met a woman who didn't measure a man's potential by his bank balance. Brynn at least had reason, given the drain of Kevin's illness on her resources. Yet somehow, it seemed terribly important that she understand something of the real Sam Court.

"Professional athletes are just ordinary men thrust into hero status, Brynn. Take me, for instance. I grew up in an old farmhouse in Minnesota surrounded by cousins, any one of whom was a more experienced skater than me." Stretching out his long legs he crossed one ankle over the other. He gave a wry smile. "Behind our house was a pond where generations of Courts learned to skate almost before they learned to walk. I hated skating when I was little. I only kept at it to please my father. And if you knew hockey, you'd know Iron Man Joe Court. For fifteen years he was one of the NHL's best players. He went on to coach a major team.''

Brynn studied him with a dreamy smile. She pictured Sam at Kevin's age amid a large, boisterous family, and she liked the image. "I see," she murmured. "So he coaches a team in California, which you eventually joined? That's nice."

Abruptly Sam stood up and crossed the room. Sliding open the fireplace screen, he knelt, adding another log. *Bingo!* Just like that, she'd hit a nerve. He'd never opened up to any woman before, but for some reason, with Brynn, he wanted to try.

"Years ago, Iron Man and I had a falling out." Hell, if that wasn't a watered-down version of the colossal row he'd had with Iron Man... But was there any tactful way to tell a woman you wanted to impress that you'd split with your father over a girl you once thought you loved and felt honor bound to marry? No—especially not if you felt guilty because the girl was having your baby.

In the end, Sam offered Brynn a more acceptable version. "I was young. Fast. Cocky. I was the Samurai. When you're a nineteen-year-old hockey ace, all that matters is wine, women and song. Iron Man detested all such displays. He was a family man who held a close rein." Sam smiled. "Rather like I am today, you might say. But getting back to my story.... One afternoon, my teammates threw me a lulu of a bachelor party. The biggest game of the year was that night and I showed up three sheets to the wind. Iron Man gave me a public dressing-down to beat all and benched me for the season. His remarks to the press included some pretty harsh statements about my choice in a wife." Sam turned back to the fire, a muscle in his jaw twitching convulsively. "An hour after the newspaper hit the streets, I married Joani and signed on with the old man's arch enemy—the L.A. Encores. The rest, as they say, is history. He and I haven't spoken since."

"Your own father?" Brynn hesitated. "But it was all so long ago, Sam. Now there's Holly to consider. He must miss teaching his granddaughter to skate, her being the next generation and all. Unless he has others." She stopped rambling, shocked by the agony that flashed across Sam's face. His love for his young wife, Joani, must have been some kind of wonderful, she thought, for him to still be feeling the pain. However, his stony expression told Brynn that she'd heard all of Sam Court's life story that she was going to hear tonight, and she dared not ask what had happened to his wife.

Sam pushed at the new log with the toe of his boot. Sparks showered out. He jumped back, more wary of the sympathy he could see forming in Brynn's eyes than the smattering of hot ash.

"Save your pity. It's Iron Man's loss. Holly is his only grandchild." Dusting his hands, Sam signaled the end of their conversation. "Enough about me. Let's talk about you now." As he closed the subject on himself, even the texture of his voice changed. "When did you start dreaming up all those...those slinky...." He outlined exaggerated body curves in the air with both hands, then pointed to her sketch pad. "I mean—" he groped for words, rubbing the bridge of his nose between thumb and forefinger "—is that how you passed the time of day? Sitting on your veranda, sipping mint juleps and designing...nightgowns and things?"

Brynn's lips twitched at the corners. Now this was the Sam Court she could deal with. This man who was uncomfortable discussing ladies' underwear. She pulled a headless doll from a drawer in the end table, along with a loose bundle of silk, satin and lace as she answered him. "My life isn't nearly so exciting as yours," she said mildly, propping her drawing against her wineglass. "I can't think of a time since I was small that I wasn't designing clothes for my dolls. Oh...that reminds me, Sam." She glanced up from sorting through squares of material. "Are you aware that Holly has expressed an interest in drawing?"

Sam kept his eyes trained on the deft way she had begun draping the miniature mannequin. "I'm afraid Holly's career interests tend to resemble the path of a jumping bean. Last I heard, she wanted to be an astronaut." He shrugged. "It would be a waste of your teaching ability." He crossed to sit beside her on the couch again. Leaning an arm along the back, he placed his chin in the curve of his palm and watched her intently.

"Of course . . ." she mumbled around a mouth full of pins, "I'm not really a teacher. I developed the series of self-esteem courses because I was such an awkward kid growing up." She edged away. Unsettled by his closeness, she pretended more interest in her handiwork than she felt.

Sam chuckled. "It's hard to picture you awkward. You almost float when you walk."

Brynn placed a final pin. Then her fingers stilled. She hadn't told Sam about her years of modeling. Even now, for some reason, she withheld the information. For one thing, she doubted Sam Court was the kind of man who would understand her blindly signing a contract with Luminaire—a contract that included a binding clause on the fifth page stating that if no design work was available, she would be required to model for her pay.

Sam watched Brynn frown, though her nimble fingers had resumed their work, nipping and tucking a panel of lace over the gown of sheer chiffon. "Come back, pretty lady," he said, tweaking her nose and closing the small gap between them. "You don't have to prove to me that you're good at what you do." He nodded toward the mannequin clutched tightly in her hand. "And frankly, I'm not sure I want Holly learning how to whip up these sexy little numbers." His grin took the sting from his words. "What kind of women buy them, anyway?" Smoothing away the frown that sprang to her forehead, he grazed one finger along her cheek in the same lazy manner.

The doll slid through her fingers and fell to the floor as she jerked away. "Women like Sunne. Or me. Normal, everyday women. If you have a problem with my work, Sam, be a little more direct. If you find my designs so reprehensible, tell me why you invited yourself to dinner." Letting her anger at his narrow-mindedness take over, Brynn reached out and snatched up her glass. Wine slopped over the rim onto her hand. Two crimson droplets stained her pale skin.

"I've been out of the dating circuit for a while, but I can certainly be more direct if you like, Brynn." Enjoying her obvious annoyance, Sam bent and gently licked off the drops of wine with the moist tip of his tongue. Then suddenly turning serious, he muttered, "Damned if I know why I'm here, Brynn Powell. Maybe because I'm intrigued by the contradictions. You look much too angelic to be responsible for those daring designs."

Brynn sucked in her breath, unable to control a convulsive spiral of longing that started low in her abdomen and spread upward in ever widening circles. No, she couldn't handle direct, she thought wildly, mesmerized by his seductive violet eyes.

"I definitely didn't come here to watch you work, Ms. Powell. When I ask a lady to dinner, which hasn't been that often lately, I like her to stay with me for the duration—up to and including dessert." Calmly taking the glass from her hand and setting it aside, Sam pulled her close in a move that brought his mouth within inches of hers.

Brynn was no match for his practiced onslaught and she knew it. Feeling her meager defenses crumbling one by one, she made a last feeble attempt at joking. "Speaking of dessert, Mr Court, it's fortune cookie time! I'll just go get the bag from the kitchen." Brynn moved fast, but Sam moved, too, and she was brought up hard against his injured ribs.

Brynn watched physical pain and something else darken Sam's eyes. A response to the something else ripped through her as her lips met his in a surprising kiss.

Sam had been holding back all evening. Now, he simply took what he'd been wanting for the past twenty-four hours.

Neither of them had time to consider what was happening.

As kisses went, Brynn expected theirs to be simple, because they were little more than strangers. Or perhaps even dutiful, because she had all but helped herself. What she got was the shock of her life.

Slanting his lips across hers, Sam drove the kiss so deep it pulled a response from the very bottom of her soul. Once she had been caught in an undertow at the Oregon coast. Brynn felt a little like that now. Her body seemed to be struggling to stay afloat. Her insides quivered, and she was afraid of being smashed to bits against a rocky shore. As the panic grew, Brynn opened her weighted eyelids a crack. It only took a moment for reality to set in. She was a fake, a sham. Brynn Powell wasn't tough, after all. She liked kissing this man—liked knowing that her worries and fears lost some of their power within the strong circle of Sam Court's arms.

Then as suddenly as the discovery came, Brynn fought against it. She began pushing at Sam's chest. It wasn't wise to want this man. No two people ever had less in common. More importantly, she'd learned long ago that men like Sam Court could never belong to just one woman. But maybe he wasn't like Anthony, she argued with herself, as Sam's tongue made a gentle exploratory forage past her lips.

In a delayed response to some desperation he could sense and feel in Brynn, Sam drew back for a scant second. "Oh, Brynn!" he breathed near her ear, dragging in the fresh scent of her hair. Burying the tips of his fingers beneath her soft curls, he cradled her head and let his tongue slowly trace her lips.

She ceased to struggle, meeting his tenderness instead with a soft, primitive cry.

Swallowing the noise, Sam took a second kiss with fierce demand. Immediately he was shaken by desire so naked and exposed—a need so powerful—for just the length of a heartbeat, it scared the hell out of him. He had wanted before, but never like this. He had taken before without giving half of what he felt like giving now. But he had only needed once. Long ago, he had needed Joani to nurture the most precious gift he had ever given anyone—Holly. And when she refused, Sam Court vowed never to need any woman again. Until now, he'd had no trouble keeping his resolve.

Deliberately, he began tamping down the hunger that crept in so insidiously, seeking instead the sensation of simply wanting. He ran his hands beneath the lower edge of Brynn's sweater, counting heavily on the basic lustful contact to defuse the reckless emotions raging inside him. Last night he'd imagined Brynn Powell's skin would feel like silk. He wasn't disappointed.

Without conscious thought, Brynn eased open the buttons of Sam's shirt and placed a flat palm on his chest. She used his solid warmth to drive away the disappointments of the day.

She let Dr. Low's verdict fade into oblivion as she molded her body to Sam's.

Sam forgot why he ever considered lust a safe alternative to need. His control slipped when her hands explored the tape circling his ribs. Time and place blurred, and Sam hovered somewhere on the outer fringe of pleasing and taking pleasure when Holly's voice floated down from upstairs.

"Dad!" The single word sliced cleanly through his passion. For thirteen years the parent in him had responded to that call. Automatically the parent in him now withdrew from Brynn, setting in motion the separation of the father from the man.

Brynn, who often slept with her head off the pillow when Kevin wasn't well, heard nothing. She was lost in a world of sensation. Sensation intense enough to dull, for the moment, the heavy burden of responsibility she'd been left to face alone.

Footsteps clattered down the stairs. Sam took a deep breath, holding Brynn away with one hand. "Brynn." Her name came out sounding like a strangled plea.

"Sam?" Her soft, husky rejoinder almost proved his undoing. Especially when her golden lashes swept up, revealing lazy passion.

"Holly's coming downstairs," he murmured thickly, trailing a kiss along her throat. Methodically, he straightened her sweater, a regretful smile curving his lips.

Brynn steadied herself, gripping his arm. She couldn't think, couldn't get her bearings. It was as though her hands were all thumbs when she tugged at her skirt, which had somehow shamelessly ridden up her thighs.

Taking her cue from Sam, she hastened to smooth her disheveled hair. "Button your shirt," she whispered. She'd gained a shaky hold on her emotions and wondered how Sam could remain so calm. For that matter, she wondered—thoroughly embarrassed—how either of them could have allowed this to happen when they knew Holly and Kevin were upstairs.

Jumping to her feet, Brynn practically flattened Holly as they met head-on in the doorway.

Sam frowned. Brynn's cheeks were stained a shade shy of poppy red. And it didn't sit well with him that she was acting as if he'd taken advantage. They'd both been involved.

Rising, he stalked to the fireplace, uncaring that his shirt hung loose and was half buttoned. Tossing a log on the fire, he rounded on Holly—knowing it was Brynn he'd rather be shouting at.

"Holly, I swear, don't you ever walk like a lady? Unless the house is on fire, you owe Ms. Powell an apology for stampeding down her stairs. And just look at those glass doodads. It's a wonder you didn't break them."

Holly paused hesitantly near the end of the couch, shifting her gaze to a classic hurricane lamp on a nearby table. Crystal droplets dangling from the top globe quivered, faintly musical.

Brynn stared openly at Sam. She, not Holly, had bumped the lamp in her haste to get away from him. He knew that. And the lamp was a long way from broken. But then they'd been a long way from "Ms. Powell," too. Yet he seemed genuinely upset. Too upset for it to have anything to do with Holly. Brynn felt the heat creeping up her neck. She lifted the mannequin and began to collect the squares of material scattered around the sofa.

"I'm sorry," murmured Holly, looking in confusion from one adult to the other. "I just came down to ask if you'd let me go to the game tomorrow with Kevin, Dad."

Sam's face lost its tightness. "Now, Holly, you know our house rules. No games on school nights."

Joining him by the fire, Holly caught him around the waist with both arms, saying diplomatically, "I'm older now, Dad. Could we please change the rules?"

Sam pried her arms away.

"You gave Kevin a ticket for a school night," Brynn pointed out. "Why the double standard, Sam?"

He rocked back on his heels. "Okay, don't gang up on me. We'll try it once, Muffet. I'll even give you an extra ticket for Stacy. You'd like that, wouldn't you?" he asked, kissing the top of her head affectionately.

"Sure." Holly's smile faded. "I suppose Stacy will want to go, too," she muttered halfheartedly. Almost as an afterthought she added, "Tuck in your shirt, Dad. It looks real tacky." Edging from the room, Holly gave wide berth to the hurricane lamp. She paused at the door. "It's really late, Dad—almost ten. I'll just go tell Kevin goodbye, then we can go home."

Her slow steps could be heard echoing down the hall as Sam turned his back on Brynn and carelessly tucked in his shirt.

No mention was made of their moment of passion, and Brynn began to wonder if she'd only dreamed it. Especially after Sam faced her and said bluntly, "Holly didn't seem overjoyed about inviting Stacy to the game."

Shocked, Brynn sank down on the cushion. But she could be abrupt, too. "What's with you, Sam? You play these kissing games like a pro. So are you saying now you don't recognize that Holly has a crush on Kevin? I'd judge it's pretty normal for her to view Stacy as competition."

"A crush!" Sam took two steps toward her, hands balled into fists at his sides. His snapping eyes denied even the most remote possibility. "She's only thirteen, for crying out loud."

"Yes, a crush," Brynn repeated soberly. "Puppy love! Holly's testing her wings. And I'm quite sure your daughter knows you have women in your life, Sam. Besides, do you expect her to believe you never had a crush by the age of thirteen?"

"I don't have women," he said testily. "And boys at almost fourteen experience hormones. That's different."

"Oh, is it?" Brynn arched a brow. "Well, girls have hormones, too." Unconsciously she rubbed two fingers over her lips, still tender from his kisses.

Sam's gaze followed her fingers. "Yes . . . so I noticed earlier."

"What's that supposed to mean?" Brynn straightened, uncurled her leg and placed her feet squarely on the floor. She glared up at him.

"Nothing. I'm sorry. That remark was totally out of line." Sam raked one hand through his hair. "Perhaps this move to

Seattle wasn't such a good idea, after all. I've never had to contend with boys. How do I deal with a crush?''

Brynn considered him a moment. Sam Court was an enigma. Was this fatherly concern all an act? If not, then she owed it to Holly to give him an honest answer.

"When I first met Holly," she ventured, "I labeled her a mouse. Shy, unsure of herself. Her new haircut has given her a taste of confidence. Sam, your daughter has emerged a really beautiful young woman. Let her enjoy it. And let her go through these stages naturally."

He scowled. "There's a lot more to beauty than the physical."

"Physical beauty isn't exactly a hardship," Brynn insisted.

Sam's jaw tightened. "That's a matter of opinion."

There he was, throwing out those famous Court double standards again, Brynn thought, resenting his tone of voice. Earlier he'd been pretty free with his admiring glances.

Holly appeared in the archway, signaling frantically for Brynn's attention. "Kevin needs you."

Brynn leaped to her feet. So many things could happen when Kevin was on the machine. "Did he say why?"

"I, uh . . . I spilled my fruit juice all over his bed," Holly stammered. "It was an accident, but he's soaked and refuses to let me help clean up the mess." She lowered her gaze. "He said if I was going to be a nurse I'd have to learn to be more careful."

Brynn accept Holly's empty tray, stacking it with hers. "Don't let Kevin bully you, Holly. The state of his room is continually a sore subject around this house. Maybe now he'll let me wash his sheets."

Sam stepped forward. "A nurse? I told Brynn you wanted to be an astronaut."

Brynn read the love in Sam's exasperated words. It was this easy camaraderie he had with Holly that she found so appealing. Unexpectedly, her stomach tightened. This was the Sam Court who sent her pulse skyrocketing.

"Maybe I'll be a doctor, Dad. A surgeon. Kevin showed me a book his doctor gave him. It has pictures that show step by step how they replace a kidney. Neat-o stuff."

Brynn shot Sam a quick look of apology. "I'll speak to him, Sam. Kevin sometimes forgets not everyone shares his enthusiasm for all the gory details of surgery. He's been in and out of hospitals so much, medical terminology is his second language."

"Sis, are you coming?" Kevin's call from above rousted them.

"I'd better hurry." Brynn walked quickly toward the stairs. "His movements are restricted when he's on the machine. Will you mind terribly showing yourselves out?"

Reaching for Brynn, Sam caught her arm. "Let me help. Kevin must weigh as much as you do, or more."

Without thinking, Brynn touched a finger to Sam's chest, running it lightly over his taped ribs. "What about your injury?"

Holly shot him a penetrating gaze. "I didn't know you'd been hurt, Dad. What if you can't play in tomorrow's game? Kevin is counting on watching you."

Sam grimaced. He hadn't said a thing to anyone about his ribs, which left only one way Brynn could have known. And he didn't want Holly figuring that out. "You're all heart, Holly," he managed at last. "So much for family loyalty."

Holly ignored him and grinned happily at Brynn. "With you and Kevin both there, it'll be like Dad having a real family rooting for him tomorrow night, won't it?"

Brynn looked aghast. She didn't want Sam to think she was fostering such nonsense. Attempting to tug her arm from his loose grasp, she muttered in protest, "Really, Sam you two go on home. Don't worry about Kevin. We've worked out a system for taking care of his needs. I wouldn't dream of risking you further injury."

Kevin called out again, clearly losing patience.

"I'm coming," Brynn yelled, rolling her eyes expressively. "Thanks for dinner, Sam. I must say..." She hesitated, choosing her words carefully. "Tonight I needed a distraction."

Sam's brow furrowed. He was annoyed as hell about her referring to their shared kiss as a distraction. His grip on her arm tightened.

When Holly ran to the bottom of the stairs to call out some final bit of encouragement to Kevin, Sam almost snarled near Brynn's ear, "You have some nerve saying I play games, Ms. Powell. Suppose we just forget that kiss ever happened?"

Brynn felt herself flush. "I hope you didn't think . . ." Her voice cracked and she wet her lips, beginning again. "I mean, normally I don't act the way I did tonight." She was determined not to let Sam see how much his curt dismissal hurt. After all, she suffered no illusions about the kind of man he was. She worked to keep her tone even. "You do recall my telling you I don't play games, Sam? If there were any games going on here tonight, they were all yours, *Mr. Court!*"

Releasing her arm, Sam yanked open the door. He was immediately struck by an icy wind that might have cooled his anger had he not been so thoroughly provoked. "And I'm telling *you,* Brynn Powell, I play one game and only one!"

"Really?" she drawled, sensing Holly's approach. "And what game is that? Post office?"

"Hockey," came his swift, taut reply. Buttoning his topcoat, Sam ushered Holly out into the chill wind without so much as a backward glance. Near the bottom step, he halted and tossed casually over his shoulder, "Tomorrow night, Ms. Powell. Seven-thirty. The arena. Be there!"

Several rude retorts flew to the tip of Brynn's tongue. However, none of them were acceptable in front of Holly. Biting them back, she heard the Jaguar's first growl before she slammed the door with all her might.

"Be there," she mimicked. The man's arrogance was unbelievable.

Another call from Kevin—a timely reminder that reality awaited.

Well, Sam Court wouldn't have to tell *her* twice to forget about his kisses. As of this moment, he could consider them forgotten!

CHAPTER SIX

BRYNN AWAKENED with a feeling of pessimism. She'd realized during the night that forgetting Sam Court wasn't quite as easy as she'd first thought it would be.

She began her regular morning exercises, refusing to examine just how she'd come to know this. She'd gone to sleep fighting thoughts of Sam Court, and a clear picture of him had accompanied the first flutter of her eyelids at daybreak. But even if she couldn't rout his image from her mind, she had to avoid the man at all costs, she told herself grimly. The last thing she needed now was involvement with another man whose emotions were overshadowed by his ego.

Stretching resistant muscles, Brynn reached both hands toward the ceiling. Then she bent swiftly and placed her palms flat against the floor. Mr. Defenseman Court had a lot of nerve insinuating *she* was playing games. As if a super jock like him was above reproach. "Ha!" Through the zing of blood rushing to her head, Brynn heard Kevin's sharp rap at her bedroom door.

"Enter," she called, trying not to lose count while increasing isometric pressure. But it would take a lot of pressure to banish all trace of what had happened between her and Sam on the couch last night. They'd been like school kids, she thought, annoyed enough—embarrassed enough—for sweat to bead her brow.

Kevin's tennis shoes and jeans cuffs appeared in her slightly skewed line of vision. "I can't find my Skyhawk sweatshirt, Sis. Have you seen it?" Kevin rested his hands on his knees, hanging his head upside down, meeting Brynn's gaze in spite of her awkward position. "Sis, did you hear me? I've got to wear my school shirt. Today is assembly."

"Try looking in the mess under your bed." Brynn huffed between words. "I noticed your stash when we changed sheets last night. Is that how you cleaned your room before Holly's visit?"

"It's not there," he insisted. "Did you put it in the wash?"

Trying to control her breathing and hold on to her patience, she didn't answer as she switched to running in place.

"Brynn!" Kevin spread his hands in exasperation.

She stopped, reaching for a towel that lay draped across the arm of a chair, and wiped the sweat from her face and neck.

"Kevin, you are going to have to assume some responsibility for taking care of your own clothes. I realize Mom hired someone at the shop while she stayed home and mothered you, but I don't have that luxury. I barely have time for the paperwork, grocery shopping and designing, and no time at all for myself. No one takes care of me, Kevin."

He took a step backward, absorbing his sister's uncustomary outburst with a shocked look. "When I get my new kidney, you won't have to take care of me, Brynn. I'll get a job. I'll take care of myself. Why didn't you just tell the folks' lawyer, Mr. Beeman, that you resented coming home?"

"Oh, Kevin!" Brynn closed the gap between them and threw her arms around his stiff body. "I didn't mean it to sound like that." She gave him a little shake before pulling away. "I don't resent it at all. If anything, I'm sick over not being here more for you. Forgive me, okay? I guess I'm still upset over not being the donor you need."

"Would you have married that Anthony character if I'd been well?" Kevin tossed the question out suddenly and without prior warning, thrusting his hands into his jeans pockets. "I know he came here after the funeral and tried to talk you into leaving. I overheard him. Did you love him, or what? I've always wondered if you resented me as much as he did."

Brynn gasped. She'd underestimated Kevin's perceptiveness. Assuming at the time that he was too consumed by grief to be aware of much else, she hadn't been discreet in her final argument with Anthony. Now, biting her lip, she chose her words carefully. "Anthony Carraras is a smooth-talking womanizer. He has such a monumental ego that he refused to believe I'd really leave Luminaire. Anything between us, other than of a work-related nature, was over long before I came home. And all I ever was to him was a commodity."

Kevin shrugged, turning pragmatic. "By that, do you mean all the two of you had going was sex? No love?"

"No! It wasn't like that. Not that kind of commodity." She bristled. "Now, listen here, young man!" Brynn draped the towel around her neck, placed her hands on her hips and glared at her brother openly. "How did a conversation revolving around your missing sweatshirt wind up discussing my... my... *me!*" Brynn flushed, waving a dismissive hand.

Laughing, Kevin rubbed goose bumps from his arms. He strode over to his sister's closet and pulled open the doors. "Wind up how, Sis? Discussing your sex life?" His tone reverted to normal as he teased her. "Is that what you couldn't say?" He snorted. "My human sexuality teacher says the real problem between men and women today is that they're afraid to use the word sex in conversation."

Presenting his back to Brynn, Kevin calmly began sliding hangers along her closet rod. "By the way, I'll confess, Sis, my sweatshirt *was* in the heap under my bed. It's a real mess," he admitted sheepishly. "I've thrown it in the laundry basket— really. So I was hoping you'd lend me yours." Pulling out her shirt, Kevin turned to face her, waving it, and grinning a winsome appeal. "And I swear, Brynn, I'll help Mrs. Flemming clean tomorrow."

"Just a darn minute," Brynn sputtered, darting around her bed. She snatched at her sweatshirt, catching instead the empty hanger he tossed away.

Kevin paused in the effort of shrugging into her clean shirt. He peered at her under the lower edge, standing awkwardly with arms tangled in the sleeves.

"Oh, go ahead, wear it." She motioned for him to finish dressing. Frowning, Brynn studied her brother, remembering the conversation she'd had last night with Sam. He'd more or less agreed to discuss the birds and bees with Kevin. So, under the circumstances, it was just as well she'd learned his help wouldn't be required. Other than the game tonight, she couldn't think of any need to see Defenseman Court again.

"How come I didn't know you were taking human sexuality this semester?" she queried Kevin. "I distinctly remember going over your registration card."

Kevin adjusted the crew trim around the bottom of the sweatshirt. Seeking out Brynn's mirror, he pulled a comb from his pocket and slicked back his hair. He pocketed the comb, then ambled across the room, lounging briefly against her door frame.

Brynn waited impatiently with her hands on her hips.

"They call it health, Sis. So parents don't get hysterical. Right now we're studying the causes and effects of sexual deprivation on human psychosexual development." Kevin gave her a measured look. "I'll bring my book home this weekend. If you ask me, you're a classic case. You've been so uptight lately. Maybe you need to get out more. You know... find a man."

As he turned away, Brynn almost choked. However, her strangled response was lost on Kevin, who blithely sailed out of the room and clattered down the stairs.

"Gotta run, Sis," he called over one shoulder. "I'll miss my bus if I don't hurry. You won't forget about Sam's game tonight, will you? Hey!" He paused halfway down. "Maybe you oughta drag out some of those jumpsuits you brought home from New York. They've got class. It just occurred to me—the Samurai might even take an interest in you! And with you being deprived and all..."

Brynn felt her smoldering indignation explode into outrage as Kevin's footsteps resumed. She raced out of the bedroom and leaned over the balustrade in time to see him hoist his backpack.

"Deprived, am I?" Brynn shot after him. "Hold it right there, you adolescent Sigmund Freud." Her voice ended in a shriek as she slid on the polished landing. She grabbed for the last newel post, missed and landed solidly on her derriere. Since she wore only the leotard and tights she'd donned for her morning workout, the parquet flooring Mrs. Flemming had waxed to such a high sheen bruised more than her pride.

Kevin grinned at her devilishly and waved. "My bus is here, Brynn. We'll talk later, okay? Health is my first-period class and Mr. Rusk is discussing our id."

Pulling herself upright, Brynn tightened her fingers on the post. She felt a slight vibration as the front door slammed, then she sagged down onto the top step.

"Mr. Rusk had better not be discussing *my* id, Kevin Powell," she ground out between her teeth. Touching her forehead to her knees, Brynn hauled in a deep breath. Then her shoulders started to shake and she began to laugh. She had to admit the situation was hilarious, once she thought about it. Had she really appealed to Sam Court for help in discussing the facts of life with the uninhibited young upstart who had just been casually tossing out words like psychosexual and id? "It's too late to give Kevin what he really needs." She groaned. A good swift swat on his gluteous maximus—to put it in Mr. Rusk's language.

Still chuckling, Brynn got to her feet. Here she was, like the proverbial circus clown, laughing on the outside and crying on the inside. What she needed was an honest-to-goodness adult-to-adult conversation over not being Kevin's donor. Strange, but Sam Court's name came to mind. Too bad she hadn't stuck to talking last night. And missed that kiss? a little voice inside her asked. "So maybe I am deprived," she remarked out loud, slowly making her way to the shower.

IN HIS NEW KITCHEN, Sam was struggling through domestic chores. Nothing was falling into place for him, at least not with the ease he'd grown accustomed to when his former housekeeper organized their mornings.

Holding ice on a finger he'd burned while testing the heat of a waffle iron, Sam stalked to the foot of the stairs and bellowed up to Holly. "For the last time, young lady, get down here for breakfast."

Holly stepped out from the upper bathroom, then immediately jumped out of sight. Sam noticed she was wearing faded jeans and her new bra, and she held a curling iron still wrapped tightly in a strand of brown hair.

"I don't have time for breakfast, Dad. Stacy is picking me up early. Did you wash my Skyhawk sweatshirt? I tossed it in the hamper last night. I need it for today's pep rally."

"It's in the dryer with my sweats, but you aren't leaving this house without breakfast, so get your tush in gear."

"Dad...gross! My new shirt will be all smelly from your sweats." Holly poked her head out again. Her new, shorter curls bounced.

Sam dropped the ice cube, then bent quickly to retrieve it from the floor. It was the second time in as many days he'd been shocked by his daughter's suddenly grown-up look. Where had the years gone? For no reason at all, he felt something was missing from his life.

"What are you doing with the ice, Dad?" Holly descended the stairs, modestly holding a towel over the demure bra. She dived into the alcove where the washer and dryer stood.

"I burned my hand cooking waffles for my ungrateful child. And by now I imagine they're stone cold," Sam muttered.

"I hate waffles." Holly emerged from the alcove waving a navy sweatshirt emblazoned with a white hawk. "You shrunk my new shirt, Dad. Why didn't you lay it on top of the dryer on a towel like Mrs. Peters used to do?"

Throwing up his hands, Sam headed to the kitchen. "Why didn't you handle it yourself, Miss Know-It-All? You have as much free time as I do. You'd have more if you didn't spend so long in front of the mirror each morning." Whipping around, Sam pointed toward the stairs. "Go! Finish dressing. I'll fix toast."

Quietly, Holly closed the alcove doors. "Boy, you sure are touchy today. I don't spent half as much time in the bathroom as Stacy. I'll just wear a blouse and buy a new sweatshirt at the bookstore. Maybe before I need it again somebody can give you lessons in doing laundry. Say, I'll bet Brynn would...if you asked her."

Sam froze. Looking over his shoulder, he eyed Holly suspiciously. A candid memory of Brynn Powell and the little scene Holly had interrupted last night had been weighing on his mind. As a matter of fact, all morning he'd been dwelling on a variety of things he'd like to explore with the lady just mentioned. Laundry wasn't one of them. Still, he wanted to put an immediate stop to any matchmaking ideas Holly might be entertaining.

"She's Ms. Powell to you, kiddo," he growled, pointing one finger toward the stairs. "You have exactly five minutes until breakfast—one of which is fast ticking away." Sam's eyebrows shot up in surprise as Holly trotted off instead of pressing her point.

The very idea of finding some of Brynn's lacy designs mixed with his laundry set fires licking along his veins. Already Sam knew he was counting too much on seeing her tonight, seated in his reserved corner at the game. It was crazy, because she would never have agreed except for Kevin. He knew that, and yet . . . Sam sighed, jamming bread in the toaster.

Holly slid into her seat at the breakfast table with only seconds to spare. Minutes later Stacy arrived and together the girls made plans to meet Brynn and Kevin after school and ride with them to the game. Brynn's name came up so frequently in their conversation that Sam's nerves were stretched to the limit by the time they left for school. Yet once they'd gone, the houseboat seemed eerily silent.

Faced with cleaning up the mess in the kitchen, Sam suffered a sharp pang of loneliness. He considered calling Brynn—to try out his newly installed telephone, he told himself. Would her voice still carry the smoky tones of sleep? He checked his watch. Was it totally unacceptable for a man to call a woman at this hour? Or did he have to be serious about her? But just how did a man know if he *was* serious?

Sam moved restlessly around the kitchen. He blew faint traces of flour from the kitchen counter and watched them slowly settle on his multicolored kitchen carpet. The tiny specks were hardly visible. A housekeeper would have cleaned it up, he thought, feeling some guilt. And he, too, would have vacuumed, if he shared the household chores with someone who cared. But Holly didn't. She was just a kid. He sighed, tightening the belt of his terry robe. He winced from the pain it caused him. Passing a hand over the bulky tape around his ribs, he stretched gingerly. His gaze slid to the telephone again. No, rather than call Brynn and find himself making small talk, he'd better take a quick run—work out some of the kinks. If he didn't, he'd be warming the bench in tonight's game.

Sauntering to the alcove, Sam opened the dryer and removed his new gray sweats. That was when he discovered Holly's navy blue Skyhawk sweatshirt had faded, leaving great blue blotches on both the top and bottom of his set. Sam stared at them for such a long time, the spots began to take shape.

Swearing to himself, Sam changed into the mottled sweats. If he was still living in southern California where everyone seemed to have a personal psychiatrist or guru, he could probably set a new trend by peddling the spotted sweats as do-it-yourself Rorschach tests. Grinning at the thought, Sam yanked open the front door, then paused to pull up his hood as a buffer against an unusually thick morning mist.

Sam jogged slowly up the ramp, ignoring the strange look cast his way by a neighbor heading off to work in a worsted wool suit and tie.

He'd only gone two blocks when a stitch deep in his side caused his steps to falter. It was raining now. Slowing, Sam sucked in great draughts of air. Many more pains like that and he really would have to leave hockey. He could work with kids new to the game—like his father did. There might be a chasm between them, but he respected Iron Man's coaching integrity. Unconsciously Sam changed his course. Instead of heading home, he limped the last few steps up the hill until he stood in front of Brynn Powell's home.

HAVING DRESSED ONCE, Brynn stripped out of a hot pink jumpsuit and chose instead one of cobalt blue. She didn't know when the idea Kevin had planted in her head had sprouted and grown acceptable, but it had. However, the pink rayon had clung indiscreetly, showing clearly every subtle line of her newly designed bra and thong bikini. Now she was trying out the blue.

"Ah!" Brynn sighed audibly. Under the slightly heavier textured weave of the blue raw silk, that mysteriously bare look she'd been striving for with the underwear design had been achieved.

Adding a gold necklace and bracelet, Brynn studied her image in the bedroom mirror, trifling with the idea of leaving her hair loose. Why? Because Sam Court had so obviously approved of that style? Brynn caught up her hair and swiftly twisted it into its usual knot, leaving perhaps a few more strands than normal loose around her face.

Next she sprayed a fine mist of her favorite perfume on her throat and wrists. After all, she wasn't dressing to please Sam Court. She checked her watch. Changing clothes had taken extra time. If she didn't hurry, she'd have to forgo coffee. She snapped off the light decisively and left the bedroom.

Catching her reflection in the glass of the framed pictures hanging along the stairwell, Brynn hesitated. Would following Kevin's advice draw Sam Court's eye at tonight's game? And speaking of Defenseman Court's eyes, they were the most expressive of any man's she'd ever met. She'd seen admiration in them last night, along with something else. Yes, she thought with a touch of smugness, for a man who held physical beauty in such low esteem, Sam Court had done his share of looking.

The doorbell chimed. Brynn's heart chilled. She didn't expect visitors at this hour of the morning. Twice before it had meant Kevin had fallen ill at school. Both times the vice principal had come to personally escort him home and gone with her to the hospital. In each case Kevin's electrolytes were way off balance. Drained of energy by the thought, Brynn threw open the door only to find Sam Court, his sweat suit wet clear through, hunched close to her door.

"Sam?" Brynn reached out to steady him with her right hand.

He'd worked up a sweat coming up the long hill, and now he could feel his body heat steaming through the damp cotton fleece of the warm-ups as he pushed back his wet hood. He almost tumbled inside when Brynn abruptly yanked her hand away. Looking up, he grimaced. A sharp pain shot through his ribs, nearly felling him.

Brynn's left hand remained pressed against her throat. His name still hung between them like a whispered question.

"Uh . . . hello." He struggled to draw a normal breath.

She was surprised—shocked, really—to see him, Sam realized. And why not? She was dressed for work; she looked chic, elegant…beautiful. He was wet, sweat-stained and all-around grungy. Joani had always thrown a fit about the way he looked after a morning run. He'd showered in their pool house to save battling. And in California, Joani had seldom had to deal with rain.

"Don't let me hold you up," Sam said harshly, backing off. "It must be later than I thought."

Brynn's hand tightened on his arm as she began to recover from the initial shock of seeing him. "Come in," she urged. "It looks as if you've been caught in a real deluge. I was just going to have coffee. Let me grab you a towel and then I'll pour us both a cup." She tugged him inside, then closed the door, never once asking why he was there.

Her floral scent reached him as she opened the hall closet. Sam closed his eyes, savoring the fragrance he had automatically come to associate with Brynn. Sweet. Intoxicatingly sweet. Narrowing his gaze, he wondered what, if anything, she was wearing beneath that incredibly sexy blue thing.

"Are you all right, Sam?" Brynn asked in a worried tone, thrusting a large, fluffy towel into his hands. "Is it your ribs?" She touched his chest lightly.

Sam's eyes flew wide when she trailed a comforting hand over his taped ribs. He felt a burst of answering heat and forced himself to back away. "I'm fine," he growled, quickly dashing the raindrops from his face. "I try to run a couple of miles every morning," he added, willing their perfunctory conversation to distract him. After all, he'd come to talk, not to touch.

"Your dues-paying, daily-drudgery part of being a professional athlete, right?" Brynn laughed, tapping his arm lightly as she said it.

Damn, he thought, staring at her. He'd be hard pressed to remain perfunctory at this rate. "I'll take that coffee now if the offer's still open." With a shrug, he inclined his head toward her kitchen. "After you."

"Of course." Brynn's smile faded. "Follow me." Leading the way, she felt her cheeks grow warm. "Frankly I'm astounded to have found you on my doorstep." She took two earthenware mugs from a rack and poured fresh coffee in each. Her thoughts were centered on how they'd parted last night.

Still clinging to the towel, Sam accepted one cup. Leaning a hip against the counter, he breathed in the aromatic steam.

"Wouldn't you rather sit?" Brynn indicated the kitchen table.

"This is fine." Sam sipped carefully. "If I sit, my muscles will tighten up and I might never make it home."

"Oh!" Brynn peered at him over the rim of her cup, letting her gaze drift slowly over every inch of him. His muscles, straining beneath the damp sweats, looked fine to her. "I could drive you."

"No." He shifted nervously under her frank appraisal, until both hips rested solidly against a cabinet. "I'd just drip all over your car."

"Here, let me take that wet towel." She reached for it, still smiling.

Sam pulled it to his chest, almost spilling his coffee. "Don't get close to me. You're all spiffed up."

"All right. Keep the towel if you like." Puzzled, she lifted one shoulder. "But you can't hurt this floor by dripping on it. It's no-wax. My parents had it installed a year before their accident."

"Holly told me what happened to them. It must have been hard on you, taking over Kevin and the household without any warning."

"Not so hard," she murmured, "except losing them like that. He's the only family I have now. I must admit there was a lot I had to learn about glomerulonephritis."

He made a face. "What exactly is that? It sounds terrible."

"I'm sorry." She shook her head. "That's the technical name for Kevin's ailment. In layman's terms it's kidney failure."

Sam studied his coffee. "We—uh—kind of got sidetracked last night. According to Sunne, you had some bad news yesterday."

Brynn lowered her cup to the counter. "Yes." She hesitated, staring into the distance. "Kevin is one hundred percent dependent on the dialysis machine upstairs to do the work of his kidneys. I was really counting on being a suitable kidney donor for him." She sighed, momentarily drawing her lower lip between her teeth before releasing it and speaking again. "I wasn't." She ended quickly, blinking hard to stem the tears.

Sam placed his cup beside hers and dropped the towel on the counter. "Hey," he said, stepping close and gently resting one hand on the back of her neck. "I can't offer my shoulder because I'm so wet it would ruin your outfit, but I listen well. Do you want to talk about his options?"

As shaken by Sam's tender touch as she was by his sympathetic offer, Brynn ran a knuckle under her lower lid to brush away an errant tear. His shoulder didn't look that damp. How would he react if she leaned on it? For too long, she'd kept things bottled up inside. "No," she managed at last.

Sam's fingers tightened briefly before he withdrew his hand. "We'll change our topic totally then. Tell me about your job in New York. Did you have a B.V.D. shop there, too?"

"B.V.D.?" Brynn repeated the letters slowly. When it dawned on her, she laughed and shook her head. "No. After college, I took a job with Luminaire. They're a big name in women's—ah, intimate apparel." She bit her lip, not wanting to get onto this subject with him. After all, he'd made his opinion of her designs quite clear. And last night, he'd been so rigid in his views about beauty. She wouldn't step into that trap again.

"We've already been over this ground, haven't we, Sam? You know I'm designing a line under my own label. Originally, Romantic Notions belonged to my mother. I took it over when I came home. Actually, both the business and the house are half Kevin's. We'll worry about splitting them when he turns twenty-one. I don't plan ahead any more. I just take life one day at a time." She shrugged. "There you have my story in a nutshell. Now it's your turn."

Sam took a long swallow of coffee. He wasn't good at talking about himself. "There's nothing to tell. Nothing I'm sure you don't already know, that is."

"Oh?" Brynn refilled her coffee, debating whether or not to bring up a question she'd asked him earlier. A question he'd never answered—like, where was the former Mrs. Court now? Sunne would tell her if she asked, but Brynn preferred to be direct. "Tell me about Holly's mother, Sam. I like to know the background on all the students who take my self-esteem classes—especially if it's something that may have a bearing on how they'll react to some of the subjects we discuss." True, but there was another reason for asking....

Sam stiffened automatically. He'd never been one to white-wash the truth about his broken marriage. He'd honored his vows, even tried holding his marriage together long after Joani had called it quits. "Holly's mother left us to join a Vegas chorus line when Holly was two." Was that too blunt? he wondered, measuring her response.

"That long ago?" Brynn was shocked and she was certain it showed in her face.

"Yes." He shifted against the counter. "And less than a year later she ended up on our doorstep broke and crying. For Holly's sake, I let her stay."

Brynn gazed at his stony features and her heart went out to him. "Oh, Sam, I'm sorry. I didn't mean to pry."

"Don't be sorry," he snapped. "When Holly was six, Joani took off again. She left because some nightclub owner promised to make her a star." All this time, and he still wasn't ready to admit his second try had stemmed more from duty and pride than love. Yet sometimes, Joani's many betrayals still hurt. "I'd help Joani out again if she needed it," he said. "But right now, she's happy on the fast track."

Brynn set her cup on the table, fighting off a sudden chill. He sounded like a man who was still in love. Her tone softened. "I didn't know, Sam. What can I say?"

"Nothing. If you have any chance to influence Holly in your class, though, just remember that I don't want her to become obsessed with her looks."

"Not every woman who's concerned about her appearance wants to go on stage, Sam. And Holly is at the age where she wants to emulate her peers. Try to remember what *you* were like at thirteen. At her age, egos are so delicately balanced."

Sam drained his cup, then slapped it on the counter. "I think I told you before that Holly's ego is my concern. We're fine. Don't create trouble where none exists."

Her eyes widened. "My mistake. I thought you asked for my opinion. Why *are* you here?" She turned to look him straight in the face. A challenging look. He was sending mixed messages again.

"It was a domestic issue—but it's not important. Don't let me keep you from your work." His tone was several degrees chillier. And in less time than it took Brynn to blink, Sam had replaced his hood and was striding for her door.

Too stunned to reply, she allowed a few seconds to pass before realizing that Sam was out the front door and halfway down her steps.

She marched to the door and shouted after him. "And what do you know about domestic issues, Sam Court? You're acting just like one of those macho jocks on TV." Brynn was furious. Her one thought was to match his insensitivity. "The next time you wash clothes, you should try separating your colors. Or haven't you been asked to make a laundry commercial yet?" Resisting an urge to find something solid to throw at him, Brynn slammed the oak door. There was a thin feeling of satisfaction in having the last word. So why wasn't it that easy to close the door on him in her heart? And how had she let someone that pigheaded worm his way in to begin with?

Stopping dead on the rain-spattered sidewalk, Sam took stock of his blotchy sweats. How had he let someone he seemed always to be arguing with get close enough to scale old barriers? Suddenly seeing the humor in her closing jab, he laughed. Just now, he'd made a profound discovery. Brynn Powell was nothing like his ex-wife. Besides the fact that she was levelheaded and caring, she had something else Joani had been missing—a sense of humor. When he married Joani, he'd been too young to know that she was a slave to her own beauty and that she'd already lost the ability to laugh at herself. At tonight's game he'd go out of his way to show Brynn how sorry he was for misjudging her.

IF BRYNN HAD KNOWN, she might not have wasted so much energy steaming over the situation. As it was, by the time Kevin and the girls arrived that afternoon, brimming over with excitement at the prospect of attending Sam's hockey game, Brynn was wishing she could stay home. If it were left up to her, she'd tell Mr. Sam Court to—to... Well, it would be a rude suggestion, anyway. "How about it, kids? Couldn't we go some other night? I've had a rough day."

Three pair of bright eyes were trained on her, three disappointed cries aimed at her ears. Guilt flashed in her head like a neon sign. "Oh, all right," she muttered. "Go get in the car." Reluctantly, she dug out her car keys.

Urging her to hurry, Kevin offered to navigate. She refused his help until she ended up mired in heavy traffic with three teenagers talking nonstop, each giving her advice. She rubbed her neck and tapped the steering wheel in annoyance.

"You've been awfully quiet, Sis," Kevin murmured. "I'm sorry we bugged you to come—you really have had a tough day." Holly and Stacy met her eyes in the rearview mirror, growing silent for the first time.

Brynn chewed on her bottom lip. It would be petty to talk about Sam to the kids, and behind his back at that. "It's just this traffic, Kevin. It's horrendous. Now I know why I never go downtown at night."

"You never go anywhere but work and home again," Kevin accused. "Turn left at the next corner, Sis."

"When would you suggest I work in a social life, Kevin? Between midnight and three o'clock? And just how is it that you know so much about this area?"

"Dad and I used to come to the games."

Brynn fell silent. Being upset with Sam was no reason to snap at Kevin.

"Hey, Sis, Mr. Rusk said anyone over thirty should read our textbook. Today we discussed the mysterious id. Neat, huh?"

"Kevin, we are not going to discuss anyone's id in the middle of five o'clock traffic. And I have a few days until I turn thirty."

"Okay," he grumbled, "but it's a fascinating subject. The primitive side of man and all that."

"Keep it up, Kevin. I'll show you the primitive side of woman. Where do you think I should park?" She deliberately changed the subject.

"Anywhere." He leaned forward to get a better view. "Wow! Look at the crowd." Kevin pressed his nose to the window, and the two girls breathed down Brynn's neck. "I'm sure glad Sam gave us tickets. In this crowd it'll pay off knowing a player."

Brynn was trying her best to forget she knew a player. But only moments later her little group was given the VIP treatment and whisked through scores of milling fans straight into front-row seats. Grudgingly, she gave Sam his due.

Upbeat music poured from ceiling-mounted speakers. A crew was making the final sweep with a machine Kevin called a groomer—used to smooth the ice. Next, he pointed out a team of referees skating out to set the goal nets. Brynn felt the promise of excitement. All of this was new to her. She relaxed, letting her tension fade away.

Family members of other players stopped to chat with Holly, who was seated near the end of the row. She was careful to introduce her friends, including Brynn, who found it hard to keep the names straight. Kevin not only knew each player by name but also by number. He was clearly in his element; Brynn hadn't seem him so openly delighted since he was a much younger child.

The Mets' opponents were listed on the scoreboard as the Vancouver Ventures. The name meant nothing to Brynn. "Is it usual for the opposition to have so many rooters?" she asked Kevin.

He shook his head and explained patiently. "Brynn, Vancouver isn't that far away. They brought buses tonight."

Holly handed Brynn a program. She curled the edges nervously, studying the pictures and biography of each team member. She was astounded to find most of the players were no older than twenty-five. Holly's father wasn't quite the old man of tonight's game, but only one player on the Vancouver team was older. Secretly, Brynn thought Sam by far the handsomest of the bunch. Of course, she'd never say that to her present company, because Holly would no doubt tell Sam she thought he was a hunk. Kevin would discuss her sexual deprivation, and Stacy would tell Sunne, who'd spread her remark all over Frontage Bay. No—she surely wouldn't want it to get back to Sam.

Brynn tore her gaze from the photos as the music broke off. The crowd sent up cheers and catcalls when the lusty Ventures skated onto the ice. Brynn craned her neck to see better. One by one the players, dressed in colorful uniforms of black, red and yellow, entered the center face-off circle. Each player's name was droned hollowly over the loudspeaker and the Vancouver supporters shrieked and stamped their approval. Then it was the Mets' turn, and the hometown fans went wild, drowning out the Venture fans' jeers.

Imbued with a touch of the win fever she felt running high around her, Brynn cheered loudly for the more conservatively dressed Mets.

When the crowd settled back into their seats, she saw that instead of hockey sticks, each Met player carried a delicate long-stemmed rose. As the lights dimmed, a hush fell over the crowd. Skating close to the Plexiglas shield in a halo of light filtering down from a single spot, each team member in turn signaled a woman in the audience and tossed her a rose.

Then out came Sam, carrying two rosebuds. Brynn hardly recognized him in his heavily padded uniform, and when she did, she scooted to the edge of her seat to gain a better view, feeling like a kid. Or perhaps more like a teen with a crush on the football captain. She felt the heat rise in her cheeks.

Without so much as looking Brynn's way, Sam signaled first Holly, then Stacy and tossed each girl a pale pink bud. Brynn leaned forward with her elbows on the railing and watched him skate away backward. She held her breath fearing he would fall. She could feel her heart slamming erratically in her throat.

Making slow circles on the ice Sam reached down and picked up a third flower—an American Beauty red—and cradled it against his cheek. The fans swooned in unison as Sam made a show of nuzzling its velvet throat. It was plain to see that he was all showman, reeling in his audience—especially the females.

And along with every woman in the crowd over twelve years of age, Brynn grew curious to see who Sam's choice would be. She didn't expect him to give it to her. Not after the way they'd parted that morning. Though she thought it would be terribly exciting to be singled out.

Then all at once a man Kevin identified as the Mets' coach beckoned Sam. The audience, primed to a razor's edge, remained tense while the coach gestured wildly with his arms and Sam shook his head vehemently.

Suddenly the Mets fans began to whisper among themselves until the noise became an insistent murmur loud enough to tear Brynn's attention away from Sam.

"Psst. Look, Sis." Kevin's elbow in her ribs pulled Brynn's focus to a man and woman standing near the end of their row. Leaning close, he hissed in her ear, "Wow! Isn't she something?" Kevin's mouth went slack as a stunning woman leaned down and exchanged words with a couple Holly had introduced only moments ago.

Brynn agreed with Kevin—she was *something* all right. The woman, a flaming redhead, would have been even more beautiful in Brynn's estimation if not for an excess of makeup. She had high cheekbones and generous physical endowments. She wore silk as though it were the only acceptable attire for a hockey game. A three-quarter-length leopard coat left the redhead looking like a new breed of endangered species. For a moment, Brynn forget Sam and his rose.

The woman's companion, a portly, balding man, was also overdressed in a European suit. He sported numerous flashy rings on his pudgy fingers. Yet he walked with an air of authority.

Brynn would have dismissed the whole thing if she hadn't glimpsed the look on Sam Court's face as he skated close to the railing, still holding the red rose. Brynn's breath escaped in a quiet hiss as the woman hurled herself at Sam.

In a dramatic gesture the lady in silk plucked the rose from his hand and followed it up by kissing Sam soundly on the lips. A long, drawn-out, high-voltage exchange.

Affected by the intimacy of the kiss and her own unwitting proximity, Brynn did her very best to hide behind her program. But she found it impossible to avoid the shrill whistles of Sam's fans and the sudden thundering drumroll that reverberated through the area. The fans stamped their feet, almost bringing the bleachers down, then begged for more as the kiss ended.

Suddenly, the house settled into silence and a whistle blew. Brynn sat stiffly watching as the chic couple joined Sam's coach in the middle of the ice. Without really considering why, she somehow felt the newfound joy had gone from her day.

"Who do you suppose they are?" whispered Kevin out of one side of his mouth.

"I have no idea," Brynn murmured. "But Leopard Lady seems to know Sam well enough."

"Doesn't look like he's too happy about it, if you ask me," Kevin said. He sprang up, pulling Brynn to her feet, as he pointed out the players who were skating into a winged V formation on the ice.

Kevin and Stacy rushed to press their noses against the glass for a better view. It was then that Brynn chanced to see Holly, still slumped in her seat.

"Holly?" She moved to the vacant seat beside the girl and touched her shoulder. When she didn't look up, Brynn bent down to find out what the trouble was.

Holly's lips trembled. She threw her arms around Brynn and whispered in a shaky voice, "That woman who took the rose from my dad . . . she looks a lot like a picture we have at home of my mother. But it couldn't be my mother—could it, Brynn?"

CHAPTER SEVEN

BRYNN HELD HER BREATH until she thought she'd pass out. Surely Holly was mistaken. Wouldn't the woman have greeted her own daughter? Why, she'd spoken with a man seated across the aisle in the same row. In the distance, over the loudspeaker, Brynn heard the announcer asking everyone to stand for the national anthems. She knew that, somehow, she and Holly had to rise.

As the players doffed their helmets, Brynn searched the arena to see where the redhead and her companion had gone. She was hoping it had been some kind of pregame hoax. Something to heat up the crowd. But no, the two were talking with the Mets coach like old friends. Off to the side was Sam looking...what? His face was unreadable. "Holly, everything will be all right, honey," Brynn murmured. "If anything as important as your mother coming to town had been in the offing, your father would have discussed it with you and made proper arrangements. You've got to trust him."

Yet Brynn wasn't sure she was telling the truth. The coach seemed to be treating the newcomers like visiting royalty. And the woman caressed the flower in loving strokes, never taking her eyes off Sam.

Accepting Brynn's reassurance, Holly scrubbed at her eyes. Without hesitation, she scrambled out of her seat and reached for Brynn's hand, holding it securely through the singing of both anthems. Was it Holly's palm sweating, Brynn wondered, or hers?

Near the end of the final stanza, Brynn sought out Sam's gaze and held it until the last note faded. Then she lowered her lashes, breaking contact. Brynn squeezed Holly's hand because she sensed the girl needed an anchor. Sam's oddly uncertain expression had given her no confidence that he would indeed have done right by his daughter. She refrained from looking up again until the referee tossed the coin and fans were asked to be seated. Stacy and Kevin came back to claim their chairs, not noticing the sudden withdrawal of the two they'd left behind. Kevin rattled on. Brynn let him.

Brynn's concern for the distraught Holly overshadowed the otherwise infectious frenzy of the crowd at the first home game of a new season. It was only after Sam entered the fray that Holly loosened the death grip she retained on Brynn's hand and began to take a halfhearted interest in the battle on the ice.

At halftime, the score was tied. Brynn watched the woman—possibly Sam's ex-wife—and her male companion fall in behind the Mets' coach and trail the team into the locker room. Oh, to be a mouse in the corner. What did the woman's arrival mean to Sam? To Holly? To her? Enough to leave a knot in her stomach; she knew that much.

"Anyone want a soft drink?" Kevin asked.

Stacy jumped up. "I'll go with you, Kev. I see some kids from school heading that way. Want to come, Holly?"

Holly slumped in her seat listlessly. Brynn answered for her. "Holly's not feeling well. Why don't you bring her back one?"

Kevin and Stacy nodded in unison and headed off to the concession stand.

"You could be wrong, Holly. The picture of your mother must be old. Sometimes one person does resemble another." But Brynn's heart sank. A woman like that would be hard to forget. And why the little performance with Sam?

Holly didn't answer, only pulling deeper into herself. Brynn was so furious with Sam she could have shaken him. The man did play more games than hockey—and they were all out of her league.

Halfway through the third period, Brynn received a note from Sam. It was brief, simply stating that although he'd planned to meet them after the game for a bite to eat, his plans had changed. Would she mind explaining to Holly and dropping her off at the Evans's home? Crushing the note to relieve her helplessness and distress, Brynn shoved it deep in her pocket and relayed the news to Holly as best she could. And yes, she did mind.

"I'm worried about my dad, Ms. Powell," Holly said a few minutes later. "He's not playing very well tonight. Something must be wrong. Do you suppose his ribs hurt more than he let on?"

Brynn glanced over in amazement. Not one word had Holly uttered about wanting to meet the woman she thought might be her mother. It was as though she had dismissed the lady in the leopard coat completely.

"He's tough, Holly," was all the encouragement Brynn could muster. She found her anger at Sam building. How could he be so insensitive? Brynn dredged up resentment enough for both herself and Holly.

And on top of everything else, the Mets lost resoundingly. Brynn and the girls were silent on their walk to the car. Kevin couldn't seem to keep quiet. He sounded like a running commentary.

"I thought the game was great," he announced for all to hear. "The score was much closer than the sportscasters predicted. After all," he allowed, "it was their first game as a bona fide team, you know."

"My dad spent half the game in the penalty box," lamented Holly, sinking into a far corner of the back seat. "Did he happen to say in that note why he couldn't meet us?"

"Not really, Holly." Brynn shook her head and started the car.

"He acted like he was really hurt that one time," Stacy chimed in. "You know, when that awful number twelve broke a hockey stick over your dad's shoulder, Holly? I thought Sam was going to deck him. Are they always that rough?"

Kevin snorted indignantly. Through a stifled yawn, he mumbled, "Stacy, you are so squeamish. You didn't see any blood on the ice, did you? Sam's the best. He operates on skill. He doesn't need to fake it. And he's never been in a brawl. But do you know how many hockey players have had all their teeth knocked out?"

"Hush, Kevin!" Brynn nudged his arm as she pulled into the stream of traffic. "We don't all share your enthusiasm for the barbaric. Perhaps you wouldn't mind changing the subject. The Mets lost. No sense rehashing a dead issue.''

Kevin grimaced wryly. "Oh, all right, Sis." Scrambling to his knees, he twisted in his seat belt until he faced the two girls in the back seat. "Holly," he demanded, "why didn't you tell me the team's getting a new owner? At halftime it was all the crowd at the concessions talked about. Do you think it's that bald guy with the *bee-utiful* lady friend? I heard someone mention the money man is a big wheel from Vegas."

Brynn shot a quick glance in the rearview mirror, in time to catch Holly's negligent shrug. She didn't want to start Holly thinking about her mother again. Could Joani Court, or any woman for that matter, be as selfish and callous toward her own flesh and blood as Sam had insinuated? Or was that sour grapes on Sam's part because she'd left him? And couldn't Kevin just keep his lip buttoned, for pity's sake? Brynn did it for him by changing the subject. "Holly, were you planning to spend the night with Stacy?"

"I don't know," she answered sleepily. "I don't usually get to stay with anyone on a school night. But Dad told Stacy's mom we'd be really late getting home, because it was their first game and all."

"I imagine *he* will," murmured Brynn half to herself, remembering the bold woman who'd snatched the rose and the kiss from Sam. Feeling a stab of animosity for Holly's sake, she turned her Volkswagen down the street of large old homes where Stacy lived. Leopard Lady had acted as though she'd like to drag Sam off to her lair, Brynn thought nastily, whipping into the Evans driveway and yanking on the emergency brake with more force than necessary. But then, maybe Sam would go willingly enough, she thought with just a little pang.

"Thanks, Brynn." Stacy lunged over the seat to give her a hug. "It's neat going to the game with someone besides my parents. I had a great time."

"Yes, thanks from me, too, Ms. Powell," echoed Holly, sliding out behind her friend.

"You're both welcome." Brynn leaned across Kevin and smiled at the sleepy girls. Gently, she added, "Holly, you can call me Brynn, too, you know."

Holly gave a crooked smile. "If you're sure it's okay. But could you maybe tell my dad? He's the one who insists I use Miss or Ms."

The front door opened and Brynn saw Sunne step into a shaft of light. "Well, Holly, I'd be happy to tell your father you have my permission, but I doubt I'll be seeing him anytime soon. Won't he just take your word for it?"

"He'll have to see you tomorrow, won't he?" Holly asked with some hesitation. "His team is going out of town and he said he forgot to give you the permission slip for my classes. Maybe you could mention it then." Shyly she turned to address Kevin. "Bye, see you in algebra tomorrow." Without waiting for his response she dashed after Stacy.

"Holly, wait!" Brynn tugged at her seat belt, giving herself more room to reach the closing door. "Tell your father to leave the form with Sunne . . ." She let the sentence trail off as the young girl slammed the door.

"I'm tired, Sis," Kevin said. "Could we just go home now? I'm not used to this much excitement in the evenings, I guess."

"Oh, Kev! I'm sorry. This is late for you. I'll just call Sunne in the morning and have her get the permission slip from Sam. He'll probably be grateful that it'll save him an extra trip." She popped the gearshift into reverse and released the brake.

"I wonder how long Sam's going to be out of town?" Kevin ran his fingers through his hair. Dropping one hand to cover his mouth, he hid a yawn.

Brynn grunted noncommittally and turned the corner. She drove the next two blocks in silence until they pulled into their own driveway.

Kevin unfastened his seat belt. "Did you know Sam had a Jacuzzi added to his hot tub on the houseboat? He said if Dr. Low gave the go-ahead, I could try it out."

Kevin sounded so eager, Brynn didn't have the heart to tell him that if the woman at the arena was Sam's ex-wife, any number of changes might be in the offing. It would be best if both Powells forgot Sam Court now. Sighing tiredly, Brynn snapped on the hall light.

"Gee, Brynn. You look dragged out, too. Maybe Sam will let you use his hot tub, if you ask." Kevin touched her arm lightly. As he headed for the stairs, he called over his shoulder, "I see you took my advice about wearing the jumpsuit. But I think maybe you'd better put it away again. At halftime I heard a couple of dudes behind us talking about how sexy you looked. One of them is on our varsity football team. I didn't like them giving you the once-over. You're my sister!"

Brynn laughed as she climbed the stairs behind him. Strangely enough, his playing the protector was just what she needed to make her laugh and forget Sam and his red-haired friend. "Well, well, Dr. Frankenstein, perhaps you've created a monster. I guess you'll just have to live with it."

Brynn made claws of her hands and chased Kevin across the landing. Beating him to his bedroom, she flipped on the light and turned to ruffle his hair.

"Sis," he growled, throwing her a pained look. "You're acting as dumb as Stacy."

"But just think, now you can set your health teacher's mind at rest." Brynn tried, but couldn't keep the mirth out of her voice. "Look at it this way, Kev. In one simple experiment you've proved that advanced age hasn't arrested the development of my psychosexual growth." Bursting into laughter, she took refuge in her room, leaping behind the door to avoid the wadded-up sweatshirt Kevin threw at her. Their playful argument provided something other than Defenseman Court to think about and was a move toward getting her life back to normal.

In the morning, Brynn's mood changed so drastically that her lighthearted banter with Kevin following the game might never have happened.

She overslept, and when she went to awaken Kevin found him glassy-eyed and feverish. Though it was highly unlikely that the late night was totally to blame for his condition, Brynn chastised herself for allowing him to become overtired. Dr. Low had warned her that his condition could deteriorate with something just this simple. She placed the blame on her selfish desire to see Sam play.

Yes, if she honestly called a spade a spade, that was the real reason she hadn't objected to Sam's giving Kevin the tickets—and now look, Kevin's temperature was over a hundred and one. She shook the thermometer down with a vigorous twist of her wrist.

"No school for you today, Kev." Cleaning the mercury tip with alcohol, Brynn stared out the window at the drizzle. "I'll call Dr. Low to see what antibiotic he wants to start. I don't think we have any on hand. But I'll go out at lunch and get what you need." Times like this, she really felt the burden of being alone.

Kevin groaned. "Would you call Holly and ask her to pick up my schoolwork?" His request was barely more than a croak.

"I thought Stacy always picked up your homework." Brynn pulled his covers up and tucked them in.

"Quit fussing over me, Sis. I can't move when you do that." He tugged at the taut blanket.

"Well, doesn't she?" Brynn demanded.

"Doesn't she what? Who?" Kevin's brows drew together as he peered at her over the covers.

"You asked me to call Holly, but I've always called Stacy before."

"Yeah, well, Holly is more reliable. She takes good notes and she doesn't giggle all the time when she deciphers them."

Brynn studied her brother. His cheeks were flushed, and he looked decidedly unwell. "All right, Kevin. I'll see if I can catch Holly before Sunne drops the girls off at school. But remember, Holly did say her father was leaving on a road trip today. They may already have other plans for after school."

"Nope." Kevin flopped over on his stomach. "Holly said they never do anything."

Brynn pressed her lips together. She was reluctant to encourage further friendship between Kevin and Holly Court for reasons that had nothing to do with Kevin. So it was with some misgiving that she agreed. "I'll call her right after I speak to Dr. Low." But she'd no more than reached for the telephone when it rang.

"Oh, no. I hope that isn't Mrs. Flemming saying she can't come today," Brynn muttered, snatching up the receiver. "Hello," she said warily.

"Brynn? This is Sam. I didn't wake you, did I?"

She clutched the collar of her satin robe, startled by the sound of his deep voice.

"No. No, you didn't wake me. I'm an early riser, but I certainly didn't suppose *you'd* ever see daybreak, especially not the morning after a late-night game. Is something wrong?"

Sam didn't know precisely how to answer that. His ribs ached like fury and he'd had a sleepless night because of her. He worried that she might have been as upset about not receiving the red rose at the arena as he'd been about not giving it to her. Was her tone cool today—or was he only imagining it? Because he wasn't sure, Sam settled on offering her a half-truth.

"I planned for all of us to go somewhere for a hamburger after the game. But after Doug Lovell clipped me with his stick, I knew the doc needed to retape my ribs and that would make it too late for the kids. Later, another . . . uh, team matter came up that necessitated my staying."

Brynn bit her lip. "It was a school night." She didn't want to hear about Sam's team matter.

"Yes . . . well, I figured an extra hour would make a difference to you, too. So have lunch with me today. I want to make up for last night."

"I can't, Sam. Kevin is sick today."

Kevin bolted upright in bed. "Is that the Samurai? Hey, tell him how much I appreciated those great seats. Darn, I wish I could go to school today and brag a little."

"What's he saying?" Sam asked Brynn. "Going to my game didn't make him sick, did it? I could bring lunch to your house if you'd like."

"Kevin, hush," she said. "I can't talk now, Sam." Brynn rushed the words. "I hear Mrs. Flemming letting herself in and I'm already late for work. I still have to call Holly over at Sunne's to see if she'll pick up Kevin's homework today."

"I'll tell her," he offered. "She's eating breakfast. But she'll want to know exactly what's wrong with Kevin."

"You didn't say you were calling from the Evans's house."

"I'm not," he said patiently. "Are you sure it isn't you who can't take late nights?" he drawled, sounding amused. "I picked Holly up around midnight and we came home. Now, about lunch . . ."

"That's really very kind of you," she cut in, thinking midnight for Holly on a school night *was* irresponsible. "Kevin's running a fever. When kidney patients spike a temperature, there's danger of infection. It means getting a urine specimen to the lab to see if he's spilling protein, and as undoubtedly he will be, it means a trip to the pharmacy for an antibiotic."

"If I can help, tell me."

His sincere offer quelled Brynn's retort.

"Are you still there?" he asked. "You lost me right after the term 'specimen.' But it sounds as though you could do with a little help in all your running around."

Brynn twisted the phone cord around and around her index finger. Then, seeing Kevin's frankly curious gaze, she abruptly let it go. "That's too generous of you, Sam," she replied stiffly. "I know you're leaving town today and I wouldn't dream of imposing. Honestly now, I must run. Thanks again from Kevin and me for the tickets. And if you'll remind Holly about his homework I'd be grateful. Goodbye."

Sam was left staring at a buzzing receiver. He dropped it in its cradle and stood a moment longer, pausing to massage the back of his neck. Brynn *was* angry about the rose. He was sure of it. But, damn it all, she couldn't be half as disappointed as he'd been. Trust Joani to catapult into his life so dramatically. Not a word of any kind from her in more than a year and then whammo—her latest mentor decides he wants to own a hockey team. And wasn't Joani just in seventh heaven because it was *his* team?

Looking through the kitchen door, Sam studied Holly as she ate her breakfast. He'd talked to her for nearly an hour about Joani, trying his level best to be fair. Holly hadn't been very forthcoming. Maybe he'd missed something. Damn!

ELEVEN O'CLOCK and Brynn still hadn't found a single friend who was free to cover the shop during lunch hour. Hanging up the telephone, she checked her watch yet again, hoping she'd misread the time. But it was eleven, all right.

In the adjacent showroom, she heard the front door open and the bell tinkle. "Drat," she mumbled. A customer—and just when it was obvious she'd have to lock up and run her errands. Dr. Low had been insistent she get the lab tests done before noon.

"Seems like we've played this scene before." Sam poked his head around the door frame and smiled. "Who's the unlucky soul you're dratting this time?"

"Sam!" Brynn hurriedly closed the telephone book, feeling her cheeks heat as it slid from her grasp.

"Well?"

Brynn was thinking how the cut on his face, now turning shades of yellow and blue, didn't detract one iota from his wonderful, sexy violet eyes. She was so busy admiring how good he looked in turquoise, the color of the polo shirt he wore beneath an open, white poplin rain jacket, that she didn't answer until he prompted her again.

"I hope it's not Kevin being dratted—especially if he's sick."

"What?" Brynn blinked. "Oh, no. I was saying drat in general. I haven't been able to find anyone to watch the store while I go out for a while."

"I'd volunteer, but what I know about ladies' underwear could be summed up in one word—nothing!"

Brynn crossed her arms and gave him a measured look. "I'll bet."

"Let me rephrase that." Sam laughed. "What I know about *selling* it . . ." He spread his hands.

"You've made your point." Brynn stood and reached for her coat. "It's been slow today. I'll lock up for as long as it takes. Unless, of course, you came to buy something."

"You have anything in long-sleeved high-necked flannel?" he asked, moving closer until he stood staring down into her eyes. "My mother's birthday is coming up." He winked.

Brynn raised one brow. "Knowing you, I'd suppose flannel is what you expect both your daughter and your wife to wear, too, Sam."

Just for a moment, she thought she saw a flicker of agitation in the depths of his eyes. Then it was gone and the corners of his mouth tilted upward in a wry grin. "Come on," he said, gripping her elbow and hustling her through the door. "Enough of this kind of jousting. I told you I only play one game, and this isn't it. I like the feeling of silk next to a woman's skin as well as the next guy. And I never claimed to be celibate, did I? Now, let me drive you where you need to go, and I'll tell you what's really on my mind. I want to talk about Holly."

It was on the tip of Brynn's tongue to refuse him—until he mentioned Holly. She'd been thinking of the woman in the silk dress. Of course he liked silk. Joani wore it well. And a man who kissed as he did would never be celibate for long. She bit her lip and flushed.

"All right, Sam. But I need to stop by my house first. And let me warn you right now. I don't have time for lunch. So no monkeyshines."

"Yes, ma'am! I know when I've been put in my place." Sam grinned, zipped his jacket, then held the door while Brynn searched her purse for the shop keys. The morning drizzle had turned into a solid rain. They made a mad dash for the car and both were buckled into his Jaguar before either spoke again.

Brynn was first. "You'd better talk fast, Sam. These are all short hops, and I've got quite a few of them."

"Okay, here goes... I'll be gone three weeks and Holly's going to be staying at the Evanses. I'd like you to let her come help out at the shop every night after school. She could stock shelves, stack boxes, clean up around the place—whatever you need doing. I'll pay you the going rate to give her, plus I'll double that amount for your time. Will you do it?"

Brynn stared at him, her mouth open. "I can't hire her, Sam," she ventured at last. "She isn't old enough for a work permit. She'd have to be at least fifteen."

"I'm not asking you to break the law. It would be more like an allowance for her and baby-sitting money for you. You did say Holly was interested in learning to draw. And once, earlier, you said if you could afford it, you'd like extra help."

By then, he'd pulled up in front of her house. Brynn unbuckled her seat belt and jumped out of the car. "And I would hire someone, too, if the place was earning enough. I didn't necessarily mean Holly. I'll be right back and we can discuss this.'' She gave the door a push.

Sam leaned over and called through the open window. ''Tell Kevin that Holly promised to pick up all his work and help him with his algebra when she brings it by.''

''If he's not too sick, he'll be delighted to hear that.'' She hesitated and turned back. ''Sam...what about Holly's crush on Kevin? How do you expect me to deal with that for three weeks?''

''I talked with Kevin, Brynn.'' Sam shrugged lightly. ''He doesn't have a crush on Holly. The way I see it, it takes two to be in crush for any problem to exist. Go on now, get whatever you need and we'll talk more when you return. Look...you're getting wet.''

Brynn nodded, withdrawing. This was all too smooth—too civilized for the questions she really wanted to ask. She wanted to know if Leopard Lady was truly Holly's mother. If the answer was yes, where had his voluptuous ex spent the night? But then, nothing gave her the right to question anything about Sam Court, she lamented, stalking into the house and slamming the door in her wake.

By the time she came out, Brynn had convinced herself Sam Court's personal life was none of her concern. Why, then, when she was back in the car and had given Sam directions to their next destination, did she blurt out, ''Was the beautiful redhead you gave the rose to last night your ex-wife, Sam?''

Sam hit the brakes. The driver of the car behind him laid on the horn, and Sam gaped openly at Brynn as his fingers tightened reflexively on the steering wheel. Almost immediately afterward, he gained control and moved on with the flow of traffic. ''I didn't *give* her the rose. She *took* it. I don't know how you knew that was Joani, but her arrival here makes no difference to our arrangement.'' His eyes met Brynn's. ''Joani's interest here is in me—not our daughter. Holly likes you, Brynn. She quotes you constantly. I'd like her to spend more time with you. Holly needs to identify with women who have solid values and the kind of stability you've got. I don't want her to think success is having her face and figure eulogized in every pulp magazine in the country.''

Brynn held her breath, taking in every syllable. Sam had fallen silent for several moments before she realized they'd arrived at her next stop. The atmosphere was still charged from his outburst. He sounded like a man who'd been badly hurt by someone he'd entrusted with his heart. Just what did he mean, Joani's interest was in him, not Holly? Weren't they a family?

But Brynn knew how it felt to be hurt and defensive. She'd believed in Anthony and he'd let her down. Though she wished there was more time to delve into Sam's pain, Kevin was the one who claimed her allegiance right now. She pressed her hand against Sam's and quickly agreed to let Holly spend time at the store after school. "And we can iron out the details on the way to the pharmacy, Sam," she added, leaving him alone with his ghosts while she dashed into the lab.

When she came back clutching a prescription, Sam greeted her with a wide smile and a bucket of fried chicken with all the trimmings. His car smelled as her mother's house used to smell on Sundays, and for an instant she felt oddly moved, almost tearful. Obviously, this couldn't continue.

"Sam . . ." she began in a scolding tone.

Holding up a hand, he interrupted. "Before you yell at me, I'd just like to say that this isn't exactly stopping for lunch. Sitting in the car waiting for you when I could smell chicken cooking was pure torture."

Brynn laughed. "It does smell good, but it's not exactly health food, Sam."

"So, I'll double my laps at practice tomorrow." He eyed her critically as he started the car. "And you need some meat on your bones, lady. If you're on a diet, you shouldn't be."

As Brynn gave him directions to the pharmacy, she wondered if he had just paid her a backhanded compliment, and if so, how should she respond? Having no ready answer, she quickly opened the box of chicken, doled out the napkins and, after giving him first choice, helped herself to a drumstick.

"I knew you couldn't resist," he teased, angling into a parking space. "Here, give me that prescription. I'll run in and find out how long before they can fill it. You dish up the rest of the food. I'll be back before you know it. We can eat while we wait."

It was almost impossible to resist a snowballer like Sam Court, she thought, watching him hunch his broad shoulders against the slanting rain as he dashed into Harris Drugs. If she didn't watch herself, she could get used to being pampered. In fact, she could get used to leaning on a man like Sam without half-trying.

"The pharmacist asked about you, Brynn," Sam remarked when he was once more settled in the front seat and had begun to eat. "He seemed surprised that I was bringing in Kevin's prescription. He really gave me the third degree—about my connection with you *and* your brother. Is Kevin sick often?"

"Well, yes and no. Actually he's been fairly well this year for someone in his condition. Colds and run-of-the-mill viruses are exceptionally hard on kidney patients, so we buy a fair amount of antibiotics. And...we're a pretty tight community here. I hope you made it clear that we were just friends. You wouldn't want Mr. Harris linking your name romantically with mine out in the neighborhood."

"I wouldn't?" Sam stopped eating and raised one eyebrow. "Maybe I should have asked much sooner—are you romantically linked with someone else?"

Brynn felt her heart flip and knew a flush was rising in her cheeks. "No," she denied. "I don't—"

Sam cut her off again. "No is sufficient. But I wonder what's wrong with all the men in Frontage Bay." He checked his watch. "Time to go get the medicine." He reached for the door handle.

"I'll go, Sam." Brynn scrubbed her fingers with a napkin. "I have to write a check."

"So you can pay me later. I want you to finish eating. They'll be feeding me on the plane tonight."

"I will repay you, Sam." Brynn knew her face was growing redder in embarrassment. "The Powells don't accept charity."

"We'll settle up out of the money I'm going to owe you for keeping Holly." His tone and the set of his lips brooked no argument.

"You bet we will." Brynn tipped her head in agreement as Sam climbed out of the car. Having the last word hadn't given her the satisfaction she thought it would. What it did was ruin her appetite completely. She folded her plate around her uneaten portion and thrust it, along with Sam's, into the sack. Very likely Sam was looking at her as a sitter for Holly and nothing more. She was blowing these innocent conversations out of proportion. It was time she stopped.

More than an hour later, after they'd swung by her house with the medicine and she'd touched base with Mrs. Flemming, Sam drove her to Romantic Notions and pulled into an empty parking space outside the store.

"If you don't mind, Brynn," Sam continued, taking up where they'd left off earlier. "I'll call Holly at your shop every night around five o'clock. Sometimes our debriefings run late, so she'll probably be in bed by the time I get a chance to phone after the game. This way, you can give me updates on how it's working out."

Brynn fished out one of her business cards and handed it to him. "I don't mind at all. I'll love having Holly's company. Sometimes my afternoons get quite hectic. She can do price tags, if nothing else."

"Romantic Notions," he murmured, letting the shop name slide off his tongue like thick honey. "If any of the guys happen to see this in my possession, the locker room will rumble for months. Has anyone ever told you that your store is poorly named?"

"Really?" she drawled. "And *you* are an authority, I suppose?"

"I know most of the merchandise I saw inside would do more than give a guy notions." He yanked gently on one of her stray curls and wound a longer strand around his index finger.

Stacking the remains of lunch, Brynn opened her door. She refused to be goaded by his innuendos this time. "Have a good trip, Sam." Her lips twitched with the hint of a smile. "Maybe if you'd quit daydreaming and stay out of the penalty box, the Mets could score. You might even end up with fewer bruises." Already half out the door and with her hands full, she turned to look over her shoulder, managing not to laugh outright.

Sam's fingers slipped from her wispy curl. "Witch," he rasped, letting his hand slide down until it circled her neck. "What I've been daydreaming about for two days is kissing you again."

Caught off balance and off guard, there was nothing Brynn could do but meet his lips with her own. And when she did, she knew that waiting for another of his kisses was what had kept her awake last night. She tried imagining why Joani Court had walked out on this man—until she ceased all thought and simply took pleasure instead.

The food bag rustled as it fell to the floor. Somehow, Brynn hadn't expected to feel the same bone-dissolving heat as when Sam had kissed her the first time. Especially since she'd blamed her response that night on bad news from Dr. Low and more than her usual one glass of wine. Clearing her mind, she slid closer to Sam and lifted her arms, now free of burden. She buried her fingers in his hair, still damp from his dash through the rain, and reveled in its cool touch. Sometimes it just didn't pay to.

Sam made a noise deep in his throat, loosened his hold on Brynn's neck and spread his palm flat across her back. He edged her closer, taking the kiss deeper.

Somewhere out on the street, a horn honked. They sprang apart wearing identical expressions of guilt.

Brynn wet her lips. "Sam, I . . ." she started, then fell silent. In her habitual gesture of anxiety, she drew her bottom lip between her teeth.

"Oh, lord, Brynn! Don't do that." He touched her chin with one finger. When he couldn't keep it steady, he faced the front windshield and draped his arm over the steering wheel for support. He heard her pick up the bag and knew she was slipping out the door. "Believe me . . . I didn't mean to attack you like that."

A gust of wind caught the door and ripped it from her loose grasp. She tried to keep her tone light and was distressed by her lack of control when her voice broke. "I d-don't want to get involved with you. It's typical of someone in your shoes—a man who blows in and out of cities—to think you have only to sweep into town and lay siege to the first local woman you meet. Well, I don't do one-night stands. I have real responsibilities and I'm not in awe of you, Defenseman Court. And I'm not a stand-in for your long-lost love, either."

"Really?" Sam barely held his temper in check. "I haven't asked to share your bed, have I? I happen to take being a role model for young players very seriously—which is something I thought we had in common, because you do the same for teenage girls. And if you'll pardon me all to hell, I did not *blow* into town. I bought real estate here, lady...and that makes me a local, too." He matched her glare for glare until a car filled with laughing, chattering ladies pulled up near the shop door, claiming their attention.

"I have to go." Brynn lifted her chin and backed out of the Jaguar. She sighed. "I don't even know what I mean any more. I certainly wasn't taking a cheap shot at your reputation as a sports figure or your relationship with younger players. Perhaps I was referring more to your double standards—the rules you expect Holly to live by are very different from those you make for yourself."

He frowned. "I'll make her rules clear before I leave. However, I'm a little confused about the accusation in general. I'll admit to having some thoughts about you that are a long way from adolescent. But I don't call it a double standard, I call it a legitimate difference. And the difference, Brynn, is that you are a consenting adult and Holly's far from it."

"I have a business to run and Kevin's sick. Let's just leave it at a chance attraction, shall we?"

"Look, Brynn," he said, running a hand through his hair. "I'll be back in about three weeks. We'll meet for a real meal someplace private where we can talk. You aren't any more surprised by this...this attraction than I am." Leaning out the door, Sam brushed a finger lightly over her lips. "Go take care of your customers," he prompted softly when Brynn opened her mouth to refute him. "Go on." He smiled crookedly. "I'll be in touch."

Brynn watched him drive away out of the corner of her eye as she acknowledged her customers. The noisy group, all friends from the neighborhood, clamored to find out who Brynn's luscious mystery man was.

"He's an old friend of Paul Evans and new in the area," she said briskly, leading them into the shop. "You'll get to meet him at the Evans's Halloween party, I'm sure. But before you go spreading rumors all over town," she admonished, "I'll tell you what I told Sunne. I don't have time for any man in my life. Sam Court's daughter is a good friend of Kevin's and that's all there is to it. End of rumor—*comprende?*"

"Of course, Brynn," they all chorused, exchanging knowing smiles.

Brynn gnashed her teeth. She was back to thinking Sam Court a menace. He was high-handed, arrogant and very sure of himself. She knew his kind. Some men couldn't help oozing charm and personality. They collected women everywhere they went. It was like a shot in the arm to their macho pride. But hadn't she witnessed the kiss last night? Only a fool would fall for a man who kissed his ex-wife like that. Judging by the length and intensity of the kiss, Sam was a man who quite obviously wouldn't turn any former lover—or would-be lover?—away.

But drat the man—when he touched her, there was no denying she puddled like a melted marshmallow. Thank goodness he was going out of town!

CHAPTER EIGHT

SAM RAPPED ON AN OPEN DOOR, then entered the room assigned to visiting team coaches without waiting for an invitation. "Hey, Coach, I came to use the phone. Those jokers are making so much noise in the locker room tonight I can't hear the dial tone, let alone anyone talking at the other end."

Coach Covington stood, folding the player roster he was working on together with a copy of his game strategy. "You got some kind of problem at home, Court? I've seen you with an ear glued to the phone every night this week."

Already dressed in playing gear, Sam paused beside the coach's desk long enough to rest his hockey stick against the front and toss his thick gloves on the floor beside it.

"No, no trouble," he said, keeping his tone even. "When we leave the hotel, my daughter's still in school. I call her once a day to see how things are. I'm using my own dime, if that's what has you worried." He lifted one shoulder in a dismissive shrug. There wasn't any love lost between himself and Covington. It was no secret that the hard-nosed coach wanted young men with the killer instinct for his new team. Sam knew he was a disappointment to Covington on both counts, but he didn't care. Still, he had to deal with the man until he decided whether to finish the season with the Mets or try to break his contract. Aside from his general dissatisfaction, another, touchier issue had come up on this road trip.

"Your daughter, huh?" Covington paused on his way to the door. "Well, make it snappy. We've got a game to win. I was coming to find you anyway. The team's new owner signed on the dotted line tonight. He called a few minutes ago wanting to give the press some pictures, and he's tagged you."

Sam glanced at his watch, remaining outwardly calm even though his heart sank. "Have Roger do it. He's the pretty boy of the club. If you recall, I told you in Philly that I don't intend to mix with the new money man. Nothing's changed."

Covington puffed his chest out belligerently. "Well, *he* wants your mug shot with his new movie queen—someone you already know intimately, right?" The coach laughed. "This deal's getting coast-to-coast coverage, Court. Nobody turns down press of that caliber."

"I do," Sam snapped. "And you can tell that bozo I said so." Inclining his head toward the telephone, he added in a steely voice, "Do you mind? My call is private."

"You have a tight contract, Court—but I can guarantee, it's not that tight." Covington gave a snort. "Right now your name packs in a crowd. But you get bad blood between you and the money man and even a name like yours is history. Better not get too uppity. You think about that." Backing out, the coach hitched his pants higher over his paunch, then slammed the door.

Sam could feel his anger tighten as he snatched up the phone. He didn't know what Joani and her latest friend were pulling, but whatever it was, he didn't like it. All of a sudden Joani had started playing cute with him, and it wasn't typical of her. He didn't like that, either. He'd become used to her predictable whining and complaints. Channeling his ire into punching out the numbers on his telephone credit card, Sam gave serious thought to telling his agent to get him out any way he could. But there were others things to consider. First there was Holly. And now . . . there was Brynn.

Sam listened to the hollow ring crossing the circuits to reach Brynn Powell's shop. He paced the length of the telephone cord and kneaded the back of his neck with his free hand. Anticipation replaced annoyance as he heard the ring break off and someone on the other end pick up the phone. That was all it took for his tension to begin receding.

Each day he found himself more eager to call home, and he was shameless about the fact that he'd taken to phoning a few minutes before Holly was due to arrive at Brynn's shop. Today, he couldn't wait that extra five minutes.

"Good afternoon. Romantic Notions."

A ripple went up Sam's spine as Brynn's slightly breathy greeting reached out to him across the wire. He sank against a corner of the desk, savoring the sultry resonance of her voice. All that was left of his tension slipped away.

"Hi," he murmured, bringing to mind home, Holly, Brynn. Somewhere between the impersonal cities on this road trip, he'd begun picturing them as a package. Tonight he needed so badly to tell Brynn how he felt—about her, about the future, about them. The words formed in his heart, but they seemed to lodge in his throat.

Brynn raised her voice, speaking sharply. "Hello! Is someone there? May I help you?"

"Brynn!" Sam croaked out her name, fearing she'd hang up before he could think of a way to share his discovery.

"Sam? Is that you? You're early and we have a terrible connection today. It must be the storm."

Sam smiled, finding it easier to talk about the weather. "The weatherman here is blaming it on the Wicked Witch of the West. They say she's gearing up for Halloween."

"Oh, ho! We heard she was riding in from the east." Brynn laughed. "Our weatherman has named her Esther the Eastern Evil."

If he closed his eyes and cradled the receiver between his ear and his shoulder, Sam could visualize Brynn's lips parted in the throaty chuckle she'd just given. He groaned inwardly.

With a trace of laughter lingering in her voice, Brynn steered their conversation in a more serious direction. "I'm sure you didn't call to discuss the weather, Sam. Your hotel must have missed giving you Holly's message. Today was the first day of my class, and one of the mothers brought tickets for the ballet as a special treat for the group. She and Sunne took the entire class. If you'll give me a specific time for Holly to call you, I promise I'll see that she gets your message."

Sam made no reply.

Clearing her throat, Brynn murmured, "Do you mind that she went, Sam? I know how punctual you've been about calling."

"I don't like being on the road, Brynn. It gets lonely as hell. Talking to you and Holly tends to be my lifeline."

Static crackled, blending with Brynn's dry response. "Lonely, Sam? Seattle isn't that out of touch. Our sports page carried pictures of the reception committee that met your team in the Philadelphia airport. The sexy blonde in the miniskirt—the one wrapped around you—looked like she was doing her best to make you feel welcome."

Sam smoothed the furrow between his brows, where he could discern the beginnings of a dull ache. "It's all hype, Brynn. Owners think it's good publicity, but that's all it means," he said, minimizing one major part of being a professional hockey player that he truly disliked.

Brynn held her breath. Wanting to hear more of his denial, she waited for him to go on, but when he remained silent, she mentioned Holly again. "If it's not convenient to have Holly call you, she'll be at Stacy's later. By the way," she added. "I almost forgot. This is the perfect opportunity to tell you what a nice thing you did, sending Holly those flowers today. I know she'll be thanking you herself, but I'm doubly impressed that you had them delivered here during her first class...especially since you originally had objections to her attending."

"What?" The receiver fell from Sam's shoulder, hit the desk with a thud and bounced. He snatched it up. "Run that by me again, Brynn. Explain, please."

"Explain?" she asked in a strained voice. "I was trying to pay you a compliment. Obviously neither Holly nor I understood your real reason for sending the roses." Her tone became guarded. "This call must be costing you a fortune, Sam. What would you like me to tell Holly? You haven't said."

Sam expelled a pent-up breath. "For starters, tell her the roses belong to you." Hearing her surprised gasp, he raked one hand through his hair. "Damn it, Brynn, wasn't there a card?"

She didn't answer him right away, and catching a glimpse of the wall clock, Sam knew he didn't have much time. "The other night, that red rose was meant for you. I wanted you to have it. The next morning Holly asked why I hadn't given you one, along with her and Stacy. Sunne Evans was quick to tell me that yellow roses were your favorite anyhow. I was trying to make amends for the game and for the other day in the car. The day I left . . ." He broke off in exasperation, knowing he was rambling and not doing a good job of explaining what she'd come to mean to him.

For several seconds the line crackled. Sam thought maybe he'd somehow offended her again and that she'd hung up on him.

"Brynn?"

"I'm still here, Sam," she said softly. "I was just thinking. You can't tell Holly, you know. She'd be terribly disappointed. The other girls envied her. She was elated to receive the flowers. Understandably so," she said quickly. "She misses you, Sam."

The door of the coach's office flew open just as Sam felt a melting of the hard knot in his stomach. Did Brynn miss him, too? he wondered.

A teammate thrust his head inside the room, issuing a terse warning. "Coach says to get a move on."

Turning his back on his colleague, Sam gripped the receiver tight to his chin. "Give me another minute, Mike." He flung the words over his shoulder.

He heard the man mutter something indistinct and close the door. Alone again, Sam cursed the miles separating him from Brynn. "Do you know how refreshing it is to find a woman who puts my daughter's well-being before her own?" There was so much more Sam wanted to say, but as he stared through a smudged window at the night sky, he was suddenly afraid of saying the wrong thing. Probably because he'd never dealt with a woman who was this selfless before, this genuine. His heart swelled.

"I'll send more roses in the morning," he whispered, clearing a tiny circle on the glass with the heel of one hand. "A bushel full," he pledged, his voice growing husky as he struggled to say what was in his heart.

She mumbled something indistinguishable. Sam closed his eyes and massaged the bridge of his nose. Pretty words didn't come easy for him. Long distance, they were even harder.

"The devil with it . . . what's bigger than a bushel?" he demanded. "Tell me and I swear I'll find it."

"Sam, don't." Brynn's plea broke on a strained note. "I'm telling you, you don't owe me flowers. My goodness, you're paying me to let Holly help out around here and already it should be the other way around. Roses are special, not to mention expensive. You can't just pass them around like...like a clown hands out balloons at the circus."

Sam's stomach tensed. She was missing his point.

Coach Covington threw open the door. "Court, get your butt out on the ice, pronto." His words were curt. "Say again who it is you're calling," he sneered. "Your kid?"

Covington's barb was the last straw for Sam. He felt his control snap. "Go to hell, Covington." Turning his back on the man, he hunched protectively over the telephone. "I have to hang up, Brynn. It's game time. Tomorrow's Saturday—will you be at the shop?"

"You'd better go, Sam." Brynn's voice wavered. "Holly has plans with the Evanses for the weekend. But I'm sure you can reach her there tomorrow morning."

"Court!" Covington bellowed like a wounded bear.

"They were only flowers, Brynn...not a bloody proposal. Go ahead and tell Holly I'll call her in the morning, but you can't avoid me forever. Sometime soon, you and I are going to sit down and talk. That's a promise." With a solid thwack he slammed the receiver in its cradle, snatched up his gloves and stick and stalked past the coach without a word. Sam knew better than to start an argument feeling the way he did. He was, after all, still under contract.

And Covington had a reputation for pushing hard enough to make a man lose his cool in a game. Sam thought the coach's method stank, but he came close to understanding how it worked when he overheard Covington's remark to a reporter hanging out by the locker room door.

"Keep your eye on the Samurai tonight, kid. He's gonna be out for blood. The guy's got women troubles. Yes, sirree! We should be so lucky, huh?"

Sam grimaced as he tried to block out the two men's bawdy chuckles.

Before, he'd always ignored any tidbits a coach threw to the news media about his womanizing. They were never true, and for Holly's sake, he'd never let the press link his name with more than one woman at a time. He didn't understand why management felt that kind of thing was necessary to the game. Iron Man groomed winning teams and he never went in for trash. Speed and skill won games—everything else was incidental. Sam felt an unexpected need to call Iron Man to thank him for his solid principles. Would the compassionate Brynn Powell appreciate the fact that he felt like burying the hatchet because of her? But just then the whistle blew, and his thoughts and energies turned toward winning the game.

BRYNN ROSE EARLY on Saturday morning, intending to get a start on her inventory. Espresso was a luxury she allowed herself only on weekends, and she took time to read the morning paper while savoring every drop in the tiny cup. Suddenly, a caption above a photograph in the sports section nearly leaped off the page at her. *Protégée of Mets' new owner says she loves hockey.* The smaller print beneath the picture caused her to choke on her coffee. *Or does the lady still have a yen for one particular hockey player—namely ex-hubby, Sam Court?*

Brynn stared at the picture. The woman she had learned was Joani Court had her arms locked around Sam's chest and her cheek nestled just beneath the number thirty-six blazoned across his uniform. Granted, Sam didn't look altogether happy, but then, his injured ribs could still be troubling him and newspaper photos tended to be grainy. Reluctantly, Brynn had to admit they made a nice-looking couple.

So much for Sam's proclamations that he wanted the woman in Holly's life to be a pillar of the community. The woman in the photo was Las Vegas showgirl all the way. The dress glittered under the arena lights, and the woman fairly dripped sex appeal. Sam claimed not to like superficial beauty, but Joani Court appeared to have it in abundance. And she was apparently traveling with him. So much for Defenseman Court's protestations. They weren't any more believable than Anthony's empty promises had been. A yawning hole seemed to open up inside Brynn at the discovery.

Resting her elbows on the table, she cradled her chin in one hand. She tried to feel happy for Holly that the article hinted at a reconciliation between her parents. After all, Brynn believed wholeheartedly in the family unit. But where had Joani Court been while Sam raised their daughter? Didn't he care? Where was his pride? The more Brynn tried to analyze, the worse she felt. Admittedly she had come to look forward to Sam's nightly calls. She'd started thinking he did, too. Why did this hurt so damn much?

The telephone shrilled and Brynn jumped, knocking over the small cup. Could it be Sam? Her heart speeded up. Why would it be? Anyway, if it was, she wouldn't talk to him. But of course she would. Smothering a deprecating laugh, she snatched at the phone as it jangled again.

"Hello, Brynn here." Her greeting was decidedly cheerier than she felt.

"Well, it's nice to find someone congenial at this unearthly hour on a weekend. Normally I don't encounter such enthusiasm, though occasionally I bear good tidings."

"Oh, Dr. Low." Brynn made a conscious effort not to sound disappointed. After all, she hadn't *really* expected Sam. Had she? Her tone leveled. "What a nice surprise."

The doctor laughed. "Now that's more what I'm used to hearing. But maybe when I tell you that I think we've got Kevin's kidney you'll treat me to just a bit more of that optimism."

Brynn drew in a sharp breath, clutched the lapels of her robe tight and sank back into the chair. A hundred vitally important questions tumbled inside her head. None surfaced.

"I know it's sudden," he said, sobering. "And understand, we aren't one hundred percent sure. Our preliminary computer check of the blood chemistries looks good. However, we can't call it a match until the final tests are in."

"What . . . I mean how—" Brynn wet her lips, falling silent. "What about the waiting list," she squeaked, finding her voice.

"This kidney came up unexpectedly . . . an auto accident in California. It happens like that sometimes. We run a nationwide check for the most compatible match. Can you get Kevin down here right away?"

Brynn shivered. Her skin felt clammy and cold. Of course they'd all discussed it before, but their conversations had always been full of conjecture. They hadn't really talked seriously. Or at least, she hadn't. And Brynn couldn't even remember if she'd told Kevin lately how much she loved him.

What she wanted to do was yank the phone out, pretend Dr. Low hadn't called, and keep her brother safe within her own comfort zone. Realistically, she knew that was impossible. She'd always known that someday they would have to face surgery. It was just that this had come when all her defenses were down. In a wooden voice, she said, "Kevin's still sleeping, Dr. Low. Is there anything I should know before I wake him?"

Even as she asked, fear, stark and real, slammed into Brynn's midriff. This kidney—this gift of life—came at a terrible price. Deeply felt sympathy for the loved ones of the accident victim welled up. She remembered the desolation she'd felt that day she'd learned of her parents' deaths. And now, someone miles away had lost a—what? A child? A brother...spouse? Who? This was real. This was no longer "what if?" They had a kidney, he said. And far away, another human soul in far greater pain than she was had made a rational decision to give a complete stranger this chance at a normal life.

Oh, Lord, was it serious! Dr. Low was talking major surgery. Risk. What if they removed Kevin's kidneys and his body rejected the transplant? In her ear, the doctor's voice droned on clinically.

"We'll attach Kevin's new kidney to the iliac artery and vein first, then we place it in his frontal abdominal cavity. The speed of such surgery greatly enhances his overall outlook." Dr. Low broke off and asked for Brynn's questions or comments.

A chill moved up her body. She could feel her teeth begin to chatter. "I understand, Doctor. He's fortunate to be given an opportunity that some people wait years for and never get. We'll be there within the hour." She wondered if her response sounded as brittle, as ungrateful, to Dr. Low as it did to her own ears. Before he said goodbye, she asked him to thank the donor's family for signing the release. She must remember to have Reverend Cline include the family in tomorrow's prayers.

Long after Dr. Low had hung up, Brynn's fingers clenched the buzzing receiver. Hanging it up at last, she held out both hands and looked at them. They weren't trembling. On the exterior, she seemed perfectly calm. On the inside, she was terrified. She wanted to scream, was afraid she'd cry, and for the first time in her life, Brynn seriously doubted her ability to cope with this alone.

It was then that her gaze happened to fall on the emergency number Sam had given her to use in case Holly needed him. Sam would listen to her fears and he would offer sound advice and maybe consolation. Brynn knew he would understand, because he'd told her about some of his own dark hours as a single parent.

She had the telephone in her hand again. But she glanced at the discarded newspaper, with the picture in the sports section looming bigger than life. Accompanied by the article that hinted at reconciliation... Replacing the receiver, Brynn dropped her hand. It didn't matter how much she'd like to lean on Sam Court's strength just now; he wasn't available for leaning.

Rubbing her upper arms, trying to ward off her chill, Brynn turned and slowly made her way up the curved staircase. What was it she'd blithely told Kevin the night the power failed? *We Powells are tough.*

Yet when Brynn pushed her brother's door open and saw how trustingly he slept, with his cheek resting childlike on one curled fist, she thought perhaps she was one Powell who wasn't so tough after all.

CHAPTER NINE

BRYNN PROWLED RESTLESSLY around the hospital waiting room. She'd brought a book to read—something light. But she couldn't concentrate even on that, and the book, along with her sketch pad, lay untouched on a modern couch, obviously chosen to blend with the room's monochromatic color scheme rather than for comfort.

Seated nearby in a matching chair, Sunne Evans sipped a diet soda and thumbed idly through a well-worn magazine, probably left behind by some other patient's anxious family.

"Why do you suppose they play such mournful music in these waiting rooms, Sunne?" Brynn stopped pacing long enough to mutter irritably.

Glancing up, Sunne marked the place in an article she was skimming. "It's Chopin, Brynn. You're simply too nervous to recognize it. According to Dr. Low, Kevin has at least six hours before they'll know much. Wearing a hole in the carpet isn't going to help him."

"I know, but..." Brynn's sentence trailed off as she pressed her palms against eyelids still stinging from lack of sleep.

"I wish Paul could have come," Sunne lamented. "He had to go pick his mother up at the airport. Even more than that, I wish this surgery hadn't come up just when we were set to go on vacation."

Brynn sank down on the couch opposite Sunne and tried massaging some of the tightness out of her stiff neck. "You and Paul have already helped us so much. In one day and a Sunday at that, you arranged for someone to mind my shop and for Mrs. Flemming to fix meals and work extra hours after Kevin comes home." She counted each item on a finger.

"Yesterday morning, Paul and his friends kept Kevin's mind occupied by moving his bedroom down to the first floor where it'll be easier caring for him." She sighed. "In addition, you promised to teach my class three nights this week. Then Midge called, offering to do the hair-care part next week ... which I also suspect you had a hand in. By the time you get back from your cruise, I should have my life in order again...somewhat," Brynn added, with a weak smile.

Sunne rolled her eyes. "Will you ease up on yourself then? Stacy and Holly have asked to run errands and pick up groceries. They're both at the perfect age to be dedicated gofers. And you have our itinerary. You'll see, kiddo, everything will be coming up roses."

At the mention of Holly and roses in one breath, Brynn's thoughts turned to Sam. She frowned. He'd called three times on Saturday and again on Sunday and left messages on her machine. She'd been out each time and hadn't returned his calls. Thank goodness, Kevin had been out, too. Further contact with Sam Court was pointless, especially with his ex-wife back in his life. Brynn could hardly have missed the feature article in Sunday's paper—yet another touching Sam-and-Joani story—and more pictures of Joani snuggling up to her ex-husband.

"Keep reassuring me, Sunne," Brynn begged. "I think I've aged about twenty years in these last few days. I don't know how Mom did it."

Sunne grinned mischievously. "Well, you know how it is when you hit thirty. After that, it's all downhill."

"Oh, really?" Brynn asked dryly. "Have you been talking to Kevin's health teacher by any chance? According to Kevin, the man seems to think my age is synonymous with arrested development." She arched a brow. "By the way, I've been meaning to ask what you had in mind making me a gift of one of my own designs. That lavender gown is hardly my style. In fact, it's downright daring."

Sunne raised one shoulder in a casual shrug. She closed the magazine, then passed one hand through her spiky red-gold curls several times before she spoke, wrinkling her freckled nose. "At the time I bought it, my friend, I had Sam Court in mind." Ignoring Brynn's gasp, she went on. "One day when I was filling in for you at the shop, I caught him practically drooling over that gown. Something he said made me think he was picturing you wearing it." She chuckled knowingly. "I was positive that by the time your birthday rolled around, the two of you would be—"

"Enough, Sunne!" Brynn leaped to her feet and began pacing again. The scenario her friend described was one she'd toyed with herself for a time—after the kisses she and Sam had shared. Now, even the suggestion left her cheeks burning. Still she felt a certain guilt for snapping at Sunne and said in a milder tone, "My nightgowns are designed for romantics like you, Sunne Evans. For lovers. Not pragmatists like me."

"Why not you, Brynn?" Sunne persisted, her gaze locked on the tense line of Brynn's jaw. "Do you only indulge in fantasy for others? Isn't it past time you slid between the sheets wearing something other than sexless pajamas? Maybe with someone who'll teach you what romance is all about?"

Exasperated, Brynn threw up her hands. "Am I a candidate for romance? Look around you." She waved a hand to encompass their sterile setting, then crossed her arms over her breasts and rubbed her upper arms, warding off a sudden chill. "Oh, I'm not just talking about Kevin and his medical problems, Sunne. He's a real trouper. And he'd probably be the first to agree with you. But think of the hours I spend first at the shop and then slaving over a design board. I have responsibilities that don't leave time for romance." She gave a tired sigh. "Besides, didn't Anthony prove that when reality sets in men opt to go elsewhere for romance? Maybe my ego is too frail for another disappointment. Just look at the years I listened to Anthony—with stars in my eyes and rocks in my head. Did you know he never intended to let me design for Luminaire? He admitted that he'd only ever romanced me to get a company model."

Sunne gave an unladylike snort. "Why doesn't that surprise me? When we met Anthony during our college career day, I pegged him as some hot young salesman with a roving eye. I just thought it was a great opportunity for you to get to New York and the big design houses. Modeling wasn't so bad, was it? You made good money during those years. And Brynn, all men aren't selfish like Anthony. Sam Court isn't like that. Forget one bad experience. Get on with your life. What happened between you and Sam to cool things?"

Whirling, Brynn stared at her suddenly serious friend. Surely Sunne and Paul knew about the recent sale of Sam's team and the arrival of Joani Court. But even if Sunne had been too caught up in her own vacation plans to be aware of either fact, this conversation had no point. "Kevin needs me," she muttered, shaking her head and letting it go at that. Turning, she gazed out the window. Even the weather was against her. It was a gray misty day. Fog shrouded the city.

"Is that a polite way of telling me to mind my own business, Brynn?" Sunne smiled. "It won't work, you know. According to what Holly says, when her father calls after school, he'd rather talk with you than her. After my experience dating Paul during those four years he went to college in Minnesota, I'd be the first to admit how hard it is to carry on any kind of long-distance romance. But...we managed." She rolled her eyes again. "And Kevin should be much improved by the time we get back from vacation. That, Brynn Powell, will be the weekend of our party. It'll be a good time to clear the air between you and Sam, whatever happened." Pausing, she gave her friend a little hug. "Besides, I understand Sam is due home the day before Halloween."

"Sam's home now, ladies. Is there something special you want me to do?"

At the sound of his deep voice, Brynn and Sunne jerked their heads around, gaping at the object of their conversation.

He stood in the doorway of the small waiting room, holding fast to a large bouquet of roses and baby's breath. He looked tired, Brynn thought, in spite of an appealing smile that slowly curved his lips. His dark hair still bore signs of the sparkling mist.

Sunne was the first to find her voice. "Sam! Whatever are you doing here? I could have sworn Holly said last night that you'd just arrived in Buffalo. Don't you have a game in New York tomorrow?"

"It's a long story," he said giving a rueful shake of his head and passing one hand over an unshaven jaw. "How's Kevin's surgery going?" Sam's gaze captured and held Brynn's as he spoke, his tone soft and husky. He shifted the huge bouquet, angling for a better look at her.

Brynn laced her fingers in front of her, refusing to acknowledge how simply seeing him made mockery of her recent declaration to Sunne. And it pleased her more than she could say that his first thought had been for Kevin. "It's a long surgery, Sam," she informed him, trying to keep her voice level. She began to explain the procedures involved, but she was interrupted by an efficient-looking nurse, dressed in surgery greens, who entered the waiting room through a side door.

"Miss Powell."

Brynn tensed and reached for Sunne's hand.

"Yes?" Brynn's voice cracked with the advent of her sudden, overwhelming fear.

Sam moved close and laid a hand on her shoulder. He gave a reassuring squeeze, and his presence seemed to fill the room.

The petite, dark-haired nurse smiled. "Dr. Low asked me to relay a message. Kevin's new kidney is in place. To quote the doctor, *Tell Brynn it pinked up right away and it's beautiful.*"

"Hooray!" Sunne threw her arms around Brynn and hugged her tight.

Tears of happiness filled Brynn's eyes. Slowly, as she released the breath she'd been holding, she realized Sam's hand had slipped to the middle of her back, allowing her to feel his relief, too, in the sudden uncurling of his warm fingers. But then, she'd always known he liked Kevin.

Patting Brynn's arm, the nurse spoke again. "Dr. Low wants to keep an eye on things before closing, so the actual surgery is approximately half over. Try to relax, Miss Powell. The doctor will stop by to talk with you after he sees Kevin settled into recovery." Approaching Sam, she added briskly, "If the flowers are for my patient, I'll take them now. Kevin will be in critical care overnight, but we have a special place for bouquets where CCU patients can view them through the glass." Before anyone could say a word, she whisked away the roses.

"They're not—" Sam spoke as the nurse disappeared through the door. No one paid any attention to his feeble objections. Brynn and Sunne had fallen together laughing and hugging one another. So with a shrug, Sam let the flowers go.

A volunteer stepped in, offering coffee, which Sam declined. Brynn and Sunne accepted gratefully, and for some time the three chatted amicably—until Sunne checked her watch.

"Yikes! I've got to run if I want to beat Paul and his mother home. I'm glad you're here, Sam, even if I don't understand why. I hated the thought of leaving Brynn by herself."

Crushing her empty coffee cup, Brynn took Sunne's, too. Walking across the room, she dropped both cups into a waste bin.

"With all you have to do before you leave on vacation, Sunne, I appreciate the time you did spend here with me today. I'll try to catch a minute with you after you've taught those classes. Just in case I don't, though, you can leave me notes. I want you to have a marvelous time on your cruise. After all, it'd be a real shame to waste all my envy."

"Well..." Sunne hesitated, glancing toward Sam. "You'll call if you need anything, right? I love Mother Evans, but..." She made a face. "By Wednesday's class, I'll be looking forward to escaping her for a few hours. She does talk incessantly." Sunne paused, hugging Brynn again. "If we don't touch base, Brynn Powell, I'll expect to see you at our Halloween party." She wiggled her eyebrows dramatically. "Sam, I'm charging you with a serious responsibility. Not only do I want you to see that this woman doesn't back out of going, but I insist that you see she doesn't wear the same horrendous costume she wore last year."

"Goodbye, Sunne." Brynn broke in, pushing her friend toward the door. "You're going to be late—remember?" Brynn hustled her through the arch. "Sam was about to leave, too, weren't you, Sam?" She turned to frown at him over one shoulder.

Grinning, he joined her at the door. "I just got here. Don't rush me. What was wrong with Brynn's costume, Sunne?"

Sunne had reached the elevators by then, but she hesitated before stepping inside the one that had just arrived. She held the door open while she answered. "It drove away the men, that's what was wrong with it. Ask her to tell you. I can't even describe it. Not one single man asked her to dance, though."

"Which suited me fine," Brynn stated firmly, as Sunne lost her battle with the elevator door and it slowly closed.

"Is this the same costume I heard you and Holly discussing the night we had dinner at your house?"

Sam leaned one hand against the door, an action that brought his lips all too close to Brynn's ear. Turning, she ducked under his outstretched arm. His mention of the evening they'd traded kisses on her couch added a measure of sexual tension to already overstressed nerves. He had a lot of gall, given the situation on his home front. And Sam's sleepy-eyed gaze, mussed curly hair and gravelly voice didn't help matters, either.

Brynn remarked more sharply than she might otherwise have done, "What are you doing home when the Mets have two more weeks of games scheduled out of town, Sam?"

Sam tossed the windbreaker he'd slung over one shoulder on the couch next to Brynn's books. Tucking his hands loosely in the back pockets of his jeans, he glanced down, hiding his gaze from her. A muscle along his jaw jumped as he worried the inside of his mouth. "I quit," he ground out shortly, lifting his lashes and meeting her eyes with obvious reluctance. "However, my agent is still hammering out the details, so that's not public knowledge, all right?"

"You quit?" Brynn didn't have to feign shock. "Whatever for? Holly says you love playing hockey."

Looking away, Sam made deliberate swirls in the plush pile of the carpet with his gray tennis shoe. The nap darkened where he ruffled it.

"I'm sorry, Sam. Your reasons for leaving the team are really none of my business." Brynn smoothed the hem of her baggy sweatshirt. Perhaps Joani Court had never liked hockey. It was rather rough at times; he had the cuts and bruises to prove it. Maybe that had been the source of their conflict. She cleared her throat and shrugged. "Holly will be delighted to have you home, Sam. She's told me how lonely she gets when you're on the road." Brynn's mind continued to reel. Sam's sudden decision to leave hockey had to be somehow related to his ex-wife's return. Had they decided to make a clean start? Maybe Joani had agreed to give up her pursuit of stardom; Brynn knew that would please Sam.

But after all, she had Kevin and his new kidney to worry about. Whatever Sam chose to do, or why, was no concern of hers.

"This road trip has been exceptionally hard on me, too," Sam agreed, flexing his shoulders. Brynn looked so drawn, he probably shouldn't tell her she was the reason he'd taken the red-eye flight from Buffalo. He didn't want her feeling guilty about that.

Studying her slender form, he thought she looked no older than Holly and twice as vulnerable. She was wearing acid-washed jeans and an oversize sweatshirt, and her hair was gathered into her regular bun—much more ragged than usual, though. If she wore one shred of makeup, it was not discernible.

Crossing his arms, Sam rocked back on his heels. Because he wanted nothing more than to take her in his arms and kiss away her worries, and maybe some of his own, he deliberately brought their conversation full circle to the party. "So what *will* you be wearing to the Evans's Halloween bash?"

"Sam, I can't even begin to think of going. Just because Kevin has crossed one mountain, it doesn't mean he's out of the woods yet." And why did Sam care what kind of costume she wore, anyway? Wasn't he planning to show off Joani? she thought tiredly.

"Going where?" asked Dr. Low, entering the room as he untied his limp face mask and deftly peeled off a ribbed surgical cap.

"To Sunne and Paul Evans's Halloween party," Brynn answered automatically, staring blankly at him for a moment. Then as if registering his presence, she jumped from the couch. "How is Kevin, Dr. Low? Does your being here mean he's in recovery?'' Nervously she twisted an opal birthstone ring around and around until Sam grabbed her hand and held it securely in his own.

"Kevin's in recovery and he's stable. Things went very well. I wouldn't recommend a party for you tonight, Brynn. You need a good night's sleep. But by Halloween, Kevin should be home and both of you settled nicely into a routine. I say go for it.''

Dr. Low gave Sam a curious glance. "I don't believe we've met, but you look familiar."

Snatching her hand from Sam's, Brynn stepped forward. "Forgive me. Dr. Low, this is Sam Court from the—" She broke off, letting Sam finish the introduction in light of his earlier announcement that he'd left the team.

"Hockey." Dr. Low grinned and reached to shake Sam's hand. "You've been getting a lot of free publicity lately. I should have recognized you right off." The doctor looked from Sam to Brynn and back again as if weighing their relationship. Then he backed away, a flush starting at his neck as if he'd just recalled the precise nature of the publicity Sam had received. "Well, uh, I have to go check on my patient." He dipped his head toward Brynn. "Get her out of here, Mr. Court. She looks ready to drop. Come to think of it, man, you don't look so good yourself."

Brynn didn't think she liked what Dr. Low was assuming. If he was labeling her as the other woman because of the touching captions he'd been reading in the newspaper, he could just unlabel her now.

"I'm staying, Dr. Low. I'll want to see Kevin the minute he comes out of recovery. But Sam was just leaving. Kevin and Sam's daughter, Holly, are good friends. Sam just stopped by for a report on my brother's condition."

"It's your choice if you want to stay, Brynn. I'll be more than happy to send a nurse to let you know when you can visit, but Kevin will sleep most of the night except for our monitoring." He turned to Sam. "Nice meeting you, Mr. Court. We don't get many celebrities stopping by here." The doctor paused. "Especially not stopping by from New York. Isn't that where the Mets are playing tomorrow night?" Touching two fingers to his brow in a quick salute, he was gone, leaving the waiting room silent. But the atmosphere seemed to churn with his implications—some of which Brynn had been trying to piece together herself.

"Why are you here, Sam?" Brynn asked as she sighed and sank into the couch. Kicking off her shoes, she tucked her feet under her. "You know what Dr. Low was reading into it, and goodness knows, I don't think either of us needs more complications in our lives right now."

Sam took the chair opposite her and stretched out his long legs. Letting his chin drop to his chest, he closed his eyes and rubbed his lids with his forefingers. She looked so breakable just now, he'd have to weigh carefully anything he said. The slightest word could make her bolt. "Why do you insist on denying our friendship, Brynn? I came directly here from the airport because I know what it's like sitting in a hospital waiting room all night alone, praying for the dawn and some sign that the nurses and doctors haven't all gone to bed and forgotten you. Isn't that reason enough?"

"Our newspapers have been full of pictures of you and Joani, Sam. Each day, some new romantic development takes up half the sports page. The reporters are having a field day."

"Which is precisely the way Joani's...friend, the new owner of the team, wants it," he cut in. "If the team plays well and gives a high return, he's promised to sponsor her in a movie. They're looking to get her maximum exposure through this deal." He sighed. "I know there's a major difference between you and Joani. And I wouldn't expect you to understand how someone like her is capable of doing absolutely anything to get this movie contract. You wouldn't understand how much Joani craves being in the public eye. Maybe it's because she was dirt-poor as a kid. As a result, she's never gained enough confidence to stop selling herself. Or maybe you would understand... Self-esteem is what you teach, right?"

She stared at him, wondering what she could possibly say. But he went on, saving her an answer.

"California is full of Joanis trying to get recognition. Women are under less public pressure here. It'll be a good place for Holly to learn some solid principles. I just want to

have this whole mess over so I can really begin a new life here.''
He reached over and tugged on one of the curls that had escaped from Brynn's halfhearted bun. A lopsided smile curved
his lips. ''You have enough on your mind, Brynn, so I won't
bore you with my life story.''

Brynn edged away from him. His words hurt more than he'd
ever know. And what would he think if he knew that she, too,
had once had her picture spread from coast to coast? Not that
it would matter to him. His real concern was in starting over
with Joani. It sounded very much as though Sam was re-
signed to waiting patiently at home until Joani got stardom out
of her system. Brynn could have told him that some women
never did.

Blessedly, Brynn was offered a reason not to examine the
Courts more closely. A nurse came to announce it was time for
her first visit with Kevin. She was allowed only ten minutes. In
the meanwhile, Sam went in search of a phone to check in with
Holly. He insisted on staying until all reports were in—in the
name of friendship. And Brynn was too tired to argue.

QUITE SOME TIME LATER, during those lonely early-morning
hours, Brynn found herself thankful for his calming presence.

In a tense moment when Kevin's breathing changed—a reaction to the lengthy anesthetic—the critical care nursing team
put her out of his cubicle without a word of reassurance until
the crisis passed. Brynn sought solace on Sam's broad shoulder, and she was grateful he'd stayed. Even though she'd told
herself a thousand times that it wouldn't be wise to use him as
a harbor, she took all the tenderness he offered, emptying her
mind of everything else.

It was nearly two o'clock before she received word that
Kevin was resting easier and she felt strong enough to leave the
snug cocoon of Sam's arms. Then she attempted to make a
pillow of his thin windbreaker, but he brushed her hands away
and pulled her against his chest, settling her comfortably.

Around a yawn, she mumbled sleepily, ''Sunne's right. You
aren't anything like Anthony. I honestly don't know how I
would have made it tonight without your support, Sam.

Thanks!'' Shifting until her head rolled on his shoulder, Brynn smiled up at him. "I'm referring to your moral support as well as physical. Thanks for holding me up."

"Who's Anthony?" he asked gruffly, tilting her chin higher with a fingertip.

"No one important," she answered quickly. "I can't imagine why I mentioned him. He was my boss when I worked in New York. There was a short time when I thought I was more than an employee to him—then I found out he'd promised rose gardens to a lot of different women. Anthony just never kept any promises. He liked his personal life and everyone in it separate and tidy. When he found out Kevin was so ill and had become my sole responsibility, Anthony didn't bother with the pretense any longer. But by then, I'd long since stopped wanting anything from him."

Bring his hand up, Sam stroked her hair. "Poor Brynn," he murmured soothingly. "You never seem to end up with roses. Did you even see the ones I brought in today?"

She nodded slowly, her cheek brushing the fabric of his shirt. A shirt that smelled of recent laundering, tangy soap and an essence that was uniquely Sam. "Kevin hasn't seen the flowers yet. He's been too sick," she mumbled, burrowing deeper. "You should have waited."

"Those roses were for you . . . again. Holly's planning on sending Kevin flowers after he gets situated in a room. Maybe you should pick another variety of flower, Brynn," he teased gently. "Unless you can figure out a way to steal this last bouquet away from the white tornado."

Brynn frowned.

"The nurse who ran off with them," he explained. "She reminded me of the white tornado in those old commercials on TV. You know . . . whish in, whish out, then poof—no roses."

This time Brynn laughed outright. Laughing woke her up. She straightened and stretched, beginning to feel better. "That'll teach you to stop wasting money on me, Sam. Just for the record, I like daisies, too. They, at least, wouldn't have thrown you into bankruptcy."

Laughing together, they talked companionably for a while about inconsequential things. It seemed to Brynn that Sam studiously avoided all things personal. But then, so did she. And it was just as well.

He also bantered with the nurses who kept her updated on Kevin's progress. And Sam had a way of keeping everyone's spirits up. His quick wit and ready humor eased her constant worry. In spite of the lumpy couch, she slept in brief, fitful stretches. Always when she awakened, Sam was there to reassure her that all was well and she wasn't alone. Brynn took what he offered, hoarding it jealously for the time when she'd be alone again.

The eastern sky was streaked with light before Sam drifted into sleep, relaxing enough to lose the troubled lines Brynn had been curious about since he arrived. Watching him in the intimate throes of sleep created an ache deep inside her. She discovered that Sam Court would be an easy man to love. She discovered something else, too—she already did love him. But how could that be? He wasn't hers to love. No one was.

Brynn's heart thudded, then grew very still. Her commitment to Kevin didn't end with this surgery. He might not be home free even afterward. Dr. Low had been careful to point out that some patients rejected their donor kidneys as much as a year following the transplant. Without question, she was looking at many more years of a double workload to meet expenses. Kevin's illness, their medical bills, would be an unfair burden to the most settled of men. Even if Sam had been free . . . but he wasn't. Besides, she couldn't imagine him leaving hockey for good. She'd give him a month of idleness, then he'd be involved again.

A man like Sam, who traveled from city to city with the team, could be in a woman's life today and gone tomorrow. That would have happened even if he wasn't still in love with the beautiful Joani Court—which by now she felt certain he was.

For Kevin's sake as well as her own, Brynn knew she dare not acknowledge this one-sided love, not even in her most private daydreams. Yet the finality of her decision was as bleak as anything she'd already faced.

CHAPTER TEN

FOR THREE DAYS following Kevin's surgery, Brynn had no time to think about the significance of her new feelings for Sam, or even her resolution to shut him out of her life. All her days and nights were spent by Kevin's side, except for the few times she dashed home to change clothes, shower and maybe sleep an hour or two. Every time her brother cleared one major hurdle, he would come up against another. And now, the anti-rejection drugs were making him sick.

In a blur, Sam became one among the many friends and neighbors who dropped by the hospital whenever time permitted. If anyone had asked, Brynn could not have said precisely what she'd discussed with a single soul. She was near sickness herself, with anxiety over Kevin's ups and downs, and overwhelmingly exhausted.

On the fourth day, the transplant team made a breakthrough. For the first time, Kevin began tolerating the drug given to combat organ rejection. Brynn cried tears of happiness. Sam, who always seemed to be hovering in the background, went out and bought her flowers in celebration.

"I checked," he said with a twinkle in his eye as he handed her the arrangement. "Today is the white tornado's day off. These are for you to take home."

"Oh, Sam." Brynn buried her nose in the fragrant bouquet. "Yellow roses and white daisies. You remembered that I said these were my favorites." She smiled at him through a mist of tears. "How did you know I needed something frivolous today? Are you psychic?"

Tipping her chin up, he gently wiped the moisture from her cheeks with his thumbs. "You want a guy to give away all his trade secrets? No way! A man has to hold some aces. But I'm here to tell you, Ms. Powell . . . yellow roses are getting scarce around this town. Don't let me find out you've taken pity on that nice old lady in room C—the one you're always fretting about because her family doesn't visit. This time, you're letting someone do something for you for a change.''

"I shall enjoy every last bloom, Sam." Looking thoughtfully at the professionally arranged bouquet, she asked, "But should you be spending money carelessly when you don't have a job?''

It was as though a shutter dropped over his eyes for a moment, then he raised a hand and curved it around the back of her neck. "Only you would be concerned about a man's finances when he's giving you a gift, Brynn. I'm also planning to spirit you away for dinner tomorrow evening—just you and me. Are you going to check my bank balance and employment status before you accept?''

"No." Brynn hugged the roses and laughed. "My mother told me never to turn down a free meal." For the moment, in her relief, she'd allowed herself to forget Sam had an ex-wife waiting in the wings. If she'd stopped to think, Brynn would never have accepted his invitation. Not even in the name of friendship. Recent news reports, which she'd only read in snatches, said the actress-showgirl was in Seattle. There had been another interview with Sam, where he again refused to comment on his private life. His *no comments* were becoming newsworthy in themselves—even though he'd told the reporter in no uncertain terms that his private life was no one's business.

Before pausing to consider all that, Brynn agreed. "I'll accept by way of celebrating Kevin's progress," she said with a weary smile. "That's provided you make it an early dinner and somewhere close to the hospital. Even then you're in danger of having me fall asleep in the soup.''

Sam couldn't believe his luck. His invitation had been on impulse. And since he'd never expected her to agree, he hadn't chosen the best day. But he wasn't going to let that stop him. "Leave the details to me, Brynn. I'll plan to pick you up around six. I have an afternoon meeting with my agent and lawyer, so I may not get back until it's time to go. If Kevin's condition changes or if you need me for anything, leave a message with Holly."

Brynn stood and slipped one arm around his waist. She matched her steps to his as he headed for the door. They'd been through so much together, she'd begun to consider Sam the way she did Paul Evans—an old friend.

"Oh, Sam, I almost forgot. Kevin should be released from critical-care tomorrow and he's scheduled into a two-bed ward. Goodness . . . the staff here must think I'm ready to file squatters' rights on this waiting room. So his move is coming just in time. If you'll check at the desk in the main lobby, they'll give you his new room number. They're not exactly sure yet who'll be losing a roommate."

"Why isn't he going into a private room, Brynn?" Sam paused near the door, waiting for her response. They remained linked together, arms loosely entwined—like a married couple, he thought, rather liking the feeling. When she didn't answer right away, he prodded, "Is it the money?"

"Partially," she murmured. "Kevin's illness alone has run us about twenty-five thousand dollars a year, at a conservative estimate, and our insurance ran out some time ago . . ." She fell silent, wishing he'd just go. Surely he had other, more pressing things to do. Why didn't he leave while she still felt this temporary euphoria? Reality was always hovering around the corner. Today, she didn't want it to intrude.

"Get him a private room. I'll pay the difference."

Brynn stared at him. "Why would you do that, Sam?"

"Because I like Kevin and because my daughter is worried about him." He shrugged and looked away. "Or, maybe more truthfully, because I like Kevin's stubborn sister and think someone should see that she slows down and puts her feet up at least once during this ordeal."

"But what would you get out of it?" Brynn persisted, trailing her fingers around his waist. Then she stepped aside, breaking contact.

Sam jumped. "Hey—I'm ticklish." Then his face relaxed in a boyish grin. "There you go, looking out for my welfare again, Brynn. I've been playing hockey a long time. The money's been good. And . . . I don't expect anything in return. Do you want to see my stock portfolio or will you just take my word for it?''

Frowning, Brynn gazed at her flowers, hugging them so tightly she almost squashed them.

Sam reached out a hand, rubbing a single petal of one rose between his thumb and index finger. "That Anthony guy really did hurt you, didn't he? What is it? Did he start off trying to buy his way into your life by showering you with flowers and underwriting Kevin's expenses? When you look at me, do you see his ghost?''

Brynn tilted her head back and laughed. "As I told you before, Anthony didn't give anyone anything—and he thought I should make Kevin a ward of the state. Compared to him, Sam, you're close to that sainthood you told Kevin you were holding out for. Let's leave it, shall we? Kevin honestly likes sharing a room. He loves to talk.''

"So be it," Sam acquiesced, throwing up his hands. "But you're the saint here, not me!" Studying her unabashedly, Sam was forced, by the arrival of the elevator, to swallow any further comment.

"Thank you again for the lovely flowers, Sam," Brynn called softly, as the elevator door closed on his heels. She stood smiling at her bouquet for several moments after his elevator had gone. But once she realized he'd actually left, she felt lost—vacant inside.

However, that night, for the first time since Kevin's surgery, she slept through until morning.

When she opened her eyes to an unusually sunny October daybreak, the first thing that greeted her was Sam's gift. As she lay admiring the bouquet, she recalled the last time anyone had given her flowers. It was in New York near the end of a difficult shoot for one of Luminaire's new lines. She and Anthony were embroiled in a horrendous argument about her wanting to design, not model, when the flowers came from her parents. Enclosed was a wonderful note saying how much they missed her and how proud they were of her accomplishments.

In a rage, Anthony had thrown the florist's box aside, demanded she act her age and spend another hour in front of the camera. It was time, he said, for Brynn to learn that life was not all moonlight and roses. But she'd learned it already by observing his self-centered tantrums. That day put the seal on her disenchantment with Anthony. At any rate, Sam Court had more sensitivity in his little fingernail than Anthony Carraras possessed in his entire body. Brynn only wished things were different—then she could say that to Sam.

But feeling sorry for herself was not a Powell trait. Long ago Brynn had learned to accept facts as they were. She settled her cheek into her palm, determined to steal an extra five minutes of sleep, not to dream impossible dreams. By the time her snooze alarm shrilled its second warning, Brynn was far readier to cope with all the tasks demanding her attention. She had a brisk shower, then dressed in a loose-fitting denim jumpsuit.

The first thing she did after calling the hospital for an update on Kevin's condition was to catch up on the paperwork at Romantic Notions. Quite by accident during a conversation with Donna, who'd been minding her store, Brynn discovered that Holly Court hadn't been coming in after school to help out. The news surprised her, as did the report from Donna that on the few evenings Holly had bothered to come, she'd chattered endlessly about her mother. It was no more than Brynn had expected, but Sam should have told her. More than likely he'd forgotten to mention the new arrangements.

Brynn dismissed the issue of Holly's hours as insignificant and centered instead on the painful truth that Joani Court was in Seattle to stay. And because of that, she was thankful there were so many other things to keep her occupied, such as the notes Sunne had left on the first two classes. They were as fragmented as Sunne's conversations. Brynn felt better after reading some of the little anecdotes involving the girls. She missed teaching and couldn't wait to take over her class again. She found tremendous reward in helping shape young women's self-esteem. Confidence and faith in oneself were paramount in getting through life—as she could well attest. Apparently Holly had improved in that area.

What Brynn planned as a quick telephone call to Sunne netted her a twenty-minute conversation with Paul's mother and the news that she'd missed saying bon voyage to her friends. Paul and Sunne were already on their way to the airport and their second honeymoon.

Brynn might have spent more than a moment on envying their Caribbean cruise, not to mention their loving marriage, if she hadn't had a thousand and one errands to run. Halfway down her list was a reminder to pick up a costume for the Halloween party. One day last week, Sam had badgered her into going. He'd flatly told her he'd reserved a cancan outfit for her at the store where he'd ordered a riverboat gambler costume for himself. No mention had been made of what Joani Court planned to wear or if he planned to take her. But surely, the lovely ex-Mrs. Court would be attending the party with Sam. Brynn chastised herself for not clearing this up, and for agreeing to go. She really *shouldn't* take the time. But Sam had been persuasive. He'd refused to take no for an answer. And…it would be fun to see Sunne's face, Brynn thought. Her friend had gone on vacation half-expecting her to wear last year's costume, or worse. Brynn chuckled as she backed out of the parking space. Sunne was in for a real surprise.

The glee carried her through most of her list. Until she glanced at her watch and knew she'd be late getting to the hospital, where an even greater *shouldn't* awaited her. No matter how many times Brynn told herself she shouldn't be having dinner with Sam Court, she found that she was eagerly anticipating the stolen evening out.

SAM TURNED FROM THE WINDOW as Brynn hurried into Kevin's new room. The tense knot in his stomach dissolved enough for him to tease her. "Thank goodness you're here at last, Brynn." He caught her hands and pulled her close for a quick hug. "I told Kevin's nurse that if you didn't show up soon, I'd take her to dinner in your place."

"Then maybe you should," Brynn admonished tartly, pulling away. She tossed her handbag into the chair near Kevin's bed, then bent over to give her brother a kiss. "I could swear we agreed on casual, and you have on a suit and tie," she accused. But what really annoyed her was the way her pulse shot up at the devastating way he looked in it.

"I came here directly from an all-day meeting. Surely you wouldn't hold that against me enough to subject me to dinner with Hilda? You should have heard her yell at me for sitting on the foot of Kevin's bed." Sam grinned. "He tells me she's a retired army nurse. I won't even try guessing which war. The way she barks and everyone jumps, I don't think anyone's had the nerve to tell her the war is over."

Kevin laughed, biting back a groan. "Don't make me laugh, Sam. It still hurts when I move. And you ought to be happy Hilda isn't giving you a shot in your backside like she does me. I think she trained under Attila the Hun."

"Well, you must be feeling better, sport. I haven't heard you complain like this all week. I just hope you two remember the poor woman is only doing her job." Brynn adjusted Kevin's pillow and brushed the hair from his forehead until he made a face and turned his head.

"Hey, you have some new flowers." She ignored the fact that he was trying to escape her mothering and reached across him to pick up a small wicker basket filled with violets. "Nice."

"Sam just brought 'em," Kevin mumbled, red-faced. "They're from Holly and Stacy. Don't read the card. It's mushy stuff."

"It's not mushy, Kevin." Sam winked at Brynn as he spoke. "It's sentimental. But I guess you have a few years before you need to figure out the difference."

Brynn rummaged in her handbag and drew out a flat brown sack. "Before this discussion evolves into another of your daily discourses from Mr. Rusk's health class, Kevin, I'll show you what I brought you. No mush here." She pulled out a crossword puzzle book, another smaller magazine of anagrams and finally the latest issue of *Sports Outline*.

Sam snatched up the magazine. "When did this come out?" He scanned the table of contents, then flipped rapidly through the pages. "I heard from a former teammate that they've given me some digs in here. I hope you don't believe everything you read in these magazines, son. Sensationalism makes them money."

Kevin nodded in agreement.

"I'm sorry, Sam," Brynn said, biting her lip. "I didn't look through the magazine. I just grabbed it in passing. What could they say about the great Sam Court that's so bad?"

He skimmed through the article, then closed the periodical and tossed it on Kevin's bed. "Controversy makes news. I guess I can be thankful they didn't spread my face all over the cover. If you're ready, Brynn, we should be leaving."

"Kevin?" Brynn arched one brow. "I don't think I even mentioned to you that Sam and I are going out for dinner tonight. Do you mind?"

"Heck, no. I don't like all this fussing. I've got TV, these—" he waved his new books in the air "—and I'm supposed to get a roommate tonight, a kid who ruptured his spleen playing soccer. You two have fun."

Sam already had his hand on Brynn's waist and had begun edging her toward the door. "See you later, Kev. I'm taking her out of here now."

"Well," she murmured grumpily, "it doesn't sound like he'll miss me." Suddenly the thought of spending time alone with Sam unnerved her. She'd enjoyed and counted on his nightly calls when he'd been away—more than she had any right to. The sharing they'd done at the time of Kevin's surgery had been comforting, too. But this was different. This was getting back to basic man-woman stuff. This was too much like a date...a date with someone who belonged to another woman. Brynn's anticipated pleasure fled. Where was Joani tonight? she wondered. Perhaps getting better acquainted with Holly. Maybe Sam planned it like that. She lagged a bit on the way to Sam's car and reminded herself he'd never really offered anything but friendship.

Sam looked at her out of the corner of one eye. "You were supposed to rest today," he scolded, unlocking the passenger door.

Brynn frowned, meeting his gaze. "So?"

"So, it doesn't look to me like you did." He shut her door and rounded the car, taking the driver's seat.

Brynn leaned back and turned her head to study him. "Do I look that bad, Sam? I mean...you were the one who said we'd make it casual."

His gaze moved swiftly over her, then his lashes swept up and he met her eyes. "There's nothing wrong with what you have on. I just think you look tired. And you've lost weight." He started the Jaguar and backed out of the parking space.

"I truly did sleep better last night." Brynn smiled. "It's funny because I thought that being alone I'd hear every noise. Instead, I was dead to the world. They could have launched a rocket outside my window and I doubt I'd have lifted an eyelid. Having Kevin off the critical list is such a relief."

Sam popped a cassette into the tape deck and when a sixties rock tune came on, he lowered the volume, allowing only light background music that wouldn't interfere with their conversation. "You know, it's funny," he mused, fitting his wide shoulders more firmly against the seat. "In California I was an insomniac. Here I seem to need an alarm to get me going. Holly says I'm getting old."

"Partly it's our cooler weather in the northwest. And partly a less frenzied life-style. When I lived in New York, life went on twenty-four hours a day. California is rather like that, too. Seattle doesn't exactly roll in the sidewalks at dusk, but in most parts of the city, nights are for sleeping."

"That sounds like a good plan to me. 'Course it all depends on the company." Grinning, Sam pulled into the parking lot of a renowned lakefront restaurant. "I hope you approve of my choice, Brynn."

Feeling her face grow red following Sam's double entendre, Brynn focused her attention on a young, uniformed valet approaching the car. She reached out to grab Sam's arm in protest. This place he'd selected was noted for being intimate and dressy. However, Sam had already handed his car keys to the youth and was skirting the front of the car on his way to open her door.

"I don't call this restaurant casual, Sam," she said through her teeth. Then she jumped almost a foot as the valet tooted the horn behind her, motioning her to move from in front of the Jag. Forcing a smile, Brynn offered a token wave as she obliged, still muttering to Sam as she surveyed the other expensive cars in the lot. "Who do you plan to tell the maitre d' I am? Your upstairs maid?"

He shot her a broad grin. "I hadn't thought they'd ask, but I have to admit, the idea does have possibilities."

When she glared, he took her elbow and broke into a laugh as they entered the building. "I'll just tell them you're my friend. Anyway, what'll you bet no one even notices what you have on?"

"Pretty sure of yourself, aren't you?"

"Do you know you're absolutely breathtaking when you're angry?" he teased, tugging her. "You're also the hardest woman to take out to dinner I've ever encountered. And if you don't want a picture of our squabbling plastered all over the morning's sports page, I'd suggest we quit sparring and find a secluded corner."

Brynn cast a hesitant glance around and followed him in. "You're just saying that to tease me, aren't you, Sam? I've noticed you've been keeping a low profile for the past few days. They're calling you the 'no comment' man."

At the coat check, Sam removed his topcoat and helped Brynn out of her jacket without acknowledging her statement.

After they'd been seated and fussed over by a trio of waiters, all of whom seemed to know Sam by name, Brynn reached out and covered his hand with hers. "This is a big step you've taken—quitting the team—isn't it? Do you know yet what you're going to do? It must be hard with your family to consider."

He turned his hand palm up and laced his fingers with hers. The frown lines on his forehead deepened. "Whatever I do, it's strictly up to me. But I can't make definite plans until I break my contract. There are a few penalty clauses and they want to stick me for every one. But, listen—" he squeezed her hand "—we came here to enjoy the evening. No shop talk. Tell me what you'd like to drink."

The wine steward came to the table at Sam's signal and Brynn tried, unsuccessfully, to pull her hand away, realizing how easily he'd sidestepped talking about Holly and his ex-wife. And she'd noticed Joani had moved from the sports page to the entertainment section. The former Mrs. Court seemed to be as vocal as Sam was silent. Though she'd never come right out and said they were reconciling, the redhead had hinted it. Cagily, once or twice. What did it all mean? *Friend,* Sam had called her. *Were they really?* She tried again to sneak her fingers away.

Sam greeted the steward casually and tightened his hold on Brynn's hand. "Do you like champagne?" His question was low, for her ears alone.

"Yes, but isn't champagne for celebrating?"

"Well, it seems to me that we have several things to celebrate." Taking control, Sam smoothly gave his wine order before listing them for Brynn. "Kevin's successful surgery is number one. Secondly, I called Iron Man and we actually carried on a conversation without shouting. My being back home early is number three, I guess. Then I heard a rumor you had a birthday coming up." His smile held her. "Doesn't the big three-oh at least rate fourth place and one glass of champagne?"

The bucket with the champagne arrived before Brynn found her voice. She'd strangle Kevin for telling Sam her age. Several heads turned at the pop of the cork, and Brynn moved deeper into the shadows, uncomfortable with the attention. She didn't want her name linked with Sam's. He couldn't afford any more adverse coverage, and she didn't relish the idea of neighbors looking at her on the street and making her the third in a triangle—the other woman.

The steward poured. Sam let go her hand long enough to taste and approve, then he waited while her glass was filled. "A toast," he said, when they were alone once more. He lifted the tulip stem above a candle flickering in a lead crystal holder.

Brynn watched the bubbles making a faint, slow trail inside Sam's glass before she shifted her gaze to meet his eyes. This wasn't the first time she'd thought Sam Court had the sexiest eyes of any man she'd ever met. "What shall we toast?" she asked, her voice husky as she touched the rim of her glass to his. The fine hair at the nape of her neck rose unexpectedly in response to the clear tone of crystal meeting crystal, and she felt the quiver run through her limbs.

"You," he said, holding her gaze. "Me," he murmured, reaching a hand across the table to grasp hers—which was nervously pleating her linen napkin. "Us." His voice fell to a rough whisper on the last word. Clinking her glass again, he drank slowly, gazing steadily at her over the rim.

A curl of need started in Brynn's toes and traveled up her spine with such lightning speed that she forgot to swallow. Was this how Sam Court treated all his friends? she wondered.

Sam arched one brow. "Is something wrong with the champagne? I could order a different brand."

"Wrong? Oh...no," she mumbled, self-consciously taking a small sip. "Sam..." She'd been about to point out the many problems this growing intimacy between them could create. She wanted to tell him to stop teasing her with the impossible term *us*. But she was interrupted by the waiter coming to take their order.

It appeared to Brynn that Sam had no trouble choosing from a menu he'd only glanced at, while she seemed to be on some roller coaster of emotion, unable to think about food at all. At last she insisted Sam choose for her, too. When he suggested scallops and the waiter nodded agreement, she began to feel a little more as though both feet were back on the ground.

"Now, where were we?" Sam added frothy bubbles to her glass, resuming their conversation.

"Enough." Brynn stayed his hand. "I'm not much of a drinker. And all week I've been eating hit and miss. I'd hate to embarrass you by falling off my chair." Inhaling a deep breath, she deliberately switched the conversation to an earlier remark of his. "So tell me, Sam, what brought about the reconciliation with your father?" She really wanted to ask if he was mending the rift in the family because of Joani, but she wasn't brave enough for that.

Below them, in another level of the restaurant, the muted chords from a baby grand piano began, tentative at first, then gaining clarity and momentum. Brynn closed her eyes and savored the sound. "Mm. Sam, you do know how to break through all a woman's defenses, don't you? Flowers, candlelight and now classical piano." She wanted to add that the woman who let him go in the first place was a consummate fool...but she dared not.

"You're a special lady, Brynn." Sam leaned forward to capture her restless fingers. "Whether you know it or not, *you* were the catalyst for my calling Iron Man. Talking with you every night when I was on the road made me think about family—made me realize how important relationships are, and how little time a man has to develop them."

"Sam, I'm not an example. Lord knows I don't have any time in my own life to give to a relationship. First, I have Kevin to consider. This surgery might be the answer for him or it might be the beginning of new problems. Second, I need to work tons of extra hours at the shop and in my design company to pay our bills. A man should certainly rank higher than third in a woman's life."

"Shouldn't you let the man decide for himself?" Sam ran his thumb across her knuckles and studied her somberly. The arrival of their salads forced him to abandon his caress.

He made her yearn to explore all the possibilities she could see smoldering behind his eyes. Did he know how much she wanted to move in on Joani's territory? She wouldn't ever permit anything like that to happen. Yet intuition was telling her that even permitting friendship to blossom between them would cost her more heartache later on.

Brynn only hoped it wasn't too late to be rational—because, the way her heart raced when Sam Court walked into a room, her fate might already be sealed. She might never find another man who measured up.

Dinner conversation remained light and impersonal after that. Brynn was surprised to find they had many things in common besides struggling to raise teenagers alone. Sam liked antiques, as did she. Furthermore, he was quite knowledgeable on the subject and enjoyed spending time poking around estate sales. With her, it was an almost forgotten passion, one she'd not had time to indulge since taking over Kevin's care. And there were other things, too. Art, literature and travel. Time seemed to slip away unnoticed as they spoke. Before Brynn knew it, she was totally relaxed.

It wasn't until they were chatting over coffee that they moved on to a subject closer to both their hearts—namely Kevin and Holly.

"So what have you and Holly been doing with the extra time you've had together since you got home?" Brynn asked. "Have you gone to the science center, or the aquarium, or the flight museum?"

"Whoa!" Sam laughed as he finished pouring a dollop of cream into his second cup of coffee. Then looking at her in amusement, he stirred it thoroughly. "When am I supposed to have done any of those things? Holly's in school three-quarters of the day, and from there she goes directly to your shop. It's dinnertime when she gets home. Lately, I've even had to hold dinner." He paused to take a sip before going on. "I assume she must be doing a good job for you." He held up a hand. "Oh, I know you've had someone filling in...but you haven't given me any complaints."

Brynn set her cup back in the saucer with a sharp clang. "Sam, I...Sam," she began, not knowing what to say.

Straightening, he set his cup down, too. "Brynn, don't look so stricken. If Holly has become a nuisance at the store, say so."

"It isn't that." She touched his arm lightly. "Donna tells me that Holly hasn't been in all week. I assumed you knew."

"That's rubbish. Of course she's been there. Where else would she go?" Shaking off Brynn's hand, he picked up his cup and drained it. He slammed it down hard, almost as though he were daring her to suggest otherwise.

Brynn bit her lip. Whenever the subject of Holly came up, it seemed that Sam resented her offering advice, almost treating it as interference. So with some reluctance, she ventured, "What reason would Donna have to lie about it, Sam?"

Sam signaled for the check. "If you're finished with coffee, we'll just go find out." His eyes had grown chilly, and his tone matched them. "Do you know what you're suggesting about my daughter?"

"I'm not suggesting anything," she protested. "Drop me by the hospital, Sam. My car's there and I want to check on Kevin before I go home. You certainly don't need me around when you get into this with Holly. I'm sure she'll have a perfectly logical explanation. You're the one who's jumping to conclusions."

He glanced at the check, peeled out several bills and threw them on the table. He stalked off to retrieve their coats, with Brynn following. "You weren't kidding? You really do mean Holly hasn't been working for you?" His lips were set in a grim line.

The woman at the coat check wished them a pleasant evening, and Brynn flashed her a warm smile as they passed, to make up for Sam's lack of response.

"Sam," she said when they were outside and alone, "Holly's a good kid. She and Stacy probably have something going on at school. Could Holly be trying out for a part in a play, I wonder?"

"Either way, she lied to me." Sam shoved a large bill at the valet who had the car parked at the curb almost before they'd descended the steps. He hustled Brynn into the passenger seat and tore out of the lot, tires squealing.

Brynn's fingers felt numb as she fumbled with the catch on her seat belt. "If I recall, you do have rather narrow ideas on things like acting. Maybe Holly was afraid you'd be angry."

His brow furrowed. "You don't know the half of it."

"Take me back to my car, please, Sam. I don't want to be forced to take sides. This matter is strictly between you and Holly."

"Come with me, Brynn," he said, suddenly pleading. "Holly has seemed so distant lately. We hardly communicate any more. I don't understand most of the girl talk that goes on between her and Stacy. I'd just like you to be there for me until I find out what this is all about."

"All right, Sam," Brynn agreed reluctantly, hating the fact that she could deny him nothing. "But I think you're overreacting." A chill ran up her spine as her eyes connected with the bleak look in his. She could see that his pain went deep, and she almost wished she hadn't mentioned Holly's absence from the store.

Feeling like an intruder, Brynn trailed behind Sam down the ramp to his houseboat. He was in the entryway shouting for Holly by the time she stepped inside and quietly closed the front door.

"Hi, Daddy...Oh, and Brynn. Is Kevin okay?" Holly's face lost all color. She jumped up from the couch where she'd been sitting, reading.

"He's fine, Holly. Just fine." Brynn glanced nervously at Sam; when she saw his thunderous expression, she couldn't help feeling sympathy for Holly.

Sam didn't mince words. "Donna, the lady who's tending Brynn's shop, tells her that you haven't been in to help out all week, young lady. What do you have to say for yourself?"

Brynn knew how hard Sam was trying to keep his voice level, so she was unprepared for the look of fear that crept into Holly's eyes before the girl whirled away.

Sam shrugged out of his topcoat and tossed it over a chair near a coffee table where Holly's books and papers lay strewn about, some spilling onto the floor. "Holly, we've always been honest with one another, haven't we?"

Brynn was touched by Sam's effort at reasoning, at a conciliatory tone. Had he, too, seen the raw emotion crossing his daughter's face?

"You wouldn't understand this, Daddy." Holly lifted her jaw stubbornly as she slowly turned toward him.

"So try me," he growled.

"Some of the kids at school have said ... Well," she stammered, "since I got my haircut and all ... some of them said I'd be good at modeling." She spoke in a rush. "At first I refused to listen, because I knew how upset you'd be. Then when Stacy's mom took over Brynn's class, she kept saying I was a natural. And another mother thinks that with practice, I could have a great career."

Brynn gasped, then quickly clapped a hand over her mouth to stifle the sound.

"No!" His one-word denial rent the air, and Brynn caught a glimpse of the old, implacable Sam—a return of the man who'd been so rigid and unyielding at their first meeting. His face was set in a cold mask.

Holly's chin came up. "Well, *my own mother* happens to think I'd be a fantastic model, too."

Brynn watched the young woman gaze defiantly at her father. "I'm meeting her every night after school and she's teaching me how to walk. Next week, she's going to help me pick out some trendy clothes. I'm not a little girl anymore, Dad!''

Sam threw up his hands. "So it's Joani. Damn it all! I should have known. Holly..." he began in a strained voice. Then his voice trailed off and he sat down heavily, letting his eyes close. Tiredly, he passed a hand over his mouth and chin. At last his lashes swept up and he looked Holly squarely in the eye. "Why didn't you tell me you were seeing your mother? How long has this been going on?''

"I didn't tell you because you don't like her being in show business," Holly shot back. "You wouldn't have let her teach me, would you? You think she's bad."

Brynn watched the pain clouding both pairs of expressive eyes. Eyes similar in so many ways, yet ideals apart just now. She wished she'd never come. She ached for Holly and for Sam. She ached for herself, too, realizing she wanted to fill a void in each of their lives. When had she let the wanting creep in? And she was thrown off balance by Sam's surprise. Perhaps Joani's return was not as certain as she'd believed.

"I've never said your mother was bad, Holly," Sam said quietly. "Consumed by how she looks, maybe. Totally absorbed in her face, her figure and her clothing... Driven to have all those things she couldn't have as a girl. I happen to think you're better off spending time with women like Brynn and Stacy's mother—women who aren't so self-centered. Lord knows, for more years than I can tell you, I tried accommodating Joani's needs. And I've never once said she couldn't see you, Holly. Never!''

Holly remained stubborn. "Well, she told me you quit the team when you found out the man who bought the Mets is backing her in a movie. She said you were always jealous of her and other men...and she said you didn't like her looking pretty. I didn't want to believe her. I tried to see your side. But I just want a mom and dad like Stacy has.'' She snuffled. "And I don't understand how you think Brynn is different." Tears filled her eyes; her chin jutted higher.

"Brynn doesn't have her head in the clouds, that's how," Sam answered impatiently. "She has more important things on her mind than how she looks."

"Well, maybe now she does, but . . ." Bending to reach under the table, Holly separated a dog-eared magazine from the jumble of papers on the floor. Tight-lipped, she straightened and thrust it at Sam. The periodical fell open to a well-marked page.

Wordlessly Sam accepted the magazine. When at last he lowered his eyes to look, a hiss of shock escaped his lips. His head snapped up and he impaled Brynn with a look of fury.

Brynn felt her heart plunge to her toes. Even from this distance, she could recognize one of her old layouts. The ad was among the last shoots she'd done for Luminaire. Overall, it had been considered her best work. The photographer had devoted hours to making her look naturally sleep-rumpled, and Anthony had chosen the setting well. She'd lain in the middle of a big inviting bed strewn with crimson roses. In marked contrast to the white satin sheets, her nightgown was black lace and quite daring. Uncomfortably, the words that sprang to Brynn's mind to describe the entire layout were words like "provocative" or "sensuous." She felt her blood chill. The magazine was out of print. It could have come from only one source that Brynn could think of—Sunne Evans. But how could her best friend have done something so thoughtless? Brynn's resentment flared, then just as suddenly, she tempered it. Sunne deserved at least a chance to explain herself. Perhaps she'd had a good reason for showing the magazine to the class. Brynn determined not to be as narrow-minded as Sam Court.

Sam's tone was glacial. "Tell me again how you don't play games, Ms. Powell. Offhand, I'd say you're ready for the majors. This is garbage."

Brynn flinched but stood her ground. "If you expect an apology, Sam, you won't get one from me. That is a tasteful advertisement for nightwear, not a centerfold, for crying out loud! Underneath those lacy trappings lies the same hard-working, dedicated, home-and-hearth person you invited out for dinner tonight. It's been said often enough that clothes don't make the man—well, neither do they make the woman. I'm beginning to wish I *had* called you pigheaded when we met. It so obviously fits. Holly isn't Joani, and I'm not playing any games, Sam. I'd say you're the one here with the problem.''

Stalking to the door, Brynn gave it a firm yank, almost losing it to the blustery October wind. ''Don't bother seeing me out,'' she said with head held high. ''I'll have the gate guard call a cab.''

She stood for a moment, feeling the wind cut through her, hesitating only long enough to let Sam come to grips with the absurdity of his outrage. With any luck, he'd realize his mistake and come to get her. But his front door remained closed, a solid barrier at her back. Still, Brynn knew she would have found it a whole lot easier to walk away if she hadn't let Sam Court and his lonely daughter get close to her heart. Love for Holly and Sam had hit her when she wasn't looking. Now, when it was too late, she'd have to deal with the resulting pain.

In her infinite wisdom, Sunne had recommended an occasional night with a good man. Brynn realized she wanted far more than one night. But the only good man she wanted was Sam Court.

CHAPTER ELEVEN

IT WAS OVER! However compelling the mutual attraction had been between Sam Court and herself, Brynn knew it was over. And she missed their daily talks more than she'd ever thought possible. Sitting now, staring bleakly out Kevin's hospital window, she found it hard to believe that by her own carelessness and undefined fear—her failure to tell him about her modeling—she'd driven him back to Joani Court. Or so she'd heard, compliments of Stacy Evans.

From father and daughter Court, she'd heard not a single word. Holly abruptly stopped coming to class, and Sam had dropped out of sight.

According to Stacy, Holly had realized her fondest wish. Her mother was very much back in the picture.

Maybe that was what stung the most, Brynn thought, as she watched the tree outside Kevin's window bend in the wind. On the basis of one layout, Sam had the nerve to compare her with a woman he described as self-centered. Yet he'd apparently gone back to that very woman. To Brynn, the differences between herself and Holly's mother were as clear as the differences between diamonds and rhinestones. As blatant as those elevating Sam Court head and shoulders above Anthony Carraras. Still, she had only herself to blame, because she'd seen the signs and ignored the fact that Sam had been deeply hurt by his glamorous ex-wife.

Kevin seemed almost as listless and preoccupied with the drizzle of raindrops sliding down his window today as she was. "I think I'll go catch up on my paperwork, sport," she said, deciding to leave him to his own devices. "And I'm behind in preparing my lessons for the girls."

"Okay," he mumbled. "I'll see you later."

Driving home, Brynn thought about how much she missed having Holly in her class. The only reference made to the girl's dropping out had been Stacy's blunt announcement that her friend's father wouldn't let her come anymore. Brynn found Sam's inflexibility unfair and depressing. Joani Court or no, Holly needed those classes.

Every night, Brynn fumed silently. If Sam had climbed down off his judgmental high horse long enough to ask why she'd stayed with modeling, she'd have shown him the huge stack of Kevin's medical bills. Couldn't he see that if their roles were reversed, he'd do the same for Holly? If not, perhaps her affections were misplaced after all.

Struggling with problems that seemed to have no answers, Brynn dragged her tired body home after a particularly exhausting class the following evening. She felt as though she'd never needed rest so badly.

In the stillness of the night, the telephone rang, jarring her from a fitful sleep. It was Dr. Low, saying that Kevin was running a fever and they couldn't isolate the offending virus or bacteria. She'd noticed Kevin seemed depressed for the past day or two, and she had attributed it in part to the stormy weather and in part to Sam's defection. Now, reading between the lines, Brynn could tell the doctor was worried.

Rain pelted the city in sheets, and the hospital looked gray and foreboding as Brynn wheeled her Volkswagen into an almost vacant parking lot. Feeling small and alone, she entered a silent waiting room, the same colorless one she'd spent countless hours pacing during Kevin's surgery. Only this time she had neither Sunne's warmth nor Sam's broad, comforting shoulder to steady her.

Dr. Low came in looking positively grim. But perhaps it was really no more, Brynn thought, than her own sinking heart or the long shadows in the vacant room.

"We've taken Kevin to critical care...a precautionary measure at this point." The doctor offered Brynn a seat, but she chose to stand and gaze out over the city, although the view was blurred both by the pounding rain and by her tears. She stared at the diffused halo of a streetlight reflecting off the wet pavement, as though its glow was her one small ray of hope.

"Well, then," Dr. Low said, shrugging, "suit yourself, Brynn...but it's liable to be a long night. Now we play a waiting game and hope he responds to the broad-spectrum antibiotic we've started. We're testing him again for HLA. To refresh your memory, that means human lymphocytic antibodies. They threaten transplant success and sometimes show up in what we call multi tiers." He rubbed his stubbled chin. "I know this sounds tedious, but I want you to understand. Sometimes these antibodies disappear and sometimes we can fight them with antibodies of our own making. If we can't and I have to remove the kidney, he'll be back on dialysis tonight. Someday we'll know enough about the immune system to manipulate it, but until then..." He shrugged again. "Do you have anyone who can stay the night with you? I know how painful the waiting is."

"There's no one, Doctor." Her chin came up. "When can I see him? Is he holding up well? You know, Kevin's really a frightened young boy inside. He just talks big." Her voice cracked.

"Kevin understands. Right now we can't risk visitors." Dr. Low squeezed her shoulder. "He's running quite a fever. Predictable, but it doesn't make our job any easier. Well, Brynn, if you're here for the duration, I'd better get back." He walked to the door, then paused. "By the way, I nearly forgot. Kevin's asking for Sam Court. I haven't seen him around here lately. Nurse Watkins said he'd called to check on Kevin's condition. But if he's in town, you might like to ask him to come."

Dr. Low's insistence that she have someone with her alarmed Brynn. Hearing that Sam still cared enough for Kevin to call threw her completely off stride. "No, no," she mumbled. "I wouldn't want to bother Sam. It's late." Hesitating, she pulled her lip between her teeth. The media had been strangely silent on Sam's leaving the team. Or maybe he hadn't left, after all. The Mets were playing out of town, so Dr. Low probably thought he was traveling with the team. "I'll get in touch with Sam if you think his being here will make a significant difference."

Crossing her arms over her breasts, Brynn massaged the icy skin along her upper arms. Tonight, the room seemed inordinately cold, the chill seeping into her body, seeping deeper than her bones.

The doctor lifted a brow. "One never knows with transplants. I don't like making promises. However, this time, I was thinking more of you. As far as Kevin's concerned, you know I'd have been happier if you had been the donor. The best I can do now is wait things out and have someone keep you posted."

Suddenly he was gone and she was alone. Soul-shatteringly alone. Lack of sleep ceased to matter as she paced the floor. The small annoyances, the stresses and disappointments and fears—Brynn forget them all. Only one thing mattered. She tried whispering a prayer aloud, keeping cadence with the tick, tick, tick of the wall clock until its steady rhythm became her personal talisman. If it kept ticking, Kevin would win the fight.

From time to time, Brynn spared a thought for Sam. He'd made her need him without half-trying—had made her miss the shoulder he'd allowed her to lean on. Depressed, she wondered just why it was that she always seemed to form these attractions for men who dropped out in the home stretch.

Almost before the thought took shape, Brynn dismissed it as unfair. Anthony had led her on, but Sam Court had never claimed to want more from her than friendship. She was the one who'd changed, who'd begun to envision marriage—who'd elevated him to that role even after swearing she'd never give her heart to any man again.

Deep down, she'd always known he wanted Joani back. In retrospect, it was easier to see. He was lonely and he was baffled by Holly's emergence into womanhood. Perhaps Holly's rebellion had made him see it more clearly, too.

Oh, but she was so tired of being strong. Strong and alone. Tick. Tick. Tick. The hands on the wall clock moved slowly on.

A little after three in the morning a nurse tiptoed in and reported that there had been no change in Kevin's condition. But neither had he thrown off the donor kidney—which was a good sign. Kevin was fighting back, she said, for all he was worth. But he was still asking for Sam. Less than half an hour later, Dr. Low sent word that if Kevin's fever dropped another degree, Brynn could visit him, at least for a few moments.

And if it didn't?

Swallowing her pride, Brynn went to the telephone in the hall, hesitating only a moment before placing a call to Sam's houseboat. For Kevin's sake, she'd beg Sam to come. He was a caring, compassionate man. Surely he wouldn't turn her down. After the fourth ring and no answer, Brynn considered hanging up. Then a woman's sleepy voice rasped out a hesitant hello, causing Brynn to suffer a pain so swift and intense it was like having the sharp edge of a knife slice a gaping hole in her heart.

So he *had* made up with Joani. For a heart-stopping moment, the pain of knowing rendered Brynn mute.

"Hello—hello?" The woman's voice held a note of panic now.

"Sorry, wrong number," Brynn mumbled, hanging up quietly and leaning forward until her forehead touched the cold metal housing of the pay telephone. It was time again for testing what Brynn Powell was made of. Until she heard Joani's voice answering Sam's phone, Brynn hadn't realized that she'd still held some hope of righting matters between them. Now there was none.

The hands of the clock moved to four o'clock and Brynn thought it must surely be the lowest hour in her life, outside of the day her parents died. A dismal hour made worse by knowing the man she'd come to love had taken his former wife into his bed. It shouldn't hurt so much—but it did.

Love? The word swam in her head. Had she been falling in love while Sam was waiting for Joani to return and warm his sheets? "No!" she whispered. Sam had never wanted just any flesh-and-blood woman, she told herself; he'd been seeking a goddess. But maybe he'd changed. Brynn hoped he had reconciled himself to the human imperfections in the woman with the sleepy voice. Otherwise, he'd never find the happiness he sought. She failed miserably in her attempt to be magnanimous.

Suddenly the long night was over and with the arrival of a gloomy dawn came a glimmer of encouraging news. At long last, Kevin was responding to treatment. Brynn was allowed five minutes with him. She vowed again before going in to see him that both Powells would brush Sam Court from their minds.

Reaching over the side rail of her brother's bed, she stroked his limp, dry fingers. Her own were clammy with relief.

"Hey, Sis," he murmured in a weak voice. "You look kinda like I feel...like you've been dragged through a knothole backward."

"You're all heart, buddy." Brynn hadn't meant to shed tears where he could see. In fact, she'd been forcing them back all night. The release came from hearing a return of the old cheeky Kevin, however feeble, and it came swiftly, like unlocking the floodgates on a dam. What did she care that she had no one to lean on? It only mattered that Kevin had *her* and she'd be there for him forever if need be. She couldn't stop the tears of joy.

"Don't get sloppy, Brynn. We Powells are tough. You said so yourself," he whispered, though his voice broke at the end.

She smiled through her tears. "You keep reminding me, sport. I don't suppose you want to hear I love you, either." Leaning down, she kissed him on the forehead.

"I dunno. I s'pose even tough guys need to know they're loved. Say, Brynn, speaking of tough guys, I gotta see Sam."

Brynn stopped short on her way to the door. She took a deep breath. "I haven't seen him, Kev. Why do you need him?"

"I promised a friend the other day that I'd talk the Samurai into emceeing our junior-senior prom. It's a pretty big deal, you know. The emcee has to be cool. All the kids have a lot of respect for Sam. Do you think he might do it, Sis?"

Brynn took in her brother's bright eyes and his chalk-white face. "Uh...I suppose so, sport," she lied. "But isn't your first priority to simply get well? After all, the prom is more than six months off."

"You and Sam have a fight?"

Brynn looked away. It amazed her how kids could cut right through to the heart of things. Seeing a nurse headed toward them, Brynn jerked open the door. "This nurse is going to throw me out, Kevin. You just rest, young man... We'll discuss this later."

For the remainder of a very long day, Brynn managed to avoid the entire subject of Sam Court, though she did some fancy sidestepping until Kevin's condition stabilized. She simply brought up a different issue each time Kevin mentioned Sam.

By the time she left for home, Brynn was dead on her feet and tense from dodging his one-track queries. She called herself a coward for not just coming right out and telling Kevin that Sam's life had changed, that he had new priorities. Maybe tomorrow's paper would be filled with the Courts' reunion. If so, it would be easy to let Kevin figure things out for himself.

Once inside her house, Brynn didn't even try to make it upstairs. Instead, she collapsed on the couch in the living room and pulled an afghan over herself. She was asleep before her head hit the pillow.

Her dreams were a wild mix of hospital scenes interwoven with ice hockey and a few images from her old magazine layouts. Somehow Sam Court loomed large in the last act, dressed in a tuxedo and carrying a microphone in his hand. But of course there were legions of teenage girls gazing at him in adoration. They all looked like prom queens.

Then all at once, her dream began to dissolve. No matter how hard Brynn tried to keep Sam in focus, he was being pulled away into the arms of some disembodied woman. A woman calling to him in a sleep-husky voice. A woman in sequins, silk and a leopard coat.

Brynn awoke with a start, her head pounding. Then she realized the pounding was really at her front door. Sweeping away the vestiges of sleep, she flew to the entrance, worry for Kevin crowding out the already forgotten dream.

She flung the door wide, taking a moment to let her eyes adjust to the dusky shades of early evening—and to the figure of Holly Court, who huddled crying on her porch.

"Why, Holly, what's wrong?" Brynn scrubbed at her eyes trying to focus, to understand.

Before she could, Holly launched her slender body against Brynn's and wailed, "My dad was right, Brynn. He said my mother never wanted me and he was r-right." Her wail turned to racking sobs.

"Oh, Holly." Brynn cradled the distraught girl in her arms, rocking her back and forth. She fought to wake up and make sense of Holly's words. "Come in," she urged, "and we'll sort through this together."

Sniffling, Holly picked up a suitcase that Brynn hadn't noticed hidden in the shadows. The situation was obviously worse than she had anticipated. And where were Sam and Joani while all this was taking place? Off in some cozy love nest? Resentment flared on Holly's behalf, as it had at her first meeting with Defenseman Court.

Brynn shepherded Holly into her kitchen. As for herself, she could use a bracing cup of tea; Holly might relax better with hot chocolate.

"Suppose you start at the beginning," Brynn suggested, offering the girl a seat before she filled the kettle.

Holly dabbed at her eyes. "I'm sorry I showed my dad that magazine, Brynn. He's stamped and growled like a bear ever since. I never expected him to get mad at you, too, though. I just thought he wouldn't be quite so upset with me." The girl's lower lip quivered.

"I know you didn't do it maliciously, Holly. Unfortunately it's something your father has to work through for himself. I knew early on how he would feel about modeling. I have to share the blame for not mentioning my background before he agreed to let you take the class."

Holly stared into space, looking dejected. "At first, I thought it'd all blow over. After you left, he started to go after you. But he stopped and went into the den to call my mother. I could hear him raising his voice. When he came out, he said it was settled. I could see her, but only if she came to the houseboat." The teakettle whistled just then and she paused, staring at the steam.

That explained Joani Court's homecoming, Brynn thought, handing over Holly's cup of hot chocolate. She let her herb tea steep a few moments. So Joani Court's visits included sleeping over, did they? But what business was that of hers? Brynn shook off a chill. She needed to forget Sam and help Holly through her anguish.

Holly drank a little of her chocolate, then stumbled on with her story. "Later that evening my grandparents arrived. It's the first time Grandpa Joe has ever come to visit. He said he'd been stewing about Dad's problems and had come to help." Holly stopped talking suddenly and asked for marshmallows.

Brynn searched through her cupboards until she found some. Taking a seat opposite Holly, she ventured, "Isn't that good—that your grandfather was willing to visit? Did he make up with your mother, too?"

Holly looked surprised. "Grandpa started out by giving orders. Dad yelled at him, said he hadn't changed a bit. Grandma said I shouldn't listen to their bad language. She said those two are exactly alike. Both hardheaded. Grandma laughed it off and took me for a walk. We looked at the other houseboats."

Brynn smiled. "Sounds like your grandmother's a wise lady." She could well imagine the two male Courts going head to head—like rams. "But surely you didn't pack a suitcase and leave because your father and grandfather were having an argument, Holly."

"No. Anyhow, that was last week. It was one of the days my mother showed up. I thought she was there to see me. We had plans to pick out my clothes for modeling. Instead, she just fussed at Dad and Grandpa. She kept saying things like . . . if dad tried to break his contract, her friend Mr. Jenkins would see he went bankrupt. That's when Grandpa really started to roar. He told her she was a born troublemaker and that he and my dad would never have fought years ago if it hadn't been for her. Mother just laughed harder, brushing it off, saying they were both stodgy old fogies who didn't want anyone having fun. She left without saying a word to me or telling me when she'd be back. Dad and Grandpa went into my dad's office and slammed the door. When they came out, they told Grandma they were going to California to see Dad's agent. It was like everyone totally forgot I was in the house."

Brynn refilled Holly's cup. Her heart went out to the girl. It was terrible—the rejection Holly must have felt. She patted her arm, wondering how she could help.

"Once Dad and Grandpa left, I started thinking about what it would be like to live with my mother all the time. She hadn't been treating me like a kid and she really seemed to care about me." Tears began to drip slowly down Holly's pale cheeks.

"Go on, Holly," Brynn said gently as she grabbed a tissue and patted the girl's tears away. "What then?"

"I've been thinking about it all week. This morning, I threw some things into a suitcase before I left for school. Grandma thinks I'm spending the night with Stacy." Her lower lip trembled. "After class, I went to Mother's hotel. That's when she told me she hadn't ever meant for me to come live with her. She said in Las Vegas it wouldn't look good if folks knew she had a thirteen-year-old kid. And besides, she had plans to make a movie. That's when Mr. Jenkins came out of the next room. He just laughed and said she was jealous 'cause I was younger and prettier. My mother got real mad at him. They started quarreling, so I ran away. I came here. I'm going to New York and become a model. Will you help me, Brynn?"

Brynn's heart grieved for Holly and Sam. To think she'd ever wasted any sympathy on Joani Court. And she'd been utterly unfair in her assessment of Sam. Brynn knew that under similar circumstances, she wouldn't be half as understanding of the former Mrs. Court as Sam had been.

Still, he wouldn't welcome her interference in this matter. He'd made it abundantly clear on more than one occasion that his family problems were off-limits to her. And right now, Sam probably considered her an unwelcome encore of the scenes he'd already played with his ex-wife. But there was nothing new she could offer to change his mind. Her past was what it was. Knowing she was back where they'd started brought a fresh stab of pain.

The most Brynn could hope to do was convince Holly that Sam had her best interests at heart. "You know, Holly, modeling is not all glamour. It's long, tiring hours under hot lights, posing for people who see you as merchandise. For everyone who makes it big, there are at least a hundred models who don't make enough to feed themselves. Finish school, Holly. Then if you still honestly want to choose modeling for a career, talk it over with your father. Research all the options together. He loves you. I do know that. You're number one in his life and he'll be worried sick if he calls you at Stacy's tonight and you're not there. Just think how many years you have left to make choices. So take your time. What do you say? I'll be happy to take you home on my way to the hospital."

A sheepish smile twitched at the corners of Holly's mouth. "Gosh, I feel better already just talking with you, Brynn—but do you suppose I could finish my hot chocolate before we go?"

The young girl's crooked smile, so like Sam's, brought Brynn close to tears. She forced herself to answer calmly. "By all means finish. Just don't tell the others in my class about all those marshmallows. It'll make a mockery of my nutrition segment."

Holly's smile was replaced by a furrowed brow. "I wish Dad would let me go back to your class. I don't think he objects to what you're teaching, Brynn. But I'm grounded for lying. Boy, I've screwed things up good, haven't I?" She drained her cup, then took it to the sink and rinsed it. "I wish you were my mother, Brynn." Holly threw her arms around Brynn and hugged her hard. "I don't see how my dad could believe you're anything like my real mother. It's funny, but you know . . . she didn't really seem like she was related to me at all today. I wonder if Kevin knows how lucky he is to have you?"

Brynn extricated herself from Holly's arms. For a fleeting moment, she, too, imagined herself as Sam's wife and Holly's mother. But it could never happen—no matter how much Holly wished it. No matter how much *she* wished it. Sam Court wouldn't forgive easily; it had taken fourteen years and a career catastrophe to mend fences between himself and Iron Man. The truth hit her hard and stung bitterly.

Somehow, Brynn dredged up the strength to deal with Holly's outrageous suggestion by injecting a little humor. "You mean Kevin didn't tell you what an ogre I am when it comes to making him clean his room? He'd be the last one to agree he's so lucky." Winking, Brynn added, "But Kevin does idolize your father. Maybe you could work out some kind of a trade on a temporary basis. I'm sure he'd love to switch for a month or so, as he covets your Jacuzzi. When you get to visit him in the hospital, you can ask. Shall we go?''

It was a subdued but happier Holly who talked Brynn into escorting her right to her front door. Then, because Brynn extracted a promise from Holly to confess all to her grandmother, Brynn let herself be talked into going inside with the girl for moral support.

The minute Brynn met Sam's mother, she was overcome with guilt for assuming that Joani was back in his life, his bed. As she and the older woman talked, a rapport developed between them. Brynn liked this woman and understood a little better what made Sam the way he was. She'd misjudged him. She felt ashamed of the conclusions she'd drawn so hastily about Sam and his motives—yet she couldn't deny a feeling of relief, too. He didn't love Joani!

For a while, Brynn and Mrs. Court chatted comfortably, about the weather and Kevin's surgery and Holly's new life. Then when Brynn was ready to leave, Mrs. Court invited her back soon to meet Iron Man. "I'd like my husband to see what a sensible woman our son has met at last. He's fretted for years over that unfortunate squabble they had." The plump woman sighed. "But some people," she said, "were never meant to be together. I believe Sam and Joani were like that. It's no wonder Holly's confused."

Brynn was quick to set the record straight. "Holly and her father are more my brother's friends." She colored, thinking how *she* obviously was never meant to be with Sam, either. Nor would she ever feel free to visit this houseboat again unless Sam gave her a personal invitation—and there was little chance of that.

After carefully explaining a second time to Sam's mother how she fit—or rather *didn't* fit—into Sam's life, Brynn decided to mention last night's phone call. She described the severity of Kevin's relapse. "So you see, Mrs. Court, I was the one who telephoned at such a late hour. But only because Kevin was asking for Sam. I wasn't prepared to hear a woman's voice so I hung up, thinking I'd misdialed." The boldness of the lie had Brynn crossing her fingers behind her back.

"My goodness," exclaimed Mrs. Court. "I wish you'd told me what you wanted. Sam did say something about keeping tabs on someone in the hospital. I had no idea. Hockey players are always getting hurt. I assumed it was a teammate. Here...let me give you my son's telephone number in Los Angeles. Anything that affects Holly affects Sam. Please call him. I can't say for sure when he'll return."

"That's not necessary." Brynn declined the woman's offer. "I'm pleased to report that Kevin has passed his crisis." She darted a look at Holly to see if the news of Kevin's latest setback had bothered her. But like most teenagers, Holly bounced back to her old self once her own crisis had passed. Teens were remarkably resilient, Brynn thought, unlike certain others who'd left their teenage years far behind.

As if to confirm the observation, when Brynn took her leave Holly was chatting happily on the phone to Stacy Evans. Pausing a moment, the girl gave Brynn her most effusive thanks and promised to explain everything to her father later when he called. She said she'd tell him about Kevin, too.

THROUGHOUT HER EVENING VISIT with Kevin, Brynn waited, more than half expecting Sam to call her brother from L.A. Though she would have been the last to admit it, every time the phone rang, her heart leaped and began a furious pounding. However, her wait was in vain.

By week's end, Kevin was showing marked signs of improvement. Brynn, however, was not only more jumpy, but thoroughly provoked over what she considered Sam's lack of common decency. Stacy had told her Sam was in town. Now Brynn was well on her way to feeling furious.

But if Kevin heard from Sam at all, as one nurse implied he had, he certainly didn't mention it to Brynn. And she decided she'd be hanged before she'd ask him. The way Kevin was progressing, Dr. Low promised he could go home within a week. So Brynn had to get on with her life, and in order to do that, she had to forget Sam Court.

Sunne and Paul dropped by the hospital the minute they hit town. If it hadn't been for all the work and stress Sunne faced in getting ready for her big Saturday night Halloween party,

Brynn would have let her friend know immediately just what she thought of her giving Holly that magazine. Surely Sunne deserved to suffer something, Brynn thought, for all the trouble she'd caused. And at the very least she wanted to hear Sunne's reasons. But it would alter nothing in the broader picture, so Brynn refrained.

By Halloween, Brynn was as hurt and angry as she could be over Sam's continued silence. But only for Kevin's sake, she told herself. He seemed lonely. His roommate had left; there wasn't a new one yet. Kevin needed a man's influence and Dr. Low and Paul were both too busy. And because he'd stopped bringing up Sam's name with each waking breath, Brynn was positive he hadn't heard from Holly's father. Kevin could never keep silent if he'd spoken to his idol. Her heart broke while he filled his recovery hours with TV, books and puzzles. Time moved slowly for both of them.

In truth, Brynn was downright bored on Saturday. She seemed to have nothing more pressing to do than rearrange Kevin's flowers yet another time.

"Sis. Don't you have work at home?" Kevin clicked off the TV and shifted on his pillow until he could meet Brynn's eyes. "Between you and the nurses, I'm beginning to feel smothered."

Brynn moved a plant to a spot she'd just moved it out of. "Are you trying to get rid of me, sport? I only want to help. I thought you liked company. And I know you miss having a roommate." She set a basket of violets on the windowsill, noting that they were from Stacy and Holly. Reaching across the bed, she passed a hand through Kevin's longish hair. "Maybe I'll cut your hair. All these girls in your fan club would take back their flowers if they could see you now."

Moving to escape her hand, Kevin stuck out his tongue. Then he bit back a groan as he leaned on one elbow. Gritting his teeth, he waved her away. "If you must know, Sam is coming later today for a visit." He paused as if testing the waters, then plunged on. "I suppose you know he's been out of town the past couple of weeks. But you may not know the Samurai's folks have been here. Now that he's got things more settled, he's gonna bring Holly for a visit. She's got homework for me.'' With a lopsided grin, Kevin managed to avoid his sister's accusing eyes as he adjusted the head of his bed with the automatic control.

Brynn's fingers stilled on a vase of cut flowers. "Why didn't you tell me this before, Kevin?"

"I figured it would be better if Sam came by when you weren't here. You've been so cross lately whenever his name comes up."

Brynn quickly snatched her raincoat off the chair. Her heart thudded wildly. Did Sam think her so terrible that he couldn't even be civil, for goodness' sake? Heavens, *she* would have been big enough to apologize for misjudging him. But after all, she thought, still smarting, he owed her an apology, too.

Shaking out the hat that matched her raincoat, Brynn willed her pulse to settle back to normal. "I suppose I should be thankful for this extra time you've granted me to catch up on my paperwork, Kevin. Will you call me when the coast is clear?"

Kevin rubbed one hand over the thick bandages covering his incision. Then he tugged on the bedspread, pulling it up until it rested beneath his chin. "Now you're all huffy, Sis. I just knew you were avoiding Sam, not the other way around. Girls can be so silly."

"I'm not a girl, Kevin. And Sam doesn't want to see me any more than I do him."

"Whatever, Brynn! I know how *you* are." Kevin gave a small shrug. "But I love you anyway," he mumbled. "So why don't you stop back to see me on your way to the party tonight? I want to get a load of you wearing that cancan outfit." He rolled his eyes.

Brynn halted by the door. "Who told you I was wearing a cancan costume?" Her heart plunged when she remembered Sam had been the one to choose it. Would he be taking some other date tonight, she wondered, now that he was footloose and free?

Kevin looked thoughtful. "I dunno who told me. I thought you did. Wasn't it the night you and Sam went out to dinner?"

Brynn lifted her chin. "Well . . . no matter. I'm not going to the party, Kevin. I've already left a message with Paul."

"Well, don't be coming back here for the evening," he blustered. "The nurses have planned a spook night for the ward. I don't think it includes family. Besides, it'll do you good to get out."

"Says who? That sounds suspiciously like a Sunne Evans idea. Has she put you up to this?"

"Hey, do I look like Sunne's mouthpiece? I happen to have hung around those parties. You know Mom and Dad never missed one. They're cool and the food is great. I'd like to be going myself. Just think about it, okay? For my sake. You've been hovering lately."

She made a face at him. "I'll think about it. But don't hold your breath. Besides, if the Courts are going . . ." Brynn didn't finish her sentence. And before Kevin could nag her, she dashed out, taking the back stairs, just in case she meet Sam and Holly on the elevator. Her heart did funny acrobatics in her chest each time she pictured meeting Sam. She couldn't bear it if he looked right through her. Forgetting Anthony hadn't been nearly so difficult as forgetting Sam.

Somehow it pricked at her conscience to know Sam *had* cared enough about Kevin to keep in touch. She really did feel guilty about misjudging him. But maybe he'd only called her brother to please Holly. Be that as it may, it altered nothing between the two of them, and she had other things to do with her life.

Brynn finished with her ledgers and was storing the last book away when she heard the bell tinkle. Before she could rise, Sunne Evans rushed through the showroom and into the back office.

"I've just come from having Midge do my hair and I wanted you to see my costume, Brynn. Tra la!" Sunne whipped off her coat and performed a slow pirouette. The brief, brightly colored sarong fitted her perfectly.

Brynn found it impossible to stay angry at someone as guileless as her old friend. Besides, they'd been friends forever. "If I'd acquired that yummy tan you're sporting, Sunne

Evans, I'd show it off, too. Sexy! I predict you'll be the belle of this ball.''

"Well, I wish I could say the same for you, Brynn. You look like death warmed over. We got your message about not coming tonight and believe me, I understand your not wanting to show up.'' Sunne slipped into her coat and moved toward the door. "Stacy told me about Holly dragging out your old layouts for Sam. A real difference from the Brynn of today. I can see why you're embarrassed.''

"Wait a minute!'' Brynn trailed Sunne into the showroom. "You gave Holly those magazines. Don't tell me you didn't expect her to show them to Sam. If anyone's embarrassed, it should be you—friend!''

Sunne smiled mysteriously. "So, maybe I wanted him to drool a little. But that was then. Now, you resemble a scarecrow. Your nails are a mess and I'll bet you haven't had your hair done in ages. Of course, we all understand... But after all, Sam's used to mixing with those gorgeous starlets and California beach bunnies. All those long, gorgeous legs. And you, my pal, are skin and bones. How could you hope to compete?'' Pausing, Sunne checked her watch. "Gad! I hate to rush off, Brynn, but I've really got a million things to finish before the party. What I wouldn't give for some witch's magic potion right now. Too bad about tonight. But maybe next year. Toodles!''

Brynn, who had followed Sunne into the showroom, blinked as the door slammed and the bell jingled in her wake.

"A scarecrow! Embarrassed to go, am I?'' Brynn ground her teeth together as she closed the shop for the night. Sunne had never been cruel before, she thought. But look how things changed.

Brynn was still seething over Sunne's callous remarks when she arrived home and saw the ruffled cancan outfit hanging in colorful splendor on her closet door. How could someone she considered practically a sister say such hurtful things? Brynn fumed until she suddenly remembered the old saying—sisters didn't get mad, they got even! She crossed the room and took a long, hard look at her face in the mirror. Dark circles, maybe. And far too serious, without a doubt! But a scarecrow? Never!

Brynn smiled to herself. Sunne really *hated* her last year's costume. Sam Court would hate her last year's costume, too! But if the man liked legs, well—she'd show him legs.

Taking the utmost care, Brynn pulled the garment bag from a back corner in her closet. This costume didn't lend itself to driving—she'd have to walk to the party—but it would be worth the trouble. Removing the outfit, Brynn studied it carefully from all angles. It would serve them right, she thought, as she reached for the telephone and dialed Kevin's room.

"If you really meant what you said, sport," she murmured, "I think I will go to the party after all. But it's so late now, I won't have time to stop by and show off my costume. Next year, though, we'll go together. You and I will think up something really clever to wear. Is it a date?"

Brynn suffered a twinge of remorse at her brother's gullible, ready agreement. Plunking the receiver into its cradle, she deliberately drew a deliciously scented bath and sank into it, still wearing a satisfied smile.

CHAPTER TWELVE

FROM HIS VANTAGE POINT in a crowded corner of the Evanses' living room, Sam Court kept one eye on the door and one hand free for introductions. He studied each new arrival with care. Watching. Waiting for Brynn.

Some pretty scanty costumes were revealed as coats were shed. Sam began to weave a fantasy about the hot pink and black cancan outfit he'd chosen for Brynn. He knew she thought he was against women wearing such things, which simply wasn't true. There was a time and a place for them. He was against obsessions, that was all. Any number of the peekaboo sensations swishing past him would suit Brynn Powell. And any one of them would be a fitting complement to his riverboat gambler attire, he decided, nodding hello to Paul Evans across the room. Except that none of the costumes swishing past were on that one special woman Sam wanted as his Lady Luck tonight.

He fervently hoped Sunne and Kevin knew what they were talking about when they said the only way to entice Brynn here tonight was to make her mad. If he'd gone with his own instincts, he would have rushed over to see her on his first day in town and thrown himself on her mercy.

Watching Paul and Sunne working companionably together in their roles as hosts, Sam experienced a deep and nagging envy for his old friend's easy, loving relationship. Lord, but he'd had a rough trip to L.A. The highlight had been making peace with Iron Man and swallowing his pride after all those years. But it felt good—really good. Sam felt good. And he'd have to give Brynn credit for showing him how much he needed that hearth and home she'd mentioned. Not just for Holly; for himself, too. Plucking a drink from a nearby tray,

Sam rocked back on his heels, listening to the talk drifting around him.

"The Dow is leveling out, don't you think, Court?" Someone nudged Sam's elbow. "I say it's time to buy, buy, buy if you want to make a million!" The speaker was a rotund little man wearing a funny chicken suit that accentuated his receding hairline and expanding paunch. Smiling politely, Sam accepted a business card thrust into his hand.

"Elwood Long, Financial Consultant," he read. Downing his drink, Sam backed away. It was too early in the evening and there hadn't been enough liquor in his first drink for him to take financial advice from a bald chicken named Elwood.

Dammit, he thought, *where's Brynn?* Kevin and Sunne assured him she was coming. But the seductive music wafting from the next room made him ache to hold her in his arms. All around him, glasses clinked and voices rose to compensate. What he needed to rid himself of this gnawing loneliness was to have his arms locked around Brynn in a slow, sensuous dance. His jaw tightened. Maybe he should have called her— yes, he should probably have called from California and apologized, but he preferred to do it in person, and he'd wanted everything else resolved first. At any rate, the others insisted this way was best.

And Paul and Sunne had, after all, created the perfect romantic setting. Candlelight flickered softly around the dance floor. A full harvest moon beckoned through a curved bay window, a welcome respite from the many days of rain. Dark clouds had blown away earlier, and Frontage Bay lay before him like a ring of jewels. Idly, Sam toyed with a pair of ivory dice he'd discovered in the pocket of his rented red satin vest. In the heart of the dreamlike swirl of dancers, he could almost see the shimmer of Brynn's ruffled gown. He could almost feel the creamy texture of silk beneath his fingertips. Could almost smell the heady aroma of wildflowers, Brynn's special scent.

Sniffing the air, Sam found the light fragrance intoxicating enough to set his pulse hammering. Then as the fine hair on the back of his neck rose, he turned—fully expecting to see her looking like the exotic vision he'd created in his mind.

Instead, Sam was sure his face registered the same shock reflected in Sunne's sharp hiss of disapproval. "How could you, Brynn? How could you!" her friend shrieked, shaking Brynn's arm. "Last year, not one man was brave enough to ask you to dance. Not one!"

Sam wished he could laugh just now. Instead, it took a supreme effort not to walk over and calmly rip Brynn right out of that damned disgusting outfit. He didn't see how anyone could get close enough to dance—with her wearing that spider costume! Over a satiny black bodysuit, she was all plump, velvety pillow body and fat furry legs sticking out at odd angles. Eight of them if you counted her own arms and legs in there. And all revolting. Sam had to agree with Sunne, who was busy ticking off a list of awfuls.

Behind him, Sam heard the music kick into an easy rock and he felt his abdomen coil from the slight vibration of throbbing drums. Very likely, Brynn was banking on being unapproachable. But she'd banked wrong. It struck him then that he'd want Brynn Powell wearing anything—or wearing nothing. That revelation set Sam wondering what she did have on beneath the skintight bodysuit. Sam tugged at his string tie and straightened his red vest. Tonight, he was a gambler.

Two strides brought him to Brynn's side. She hadn't seen him; in fact, there was very little she *could* see, with that hood covering her face. It took him less than a minute to identify her arms from the bobbing spidery legs. No wonder the men hadn't asked her to dance last year. Getting his arms around her would be a major challenge. Sam pasted on his most winsome smile, caught her hand and slapped the pair of dice soundly into one of Brynn's black-gloved palms.

She jerked her head around, surprised. Her eyes met his through narrow slits cut in the black hood. She was forced to angle her head to see the ivory squares lying in her palm.

Sam looked, too, and grunted in satisfaction. A five and a six winked back. A win at craps. His luck was holding. "Eleven for me, Brynn. You lose," he said silkily, grasping her other hand in a punishing grip.

"Leave me alone, Sam," she said coldly. "I've had quite enough of your games. Go play with one of your little starlets . . . or beach bunnies."

Sunne stood nearby, wringing her hands. For once, she was speechless.

Sam flashed her a reassuring grin. Without a word, he turned and strode toward the dance floor, ignoring the fact that Brynn was resisting him. The guests in more normal costumes giggled as they passed. Sam ignored them, too. And when he reached the edge of the dance floor, he deftly insinuated his body between the wire legs and swept Brynn into the dense throng of dancers.

"Wait just a darn minute," she blustered. But being somewhat out of breath, she soon gave up holding her back ramrod stiff. Still clutching the dice, Brynn swallowed her last feeble protest as Sam issued a single expressive expletive and yanked her, velvety pillows and all, tight enough to bend some of the legs.

"Where did you get this ridiculous costume, Brynn?" he asked, a chuckle rumbling somewhere inside his chest.

Relaxing a bit, Brynn shrugged carelessly and made a point of watching her spidery appendages curl around Sam's shoulder. It *was* rather comical, she thought, wanting to join in his laughter. Determined not to, she muttered, "Louise Cavanaugh does children's plays. This was Miss Muffet's spider."

Sam threw back his head and laughed heartily. Dancers edged away and opened up a larger space for them. "I'm surprised parents didn't object. Costume or not, this damn thing would scare a kid out of ten years' growth."

Brynn gave in to her own mirth then. "It did . . . which is why she gave it to me." For a moment they clung together, laughing.

"So—" his teeth flashed wickedly "—who'd mind if I dismantled the damn thing limb from limb?"

"Sam!" Sobering, she inched out of his grasp. She wanted to stay mad at him, but found it hard. One of her spider legs knocked a pretty witch's hat askew, earning both herself and Sam dirty looks. "Tell me what all this is about," she finally demanded in a frosty tone. "I hadn't thought we were even on speaking terms."

"I'm not good at admitting I've handled our whole relationship badly, Brynn. But by now you probably know I'm not good at apologies. Here tonight, though, I'd planned an entire evening of seducing you properly while begging your forgiveness. For starters," he said with a crooked grin, "I went out and bought you a whole bushel full of roses. But there's something difficult, not to mention peculiar, about offering roses to a giant spider." Leaning back, Sam studied her at leisure. "How did you wiggle into this thing anyhow?"

Seeing his look of pure male frustration, Brynn erupted in musical laughter. All trace of anger evaporated then—he looked so thoroughly chagrined.

"Do you have any idea what's bigger than a bushel full of roses, Brynn?" he asked, trying to nuzzle her ear through the gauze hood. Deftly he enfolded her hand, still clutching the dice, against his chest.

Brynn made a concentrated effort to keep her dance steps in perfect order as she slowly shook her head. She was thoroughly mesmerized by the violet eyes turning indigo with what could only be desire.

"A bed full," Sam grated softly near her ear.

Brynn drew in a sharp breath, stumbled and landed on his foot.

Unconcerned, Sam went on smoothly. "A bed full of roses and a bucket of champagne. I intended for us to celebrate tonight, because our last celebration was interrupted rather early, if you recall. Also... I was successful in breaking my contract, Brynn." With a little pride, he added, "I have a new job in Seattle, too. Coaching a high-school hockey team. It's something I've always wanted to do—train a young team right, from the ground up." Staring into her upturned face, Sam wiggled the fingers of his left hand behind the pillow that made up the spider's body. Wiggled them until he could spread his fingers flat along her rigid spine.

Brynn skipped a second step. "I'm happy for you, Sam. Holly told me about the reconciliation with your father. How is she, by the way? I've missed having her in class."

"I'm sorry about the class, Brynn. But Holly broke a house rule when she lied to me. It's a separate issue entirely. However, I am remiss in not thanking you for being there for Holly when her mother let her down. All along, I knew it was bound to happen. No matter how much I wanted to cushion the blow, there are some things kids just have to find out for themselves." He paused and tightened his hold. "But it seems that stubbornness isn't limited to teenagers, Brynn. Don't you know that all you had to do was call and I would have dropped everything and come home from L.A. to be with you and Kevin? I kept calling, but could never reach you. Your recorder wasn't on and the hospital wouldn't tell me a thing. When they finally let me talk with Kevin, he told me you wouldn't even say my name." Abruptly, Sam pulled her closer. "Have I told you yet how good it feels to hold you like this?" His voice growing husky, Sam slid his hand higher up her back, where he toyed with the zipper on her costume.

Brynn's eyes widened when he edged it down a scant half inch, but her head was reeling from the things he'd said. "I don't think I understand, Sam. Are you saying you're not angry over my magazine layout? I couldn't have imagined your reaction. You do remember... it's the picture of me sitting on a rose-covered bed. I was wearing a rather—"

He broke in. "I've thought of nothing but that damned layout since Holly gave me the magazine." He smiled into her eyes. "Before you rub the spots off those dice, Ms. Powell, why don't you just smile sweetly and tell the good folks of Frontage Bay good-night. I'm offering my bed or yours, Brynn. One has roses, one has daisies...and neither place has kids. If it takes the two of us all night, I swear we'll get you out of this and into something more...comfortable," he teased, a gleam coming into his eyes.

Brynn tried her best to stifle the quiver that ran along her limbs. Marshalling a stern look, she lifted her chin and arched a brow, determined to give as good as she was getting. "Is this bold man the same Sam Court who recently proclaimed my Sweet Dreams line of lingerie fit only for ladies of the night?"

"Ouch! You have me dead to rights. Strange how enlightened I've become in such a short time, isn't it? But I'm prepared to spend a lifetime making amends for that thoughtless remark. In fact, I have a complete list of my somewhat narrow-minded statements. The list is on my houseboat, if you'd care to see it.'' He wiggled his brows.

"What's this really all about, Sam? If this is just a variation on asking me over to see your etchings, I'm not impressed."

"You certainly don't make it easy on a fellow, Brynn. I must admit, it would've been more enjoyable proposing to a dancer from the *Folies Bergère*…" He paused and grinned. "But hey, if you want to be the whole front chorus line with all these legs, I'll go for it." His grin faded. Growing serious, he said, "Brynn Powell, I love you and I want you for my wife."

"Your w-wife?" Brynn stammered. "You're asking me to marry you?"

"The very second Kevin is released from the hospital." The teasing glint fled Sam's eyes. "If it was up to me," he said gravely, "I'd nab that preacher over there and tie the knot tonight, but both Holly and Kevin made me promise to wait until Kevin's well enough to give you away."

Brynn lost her step totally. She stumbled and dropped the dice. They bounced to the floor as she dared to hope for the first time in weeks.

Bending swiftly, Sam scooped them up. "Snake eyes. You lose again, Brynn." The eyes he turned on her smoldered dark and dangerous. "But I'm almost sure we could make these stakes more interesting on my houseboat. Especially if we had to work our way down to *the barest by Brynn* before I get a return admission of love and a yes out of you."

"You'll sleep alone in your bed of roses tonight, Mr. Court," she answered tartly. "I'd say we've got a way to go to get back to being friends before we become lovers."

"How long do you think that'll take, Brynn? I'm not a patient man." Picking up her hand, he drew a ring from his vest pocket and attempted to slip it on over her gloved finger.

"Quite some marker you're handing out, Mr. Court," she scoffed self-consciously. "But I wouldn't gamble on its being real any more than I would on that being a preacher over there. Or haven't you two been introduced? He's our local vet."

Pulling abruptly out of Sam's loose grasp, Brynn turned and resolutely made her way toward the bay window, her heart hammering.

Undaunted, Sam followed less than a step behind. "I'm serious, Brynn. The diamond's real."

"Sam!" Brynn's voice faltered and her smile faded.

"I tried telling you how I felt over the phone that last week I was on the road. When I returned, Kevin was undergoing surgery, and after that I decided to take the extra time to romance you right. You seemed to need some tenderness. Then too many things got in the way."

"Those *things* haven't gone away, Sam. Since I believe you mean Kevin's illness, your ex-wife's intrusion and my having modeled in New York." Stripping off the close-fitting hood, Brynn shook her hair loose. Her eyes clouded sadly.

Sam reached out and smoothed an errant strand of gold behind one of her ears. He watched as she peeled down long, ebony gloves, amazed how those two steps neutralized the effect of her whole costume. She looked vulnerable now, and his heart swelled, warning him to say the right thing this time.

"You hadn't been gone from my place more than a minute when I knew none of those things mattered and I wanted you back. But first, for Holly's sake, I had to take on Joani. Then my parents arrived unexpectedly. One thing led to another... but I guess you know the rest." He lifted both her hands and rubbed his thumbs over her knuckles. Looking deep into her troubled eyes, he said distinctly, "I'm trying to say I love you, Brynn, and I'm not doing a very good job of it. But I want you to know that I believe—with all my heart—there are no hurdles out there too high for us to clear if you feel the same about me."

Her fingers trembled. The solitaire winked in the shimmering light of the golden moon that hung almost within touching distance outside the tall window. It seemed to promise strength and permanence, as did the man facing her. Brynn chewed at her lower lip. "So many problems, Sam... it wouldn't be easy."

"Life's a gamble, Brynn." His eyes didn't waver.

"You're serious!"

"So I've been trying to tell you."

"Kevin and Holly..."

"Will love the idea," he finished for her.

"But you'll be the loser, Sam. I've used up my savings. I've already told you our insurance ran out, and Kevin's surgery costs even more than college."

Releasing her hands, Sam cupped both of his behind her head and pulled her into a breathtaking kiss that silenced her. Slowly he straightened, and with his gaze focused on her parted lips, he murmured, "But do you love me?"

"Yes, but—"

Quickly, Sam laid a finger across her lips and smiled. "A simple yes will do. And—" he grinned wickedly "—if Miss Muffet's spider gives me the correct answer here, she'll have won a once-in-a-lifetime shot at the grand prize."

Though she tried not to, Brynn laughed out loud. "Which is...a free night in either a bed of roses or a bed of daisies, right, Mr. Court? To win this wonderful prize, I suppose you'd expect a lady to put *all* her cards on the table. That's asking a lot, I'd say."

"Ah, well." Sam sighed, pocketing the dice and slipping out a white business card. "You can't fault a guy for trying." He waved the card under her nose. "And you may be sorry you didn't select either the roses or the daisies and quick vows from our good veterinarian tonight, my lady. Because your third choice is to come with me and meet a bald chicken named Elwood. We'll just give that lucky fellow a chance to net us enough in the Dow to subsidize a month-long honeymoon for four. I swear, Brynn Powell...if you turn down the first two, it's the next best game in town."

Catching Sam's face between her hands, Brynn stopped his lengthy discourse with a solid kiss. And when Sam would have taken the kiss deeper, she pulled back, aware of their audience. "Not to change the subject here, Sam, but I have the perfect design in mind for that honeymoon you mentioned."

"Really?"

His eyes lit up, then darkened appreciably, turning the violet irises a deeper purple. "Yes," she purred, smiling up at him. "White, the finest cotton. High necked. Three hundred pearl buttons down the front."

"Hmm," he murmured, edging close enough to nip her bottom lip. "I can see it has possibilities. A gown like that could offer a man a lifetime of romantic notions...wouldn't you say?"

Brynn shivered and followed his lips. "Only if you're playing for keeps, Defenseman Court. Only if you're playing for keeps."

Suddenly, the two of them were so involved in a tangle of arms and springy, fur-covered spider legs, as Sam sealed his promise with a kiss, that they missed the thumbs-up signal passing between Sunne Evans and Holly Court. The prearranged sign clearly told Sam's daughter to call Kevin Powell right away. The reverse psychology suggested by his health teacher, Mr. Rusk, had indeed worked.

HARLEQUIN
Romance

is

 contemporary
and up-to-date

 heartwarming

 romantic

 exciting

 involving

 fresh and
delightful

 a short, satisfying
read

 wonderful!!

**Today's Harlequin
Romance—the traditional
choice!**

HARLEQUIN

Romance®

Delight in the exotic yet innocent love stories of
Harlequin Romance.

Be whisked away to dazzling international capitals ... or
quaint European villages.

Experience the joys of falling in love ... for the first
time, the best time!

Six new titles every month for your
reading enjoyment!

HRG-1

"Okay," he mumbled. "I'll see you later."